Other I

MW01088706

FRONTIER
JUSTICE
DAN BURLE, SR.

Three
for Hire
GUNSLINGERS
ON THE SANTA FE
DAN BURLE, SR.

Three
for Hire
THE SHADOW
ASSASSINS
DAN BURLE, SR.

Three
for Hire
REVENGE OF THE
MESCALERO
APACHE
DAN BURLE, SR.

Three
for Hire
TOMBSTONE,
THE LETHAL
CONNECTION
DAN BURLE, SR.

Other Books by Dan Burle, Sr.

FRONTIER JUSTICE

ACROSS THE RIO GRANDE (EPISODE II)

DAN BURLE, SR.

Wasteland Press
www.wastelandpress.net
Shelbyville, KY USA

Frontier Justice:
Across The Rio Grande (Episode II)
by Dan Burle, Sr.

First Printing – April 2017
ISBN: 978-1-68111-172-8
Library of Congress Control Number: 2017935597

Printed in the U.S.A.

0 1 2 3 4 5 6 7 8 9

Dedication

This book is dedicated to my friend, Dr. Jay Davis Clark, otherwise known as "Dr. Jay". I consider him to be Tombstone's Historian.

During January of 2016, I was in the process of writing the book, *Three for Hire: Tombstone, The Lethal Connection.* One evening when I was flipping through the TV guide just before dinner, I noticed that there was a documentary scheduled to be on in just a few minutes. It was entitled *Gunslingers: The Tombstone Vendetta.* Well, I told my wife to "put the meatloaf and mashed potatoes in the oven and turn it on warm, because there is a show coming on that I just have to watch." Now normally at this point a wife would kick her husband out of the house for obvious reasons. Not my wife – she understood – we are Old West historians.

We ate one hour later than normal, because we watched the documentary about the Earps, Doc Holliday, and the cow-boys, as they were called back then. We enjoyed the show because it was factual. I knew this because of all the research I did for my book.

I recognized one of the narrators. He was Kurt Russell who played Wyatt Earp in the movie, *Tombstone.* However, there was one person who I was really impressed with who I thought stood out among the others. I told my wife that he was special. There was something about him. It was his quiet passion for the story he conveyed. I could see it in his eyes - I could hear it in his voice. His name was Dr. Jay Davis Clark.

When I finished writing my book and it was published, I told my wife that we should introduce it by doing a book signing in Tombstone, Arizona. She agreed, so I lined it up. In my research of the present day Tombstone, I discovered that the same person Bernice and I saw on that documentary did a Historical Walking Tour in Tombstone. So there was no question about it; we scheduled a tour with Dr. Jay, and we are glad that we did!

I can tell you from our experience, Dr. Jay's highly acclaimed Walking Tour is a must if you visit Tombstone. His ability to combine history with humor will make your tour as memorable an experience as it was for us– his story telling will transport you back in time to October 26, 1881 as you stroll down the very same streets that the Earps and Doc Holliday walked on their way to the Shootout at the O.K. Corral. Dr. Jay's Tombstone Walking Tour has been honored by being named "the number one activity" in Tombstone by Trip Advisor.

From the very first day we met, we became friends. On our second day in Tombstone, Dr. Jay brought his lovely wife Linda over to our book signing to meet us. That was really special. After talking for a while, I discovered Dr. Jay and I both have a lot in common: we are the exact same age, we both grew up watching Westerns on TV, we both can't get enough of the Old West, and we both have wonderful wives.

I have always admired people who have a passion for life and for what they do. Dr. Jay is one of those people. His passion for the Old West is off the chart. His knowledge about the events in Tombstone is unmatched. The enthusiasm that he conveys, through his unique presentation style which he dubs "edutainment" as he guides groups on his daily tours around "the town too tough to die", is contagious. Dr. Jay's parting message to his tour group each day is worth repeating – "yesterday is history, tomorrow is a mystery, and today is a gift...that's why we call it 'the present'."

Dr. Jay's resume is amazing. He's a real-life dentist/forensic dentist (retired). He now splits his time between guiding tourists on a behind the scenes history tour of Tombstone, Arizona (TombstoneWalkingTours.com), acting, and along with his partner of thirty years (Linda R. Young) officiating their own brand of unique and customized weddings and vow renewals in Tombstone (TombstoneWeddings.com).

Dr. Jay and Linda are also gifted actors, with many stage and screen productions to their credit.

It is my honor to dedicate this book, *Frontier Justice: Across the Rio Grande* to my friend, Dr. Jay, a man of passion, sincerity, humor, and spirit – a man who enthusiastically continues to tell the story – the story of the Old West.

Disclaimer

Author's Foreword

The Wild West – hundreds of thousands of novels have been written about this remarkable time period in our country's history. After all, the mid to late 1800's gave authors a plentitude of topics to choose from.

However, it was the newspapermen of those days who gave these captivating events a resounding heartbeat, and brought them to life. Many times they conveyed the accounts based on their own Northern or Southern heritage, political party affiliation, and the likes – some made heroes out of the outlaws and others made outlaws out of the heroes.

Jesse James

On April 3, 1882 the notorious outlaw, Jesse James, was gunned down in coldblood by one of his own trusted gang members, Bob Ford. Jesse was a murderous criminal all right, a no-good to say the least, but he was a hero to many Southern sympathizers who never abandoned the rebel cry in their hearts and souls. The news of his death traveled across the wires and spread faster than a sagebrush fire in the Texas Panhandle.

The headline for the *Evening Bulletin* out of Maysville, Kentucky on May 4, 1882 read:

THE MURDER OF JESSE JAMES

"Let not Ceasar's servile minions,
Mock the lion thus laid low;
'Twas no foeman's hand that slew him
'Twas his own that struck the blow."

This reporter attempted to justify Jesse James's criminal actions as being a victim of the times. Here is the verification for my assertion. He wrote:

"Not one among all the hired cowards hard on the hunt for blood-money, dared face this wonderful man, one even against twenty, until he had disarmed himself and turned his back to his assassin, the first and only time in a career which has passed from the realms of an almost fabulous romance into that of history. We called him outlaw, and he was; but fate made him so. When the War came he was turned of fifteen. The border was all aflamed with steel, and ambuscade, and slaughter. He flung himself into a band which had a black flag for a banner and devils for riders. What he did, he did, and it was fearful. But it was war. It was Missouri against Kansas. It was Jim Lane and Jennison against Quantrill, Anderson, and Todd. When the War closed Jesse James had no home…"

The Shootout at the O.K. Corral

This was the most notorious Old West gunfight of all times. It occurred in a southwestern silver mining boomtown named Tombstone, in the Arizona Territory. The gun battle became known as the Shootout at the O.K. Corral. It happened on October 26, 1881. It was a cold day in the desert on that infamous day. Old timers say that there was a dusting of snow on the ground that morning. Wyatt Earp would later refer to the afternoon shootout as a street fight because it culminated on Fremont Street.

Two Tombstone newspapers leaned the story different ways. The *Tombstone Daily Nugget* was of Democrat influence – a southern lean. *The Tombstone Epitaph* had a northern Republican lean - the Earps were from the north – the owner was a good friend of Wyatt - enough said.

The headline in the *The Tombstone Epitaph* on October 27, 1881 read:

YESTERDAY'S TRAGEDY

Three Men Hurled Into Eternity in the Duration of a Moment

Here is a short excerpt. Note: The Earp mentioned here is Marshal Virgil Earp.

"Marshal Earp says that he and his party met the Clantons and the McLowrys in the alleyway by the McDonald place; he called to them to throw up their hands, that he had come to disarm them. Instantaneously Bill Clanton and one of the McLowrys fired, and then it became general. Mr. Earp says it was the first shot from Frank McLowry that hit him."

The headline in the *Tombstone Daily Nugget* on October 27, 1881 read:

A DESPERATE STREET FIGHT

Here is a short excerpt. Notice the subtle difference in where the blame fell compared to the above article.

"...the Marshal said to the Clantons and McLowrys: 'Throw up your hands, boys, I intend to disarm you.' As he spoke Frank McLowry made a motion to draw his revolver, when Wyatt Earp pulled his and shot him, the ball striking on the right side of his abdomen. About the same time Doc Holliday shot Tom McLowry in the right side, using a short shotgun..."

Newspapers all around the country picked up these two stories and they were published for weeks from the West coast to the East coast. Some saw the Earps as heroes; others claimed they were street murderers. Eventually the Earps became the heroes, because some say years later, Wyatt himself made it so.

Note: Both newspapers spelled Frank and Tom's name "McLowry". Their names on their gravestones are spelled McLaury.

Custer's Last Stand

History has not been generous to Custer's decision to audaciously attack the Sioux when he did. But one cannot argue the courage and valor of Lieutenant Colonel Custer and the intrepid men of the 7th Cavalry. They fearlessly charged into the annals and pages of American history and military books on that infamous day in June of 1876.

The headline from the *Bismarck Weekly Tribune* out of Bismarck, Dakota Territory dated July 12, 1876 had a middle-of-the-page, front page story on the events that occurred at the Little Bighorn on June 26, 1876. The long headline stretched out two-thirds of a page.

It read:

MASSACRED.
GEN. CUSTER AND 261 MEN THE VICTIMS
No Officer or Man of Five Companies Left to Tell the Tale
Three Days Desperate Fighting Under Maj. Reno

Full Details of the Battle
LIST OF KILLED AND WOUNDED
THE BISMARCK TRIBUNE SPECIAL
CORRESPONDENT SLAIN
Squaws Mutilate and Rob the Dead
Victims Captured Alive Tortured in a Most Fiendish Manner
What will Congress do About it?
Shall this be the Beginning of the End.

"It will be remembered that the Bismarck Tribune sent a special correspondent with Gen. Terry, who was the only professional correspondent with the expedition. Kellogg's last words to the writer were 'We leave the Rosebud tomorrow, and by the time this reaches you we will have met and fought the red devils, with what result remains to be seen. I go with Custer and will be at the death'."

That was just a short piece of the long three column front page article about the events of that infamous day.

These three examples and many others from the Old West are well-known to this day because of saved newspaper articles from that time period. They have literally become cherished treasures and journal entries into the American archives. Tales of the Wild West have also become well-known because authors and historians continue to write books and documentaries about the so-called intriguing and romantic era of the cowboys and frontiersmen, who courageously blazed new trails in the uncivilized West.

Make no mistake about it though; there was nothing glamorous about living in those days. Streets in the Old West towns were filthy, muddy at times, and reeking with the smell of horse manure and equine urine.

Cow towns were noisy and unsanitary. Trains rolled right through the middle of town. Large herds of longhorn steers up from Texas, which were sometimes carrying tick fever, were paraded down the middle of Main Street to their corrals next to the railroad spurs. Gambling houses, saloons, and brothels sprung up in every town that became a railhead and trail's end for Texas drovers. Lawlessness often ensued.

Cattle drives which are glamourized in movies were far from being gratifying. They were hard on the Texas drovers: hard on their backs and their entire bodies. Cow punchers rode long days for months on stiff leather in the heat, cold, rain, and snow. At times water holes were few and far between, separated by many miles of dry barren land.

The cowboys ate mostly beans and bacon and when they ran out of Arbuckle's, they boiled horse grain or acorns for coffee. Sometimes they fought Indians, cattle rustlers, and even farmers along the way when their herds crossed plowed or planted fields as they approached the cow towns.

Early settlers had hard times as well, trying to survive Indian attacks from Comanche, Apache, Sioux, Cheyenne, Ute, Crow, and other Native American tribes which resented losing the land of their forefathers and their century's old way of life.

Frontier diseases killed many in those days. Tuberculosis, or consumption as it was known, eventually snatched the last breath of life from the disreputable Doc Holliday at age 36 on November 8, 1887. It spread easily from person to person. It is believed that he contracted the disease from his own mother when living in Georgia.

Typhoid fever, dysentery, and smallpox seized the lives of many. Those dreadful diseases did not discriminate between the wealthy and the poor, the high society and the homesteaders, or the westerners and the easterners. During the Civil War over 81,000 Union soldiers died from typhoid or dysentery, far more than died from battle wounds. Typhoid fever took the life of Stephen A. Douglas on June 3, 1861, and even the young 11 year old son of Abraham Lincoln, William Wallace Lincoln, on February 20, 1862.

There were no antibiotics available back in the days of the Old West - penicillin wasn't discovered until 1928. If you were wounded by a bullet or by a Comanche arrow, or even cut yourself on a rusty barbwire fence, chances were you would lose a limb, or die of blood poisoning or gangrene. Charles Goodnight's partner, Oliver Loving, was seriously wounded at Loving Bend on the Pecos River during a Comanche attack. He soon died from gangrene on September 25, 1867, at the age of 54. He was traveling ahead of their cattle drive for contract biddings.

Many also died from lawlessness in the new frontier. Where there was no law around for miles, frontier justice prevailed. Cattle rustlers were hung on the spot from the nearest tree, and vigilante groups took the law into their own hands and strung up criminals even if they were already jailed and awaiting trial. Some unruly gang members killed their own when they were doubled-crossed or crawfished on.

All of these things have been written about in hundreds of thousands of Western novels over time. But there is one subject that has evaded most Western novels, and that's the subject of secret societies.

That is very peculiar to me because in my research, I have discovered that between the years of 1859 and 1885, there were over 500 mentions in articles referring to secret societies of all kinds.

In the *National Republican, Washington, D.C., Monday Morning Newspaper*, April 2, 1883, on page 1 of 8, column 3 the headline read:

APACHE ASSASSINS, A SECRET SOCIETY FORMED TO EXTERMINATE THE RED MAN – ADDITIONAL MURDERS – INDIANS FLEEING.

In the same column a sub-headline and story read:

A SOCIETY TO EXTERMINATE INDIANS

"San Francisco, Cal. April 1. – A gentleman just returned from Arizona confirms the report that a secret society exists among the whites of Arizona to exterminate the male Apache on the San Carlos reservation and all found roving north of the frontier. The reservation is looked upon as a mere refuge for the Indians, where they may retire when hard pressed and obtain arms, provisions, and such for another raid."

The secret society this article referred to was known as "Shakespeare's Guards" with Captain Black as their leader.

Secret societies have existed for hundreds of years. Various ones have been thought of as controlling and manipulating historical events from the shadows. Because of the fact that secret societies held meetings behind closed doors, it was thought that they had something to hide, and were not to be trusted. Many people thought secret societies were out to destroy governments and religious institutions. At one time, if you were a Roman

Catholic, you could be excommunicated from the church if you belonged to specific secret societies.

Some secret societies had religious components like the Knights Templar. Another one wanted to control certain world commodity markets and use African slaves as their labor force. They were the Knights of the Golden Circle. John Wilkes Booth and Jesse James were two notables in history who belonged to the KGC.

One of the oldest and still existing secret societies goes all the way back to Solomon's Temple – some say it even goes further back in time - to the building of the pyramids. The fact is that it grew out of medieval craft skills. It is known as the Masons or Freemasons. Today some claim the Freemasons are no longer a secret society but a society with secrets.

There are several appendant bodies of Freemasonry. One is the Shriners. They are described as "a fraternity based on fun, fellowship, and Mason principles of brotherly love, relief, and truth."

The Shriners' charitable arm is the Shriners Hospitals for Children which is a network of 22 hospitals in the United States, Canada, and Mexico. They have hospitals that specialize in orthopedics, burn care, cleft lip and palate, and spinal cord injury.

They give millions of dollars in free medical care for children. They are a great organization.

There were many notables who were Freemasons from the beginning of our country to the frontier days of the Old West. Here are just a few: 14 Presidents of the United States, 9 men who signed the Declaration of Independence, 8 who signed the Articles of Confederation, 13 who signed the Constitution of the United States, in addition to William Clark, Wm. "Buffalo Bill" Cody, Meriwether Lewis, Stephen F. Austin, Davy Crockett, Kit Carson, James Bowie, Wyatt Earp, Sam Houston, Colonel William B. Travis, Samuel Colt, Paul Revere, Turkey Creek Jack Johnson and Texas Jack Vermillion, just to name a few.

When you think of Tombstone, you think of the Earps, Doc Holliday, the Clantons, the McLaurys and the O.K. Corral. If you are familiar with the history of Tombstone, you may also think of the Schieffelin Hall. It was a two story adobe building built in 1881. The bottom floor was used for dining, dancing, and as a theater. The top floor became the Freemason's King Solomon Territorial

Masonic Lodge #5. They moved into it when the building was completed.

The Schieffelin Hall is still standing today and the second floor is still the Freemason's Lodge.

The first Master of the King Solomon Territorial Masonic Lodge #5 was Wells Spicer. He was the judge who presided over the hearing regarding the Shootout at the O.K. Corral. After hearing all of the testimonies and evidence, he saw no need to hold a full blown trial. The Earps and Holliday were not charged with a criminal act.

An interesting story about this lodge is that Virgil Earp, U.S. Marshal in the Tombstone area, petitioned the lodge for membership in 1881. Spicer along with another member recommended him, but the membership voted him down.

There is another factor that has created great interest as it relates to secret societies. Over the years they have been known to have had hidden treasures which have been sought after for centuries by treasure hunters from all walks of life. Lost treasures have also become the subject of many present-day novels of various genres, documentaries, and movies.

And Now My Book

Frontier Justice: Across the Rio Grande, is the second episode of my Frontier Justice series. The first episode, *Frontier Justice*, should be read before reading this book.

In this new Frontier Justice episode, I have introduced and made a major part of the plot that which has evaded most Western novels of the past: secret societies, and their hidden treasures. This book is filled with intense moments, Wild West action, mystery, intrigue, twists, and many surprises. What is fact will sometimes seem to be fiction; what is fiction will sometimes seem to be fact.

Find a nice quiet location in your home and enjoy *Frontier Justice, Across the Rio Grande.* However, be prepared for another wild ride in the Old West.

Dan Burle, Sr.
"Keeping the Spirit of the Wild West Alive"

Fictional Characters

Dakota Wilson
Pecos Fransisco
Lillian Langtree (a.k.a. Diamond Lil)
Luke Barnes (a.k.a. Rusty Blake)
Jerod Brinkman
Kathleen Brinkman Barnes
Johnny Dane
Kenny Burkley
Doctor Eddie Hawkens
Tom Kiefer
Marshal Ben Richards
Slim
Jimmy
Colorado Jackson
Brisco
Matt
Carlos Bautista, Ben Harrington
John Short
Bobby Green
Tom O'Hara
Bret Stone
Cole Brinkman (a.k.a. Burns)
Deputy Marshal Jake Lucas
Deputy Frank
Mr. Franks
Jerry, the telegraph operator in Pueblo
Matt Brinkman
Bob, Mrs. Bains, Johnny Sullivan
Jonathan Mueller and family
Billy and Sam Lane
Mr. Brennen
Steven, the Interior Designer
Robert, the Architect
Michael the teller, Jodie
Mrs. Dempsey, Jasper

Table of Contents

PROLOGUE

"My dear friends, I can't tell you how much my wife Kathleen and I appreciate you allowing me to serve you as your minister here at St. Patrick's. Kathleen and I have come to love this town of Hays City, Kansas.

In Proverbs 11:10 it is said, 'When it goeth well with the righteous, the city rejoiceth: and when the wicked perish, there is shouting.'

Yes my dear friends, there is jubilation in our hearts and in our streets today.

The Good Lord has transformed this once wicked town of vice and gunplay to a God fearing town of righteous hard working men and women; men and women who are raising beautiful families in the eyes of the Lord. Yes, we all know that the family is the cornerstone of society. As I look around in God's house today, I must say, I am proud to be a part of this wonderful community I call my family.

Since our church social and luncheon is today, and I see the sun shining brightly through our newly installed stained glass windows, it seems appropriate to end this service with Psalm 1 which is entitled,

'True Happiness:

Blessed is the man that walketh not in the counsel of the ungodly, nor standeth in the way of sinners, nor sitteth in the seat of the scornful.

But his delight is in the law of the Lord; and in his law doth he meditate day and night.

And he shall be like a tree planted by the rivers of water, that bringeth forth his fruit in his season; his leaf also shall not wither; and whatsoever he doeth shall prosper.

The ungodly are not so: but are like the chaff which the wind driveth away.

Therefore the ungodly shall not stand in the judgment, nor sinners in the congregation of the righteous.

For the Lord knoweth the way of the righteous: but the way of the ungodly shall perish.'

My dear friends, that ends our service for today. Now from what I understand, our special luncheon will be served outside in just fifteen minutes. The tables are already set up and I can smell the aroma of that delicious fried chicken wafting through the open windows of our beautiful church. I don't know about you, but I am ready for a Sunday afternoon meal," Preacher Luke Barnes said as he put a slight grin on his face that displayed a high degree of satisfaction and pride.

Everyone stood up as Preacher Barnes moved away from the podium and stepped down from the elevated platform. He then walked down the middle aisle toward the back of church, where he stood while he greeted everyone as they exited.

Thirty-six families were in attendance at this late Sunday morning service. Several of the ladies and a few of the men skipped the service to prepare the outdoor feast. And a fine spread it was: crispy fried chicken, mashed potatoes with white gravy, creamed peas and carrots and cornbread baked in Dutch ovens right on site. Many of the women brought their favorite pies and cakes. There was enough dessert to feed the entire town of both churchgoers and non-believers – hopefully future converts of Preacher Barnes.

The food was placed in bowls on twelve foot long tables. There were benches on both sides of each table. The town carpenters made the tables and benches specifically for this function.

A few of the ladies made special red and white checkered tablecloths for the occasion, while others were in charge of gathering wildflowers from around the countryside, and then: making bouquets, placing them in mason jars, and positioning them on the tables. Oh it was quite a spread to behold all right - the outing had the appearance and the feel of a large family reunion.

Preacher Barnes said grace, then he and his lovely wife sat in the middle of one of the long tables – a great way for him to intermingle with his parishioners. While the food was being passed around and everyone was filling their plates, the telegraph operator came walking over to Preacher Barnes's table with a telegram in hand – he had a strange look on his face – a worried look one might surmise.

"Preacher Barnes, I have a telegram for you which you need to read."

"Well I can't right now Bob. Don't you see I'm filling up my plate with these delicious foods which these lovely ladies cooked for us? Why don't you read it to me."

"I don't believe I should Preacher. It looks to be personal."

"Nonsense Bob, I don't have any secrets. Go ahead, read it out loud. What does it say?"

"Well, OK Preacher, it says,

'They're gunning for you, Preacher'."

CHAPTER ONE:

Ride Hard to Cimarron

"Good afternoon Mrs. Dempsey, how can I help you today?"

"Hello Michael, I'd like to withdraw $350 please."

"$350 – no problem – sounds like Mr. Dempsey decided to buy that fancy bull from Jasper after all."

"Yes he has. I don't for the life of me know what he sees in that overgrown hornless black beast from Scotland - but my husband is a good cattleman you know - always has been - so I guess he sees something good in it, I suppose."

"I reckon he does ma'am…Here you go Mrs. Dempsey: $100, $200, $300, and $350," Michael said as he counted out the money for the middle-aged lady.

"Tell Mr. Dempsey I said hello and I wish him luck with his new Aberdeen Angus."

"I'll do that Michael. Have a good day now."

"Yes ma'am."

Mrs. Dempsey placed the money in her purse, turned around, and walked out. The next person in line stepped up to the cashier's window.

"Hello Paul, what can I do for you today?" Michael asked.

"Hey Michael, I want to deposit my weekly store revenues. There's $450 in this envelope," Paul said as he handed it to Michael. "I'm closed now for the holiday. Mildred and I are looking forward to Thanksgiving tomorrow with my ma and pa and my sister's family out at the old homestead."

"Know what you mean, Paul. Looks like there is one more customer after you, then we're closing down too," Michael said as he looked around and behind Paul.

"The boss left early today so I'm in charge of locking up. It's actually the first time he's honored me with this responsibility. I'm really looking forward to this Thanksgiving," Michael said as he was counting Paul's deposit.

"Why's that Michael?"

"Well because I'm staying in town this year. I'm invited over to my fiancé's parents' house tomorrow."

"I heard your fiancé is quite a cook."

"Jodie? You must be talking about somebody else," Michael replied as he finished up writing Paul's deposit in the ledger.

They both got a laugh out of that at Jodie's expense. The truth was – Jodie was known around town as a better than average cook. Maybe even a cut above some of the café cooks in the entire state.

Her homemade cherry pie came in first place at the county fair the last two years and she took first place with her apple pie this year. It was the best out of 21 entries.

"Here's your deposit slip, Paul. Have a great Thanksgiving."

"Thanks Michael."

"By the way Paul, will your store be open Friday?"

"Yes, it's a sure bet I'll be there bright and early as usual. I'll open at 8:30 like always. No sleeping in after this holiday. Cold weather has arrived early this year, and I suspect the folks will be stocking up early as well."

"I'll stop by before work. I need to order one of those fancy New York derby hats out of your catalogue for my wedding."

"Good enough, see you Friday, Michael." Paul turned and accidently bumped into the man behind him and said, "Pardon me for my clumsiness, mister."

The drifter said nothing, nodded and stepped forward. Paul didn't notice that the stranger was packing a couple of fancy six-shooters.

"Now, how can I help you sir? Sorry I took so long," Michael said.

"That's OK young man. You can help me by doing exactly what I say," Dakota said as he skinned his Colt and pointed it at Michael's forehead – right between his eyeballs.

Michael jerked his head back – an involuntary reaction caused by the barrel of a .45 being positioned just six inches from the bridge of his nose.

"Slowly walk around the counter, close the front door, lock it, and pull down the shade. Don't do anything stupid. That Mexican standing over there has an itchy trigger finger," Dakota said as he nodded toward Pecos. At that point, Pecos drew his Smith & Wesson and aimed it at Michael as well while giving Michael one of those wily south of the border grins.

Dakota kept his pistol aimed at the head of the terrified teller as he walked down the counter on the inside, passed two cashier windows, pushed open the swing gate, and walked toward the front door.

At this point, Pecos holstered his pistol and pulled out his twelve inch double edged blade and held it to Michael's back and followed behind him all the way to the door. Michael could feel the sharp point of the knife poking him in the back.

"Say one word amigo, and I'll cut your spine," Pecos threatened.

Pecos knew if Michael did anything foolish, a knife would be much quieter than spending a .45 slug – the razor sharp blade would definitely accomplish the same desired result.

Pecos was famous for using his Arkansas toothpick. He cherished it because it was made especially for him by James Black, the same man who legend has it, made Jim Bowie his famous Bowie knife.

Michael didn't have time to think about it at first when that six-shooter was initially pointed at his head; but on what seemed to be a long walk to that front door with the point of a large blade jabbing him in the back every step of the way, realism set in. This young, good looking, twenty three year old, clean shaven, well-groomed man began sweating profusely. All he could think about was Jodie, his first love and bride-to-be.

Dakota waited until the front door was closed, locked, the shade pulled down, and then he said,

"Now young man, walk over to that safe and open it. And by the way, don't tell me it's on a time-lock. That got a teller like you shot in the head up in Northfield, Minnesota, compliments of Frank James. Now I'm not a James boy, but some say I'm twice as mean and I'm a dang straight shot too."

"Si amigo, and some say I am twice as mean as my pard," Pecos said with that wily grin on his face once again.

Michael walked over to the safe – his forehead was dripping with perspiration – his hands were becoming cold and clammy. The safe was indeed locked; but the type of lock was rudimentary at best. It was nothing more than a simple combination dial lock. Luckily, Michael knew the combination. However his nerves were about shot. Since his hands were sweating and then shaking like a rattle on the tail end of a sidewinder, he missed the second number three notches to the left - the safe did not open. Dakota showed patience with the young man, even after the second failure. But after the third – well, that was a different story. Pecos walked behind Michael, who was kneeling down on one knee in front of the safe, and pressed his razor-sharp blade across the front of Michael's throat and said,

"If you miss it just one more time Senor, your throat will be smiling from ear to ear. Do you understand, mi amigo?"

"Yes sir."

"Bueno. Now think, take your time, and open this safe right now," Pecos said. This time the Mexican bandit wasn't grinning - no sir - not this time. His patience had run out.

Michael's eyes started tearing up. He wiped them to see more clearly. He turned the dial to the right to number 33. Then he turned it to the left to number 22. Lastly, he slowly turned the dial back to the right to number 18. He took a deep breath, grabbed the handle, pulled it downward, and then yanked the safe door open, letting out a sigh of relief.

Dakota then handed over his and Pecos's saddlebags and told Michael to fill them up with paper money only, and to do it straightaway. While Michael was stuffing the bags with greenbacks, Dakota told Pecos to peek out the window and see how busy the street was outside. It was pretty much vacant. Most businesses in this small town of Medicine Lodge, Kansas closed early with Thanksgiving being the next day.

Dakota and Pecos were running from the law. They were members of a notorious gang out of Abilene, Kansas, a gang of professionals who had just pulled off one of the most daring heists in criminal Old West history. Their gang successfully robbed the Carson City Mint in Nevada and got away with millions of dollars in gold.

That is until Allan Pinkerton and his detectives caught up with them at their hideout along the Smoky Hill River just outside of Abilene. Dakota, Pecos and a crooked lawman hightailed out of town before the raid began and got a clean getaway. At least, that's what they thought.

Dakota and Pecos decided to ride to a small town in Texas and hide out there for a while until the dust settled and the proverbial storm blew over. But since they left in a heap of hurry, they rode out with nothing to their names but horses, tack, firearms and a couple boxes of cartridges.

So on their way out of Kansas, they decided to stop in this small town to rob a bank, steal some grub and more ammunition, and then ride hard to Cimarron, and then to El Paso, instead of Laredo as they originally planned. Pecos was more familiar with El Paso, and it was wide open for outlaws.

They learned from their previous gang leader, who found his demise back in Abilene, that the best time to hit a bank is right at closing time the day before a holiday.

The bank they chose to hit the day before Thanksgiving was the Mercantile Bank of Medicine Lodge, Kansas. This quaint little town, located in south central Kansas, was well known throughout the state and in some of the territories nearby. But its fame didn't come from being a cow town the likes of Wichita, Abilene, Ellsworth or Dodge City. No sir, its prominence came from other means which made this area so interesting.

In the summer of 1866, a Kiowa Indian tribe built a medicine lodge; some say a sacred tabernacle, near a river. That river was eventually named Medicine Lodge River. The lodge was built of tree trunks and leafy branches. It was used by the Kiowa people for the celebration of their annual sun dance.

The Kiowa Indians considered the site sacred because of the high content of Epsom salts (magnesium sulfate) in the river. It was considered a healing substance for both internal and external health issues.

However, the incident that put Medicine Lodge on the map was the Medicine Lodge Treaties which were signed by the United States and several Great Plains Indian tribes in October of 1867. They were the Kiowa, Comanche, Kiowa-Apache, Southern Cheyenne, and the Arapaho tribes. The site of the signing was actually about three miles north of what would become known as the town of Medicine Lodge. There were three treaties signed. The first was on October 21, 1867 with the Kiowa and the Comanche. The second treaty was with the Kiowa-Apache on the same day. The third was signed on October 28th with the Southern Cheyenne and the Arapaho. The purpose of the treaties was to bring peace to the area by relocating those tribes to reservations in the Indian Territory and away from the white settlements.

This set the stage for the founding of the town of Medicine Lodge. It was established by settlers led by John Hutchinson in February of 1873 and was located north of the convergence of Elm Creek and the Medicine Lodge River.

The town grew rapidly within a year of its founding. Immediately, buildings were constructed and businesses opened their doors for commerce: a hotel, retail stores, a post office, and yes a bank – a bank too tempting for Dakota and Pecos to ignore.

Pecos again slightly moved the pull-down shade to the side and peeked out the window. This time he saw the town marshal walking across the street checking doors of closed businesses. He quickly moved his hand away from the shade when he saw the marshal turn and begin to walk toward the bank.

Pecos hurriedly walked over to Dakota and said,

"The marshal is heading this way."

Dakota looked at Michael and told him to stop what he was doing and to be real still. He pressed the cold steel barrel of his pistol deep into Michael's left cheek. They waited and waited. Pecos's eyes were fixed on the front doorknob with the concentration as if he was watching a big ole South Texas venomous rattler making ready to strike. Dakota was glancing between the front door and Michael. His eyes had the intensity of a predator hawk deciding which prey to pounce on first.

Then they saw the doorknob turn and the door shake in and out several times. The marshal was testing to make sure it was indeed locked. It was a tense moment for everyone inside. Dakota shoved the barrel deeper into Michael's cheek. But then the shaking stopped, and they could hear the marshal's footsteps on the wood platform moving away and traveling to the saddlery shop next door.

Tensions eased and then Dakota ordered, "Continue filling the saddlebags, young man."

When the bags were bulging with thousands of dollars in paper money, Michael handed them to Dakota. Dakota buckled them shut and slung one over his left shoulder and then one over his right. With his gun pointing at Michael's head, he told him to lie on the floor – face down.

Pecos asked Dakota, "What are we gonna do with this gringo? He can recognize us."

Well it wasn't until about 4:00 the next afternoon, Thanksgiving Day, that Michael's fiancé became anxious. She drove her buggy over to Michael's home but he was nowhere to be found. Then, sensing something was horribly wrong, she rode over to the marshal's office. The marshal wasn't on duty but his deputy was. She knocked on the door, opened it and walked in.

The deputy was sitting at the marshal's desk leaning back in the chair with his size fourteen clodhoppers propped up on the desk. The town dimwit forgot he had his spurs on but the marshal would know the next day by the six inch scratch mark he left when he hurriedly removed his boots when Jodie entered. The deputy stood up, pulled his gun belt over his pants' belt, straightened his holster, tucked in his shirt, and said,

"Howdy Miss Jodie, what can I do for you today? It's Thanksgivin', don't you know. You ain't supposed to be out and about today. You should oughta be home with Michael. Heard y'all were having a holiday meal over at y'all's house. Michael told me so anyway. He said..."

Deputy Frank was in one of his yammering moods – some around town called it a "talkin' spell". But Jodie jumped right in and said,

"Something's wrong Deputy. Michael was supposed to come for dinner today but he never showed up. I went over to his house and he's not home either. Something's not right. He was scheduled to close up the bank late yesterday afternoon. I guess he did, but I'm really concerned that something's wrong."

"Well Miss Jodie, the marshal came back yesterday afternoon and said all the businesses were locked up OK. I'm assumin' he meant the bank too. That's usually one of the last doors he checks. Maybe Michael was called out of town. Maybe his ma or pa got sick and he left as quick as lightnin'. Betchya that's it all right. I'd bet money on it. I wouldn't fret Miss Jodie. He'll show up sooner or later."

"Maybe so Deputy."

Jodie was standing in front of the marshal's desk while they were talking. Before she turned around to walk out, she looked down and saw that big ole nasty scratch the deputy's rowel left on the top of the marshal's polished oak desk.

"The marshal is going to be none too happy with that huge scratch you left on top of his desk," Jodie said as she nodded toward the deep mark.

The deputy looked at it, raised his eyebrows, then bent down, spit on it and rubbed it with the cuff of his sleeve thinking he could make a six-inch-long, quarter-inch-deep scratch disappear with his miracle saliva – didn't work – no sir – didn't work one bit. When Jodie left, the deputy quickly placed a sheet of paper over the scratch hoping the marshal would never move it in his lifetime and discover the thoughtless blunder.

It wasn't until Friday morning when the owner of the bank unlocked the front door and walked in, that he found Michael's body lying in what was a dried up pool of blood next to the safe with the door wide open. Michael was gored three times. It was a cold-blooded murder by Pecos, whose morals would seem to flee with each passing day.

Jodie's heart was broken – she was grief stricken. They were to be married in three months. There were no witnesses to the murder and no one even caught a glimpse of the getaway Wednesday afternoon. The streets were empty. The entire town had closed down early that day for the holiday.

Oh there was a saloon still open late into Wednesday evening all right, but it was located on the other end of town. Most of the hombres in the saloon were all blurry-eyed as a result of bending elbows for a better part of the afternoon. And at that point, most of them couldn't tell the difference between a prospector's long ear jackass and a two-horned billy goat.

On Friday morning a local store owner reported to the town marshal that his store had been burglarized. Indeed it was. Dakota and Pecos broke into Murphy's General Store before fleeing town Wednesday evening - they busted in through the back door. They stole grub, ammunition, and a few shirts and trousers. They stuffed the stolen goods into 2 gunnysacks they found in the storage room. Each toted a sack as they rode hard and fast to the west and then south toward the Indian Territory panhandle.

The area they headed for was known as "No Man's Land". It was the region which would later become Cimarron County. It was a lawless area – a place with no organized government. It was a great place for outlaws to hide out for as long as they wanted - until the "move-on" itch compelled them to saddle up and, well, move on.

Pecos and Dakota camped along the North Canadian River which was also known as Beaver Creek. They decided to hang around there for several days before riding into the Texas Panhandle. The location was a few miles away from the old Santa Fe Trail, the part known as the Cimarron Cutoff. The trail was rendered obsolete with the building of the railroad to Santa Fe, New Mexico Territory in 1880.

There was still an old ramshackle trading post nearby - just off the main trail apiece which sold grub, camping supplies, and cheap liquor which you could drink if you could stomach it. There weren't any warning labels on the jugs but if there were they would probably read, "Drink at your own peril" or "Could be hazardous to your health and your horse's too". It was widely surmised that some of that homebrew tornado juice could burn a hole in a hip flask in the same time a Missouri mule could chow down a half bucket of grain.

Before leaving Murphy's General Store back in Medicine Lodge, Dakota picked up a newspaper from the counter. He noticed a headline that caught his eye, so he stuck it in the gunnysack to read later. Pecos saw the same newspaper as well. But being illiterate, he gave it no mind.

The newspaper was the *Dodge City Times* which was a weekly publication circulated throughout Ford County and southwest Kansas. It went into production for the first time on May 20, 1876.

It was late in the evening – the sun had already disappeared from the western horizon but there was still a tad of light left for campsite chores – just enough to gather some firewood for the campfire, get that wood burning, and cook up some bacon and beans.

The two desperados had made a quick stop at the old trading post along the Santa Fe Trail and picked up a jug of homebrew firewater, and biscuits the owner baked that morning. The biscuits were as hard as granite, but cut in half and dipped in red-eyed gravy solved the problem, and would be the makings for a respectable biscuit and sowbelly sandwich.

Dakota was the grub slinger on that evening. In fact he would do most of the cooking while they were fleeing from justice. Reason being – ole Pecos liked to slip in some of his extra hot chili peppers into every skillet of anything. Dakota's Yankee innards were not suited for the likes of blistering hot chopped chili peppers. Oh he was sucker punched once all right, but Dakota learned fast – fast as lightning. He knew enough not to be mule kicked a second time.

After dinner, Dakota threw a few more branches on the fire and he popped the cork on the jug of that gut warmer juice they bought back at the trading post. The night was becoming very dark, chilly, and a bit blustery. The heavy thick cloud cover concealed the light, what little there was of it, from the quarter moon.

Dakota poured some whiskey into a tin cup for Pecos and then in one for himself – to warm up their innards no doubt. Then he walked over to his horse, opened up the gunnysack tied to his saddle horn and removed the *Dodge City Times* he snatched back in the general store in Medicine Lodge. It had his curiosity up and soon would have the hair on the back of his neck standing up as well – so to speak. They had set up their camp near a downed tree – the trunk made a good bench to sit on.

"Whatcha got there amigo?"

"It's that newspaper I picked up in Medicine Lodge. I think our gang is mentioned in it."

"Can you read?" Pecos asked.

"Of course I can."

"Well then read it."

Dakota began skimming the article – not reading it out loud but to himself.

"Why that no good yellow belly skunk."

"Who's a yellow belly skunk?" Pecos asked in an impatient sort of way.

"Rusty! That's who."

"Rusty? Our Rusty?"

"Yeah, our Rusty. Listen to this. It says here:

DODGE CITY TIMES
ABILENE, KANSAS GANG BUSTED

A murderous outlaw gang which hid in the shadows of the cottonwood trees along the banks of the Smoky Hill River, just outside of the once booming cow town of Abilene, has been disbanded. A Pinkerton agent, under the guise of a safecracker, infiltrated the gang and single-handedly brought the murderous desperados to their demise. The Pinkerton agent was Luke Barnes, a.k.a. Rusty Blake. He led the Pinkerton detectives to the hideaway with a secret message that was hidden and found at the gang's last robbery."

"What…you mean to tell me Rusty was a Pinkerton agent?" Pecos asked.

"That's what it says – says it right here."

"What else does it say?"

"Says,

The gang, which was sometimes referred to as the "Professionals", was raided at their hideout by Allan Pinkerton and his army of agents. The gang earned their name the "Professionals" as a result of the specific individual notorious talents of its outlaw members: gunmen, snipers, explosive experts, and the likes. They were all fugitives from the law.

The leader of the gang was Jerod Brinkman, a local banker and a retired Confederate officer who led the rebel charge at the First Battle of Chattanooga. He was shot and killed in the hideout by his adopted daughter who was not previously aware of Brinkman's infamous activities until that very day. Also killed in the raid were Bobby Burkley, Cole Fletcher, The Kansas Kid, and Arizona Palmer."

"Ay, chihuahua! They were all killed?"

"Not all… listen to this:

Barnes single-handedly captured alive Johnny Dane, Kenny Burkley, and Doctor Eddie Hawkens. Their Chinese cook named Chan was captured by the Pinkerton agents inside the criminal's lodge. He was found hiding in the walk-in pantry wielding a cleaver. Chan was also wanted for murder in Arkansas for slicing up and killing his helper with that same meat cleaver. They say his helper called him a Chink. Chan did not like the tone and meaning of that slur. He considered it a vulgar term of hostility and contempt. He subsequently thereby turned his meat and vegetable kitchen tool into a vicious murder weapon. Dane, Burkley, and Hawkens will be tried in Abilene. Chan will be tried in Arkansas. Trial dates have not been announced yet.

Barnes informed authorities that two gang members were not captured. They were in town at the time of the raid and speculation is they are long gone. Their names are Dakota Wilson and Pecos Fransisco.

Pecos Fransisco is described as a Mexican man, 5'5" tall and weighing about 190 pounds. He has black hair, dark eyes, and a full rounded face with a thin black mustache. He is said to be extremely dangerous. He is very fast with a gun, carries a large knife which is his weapon of choice, and he angers easily.

Dakota Wilson is about 6' tall and slim at 175 pounds. He has sandy colored hair, green eyes, and a thin face with a handlebar mustache. He is known as the fastest gun north of the Red River. There is a reward of $1,000 each for their captures, "Dead or Alive"."

"Ay, Dios mio, somos famosos," Pecos said.

"For God's sake Pecos, speak English."

"I said, oh my God, we are famous."

Dakota began skimming through the rest of the article. Then he said,

"Listen to this. Now we know who Brinkman's boss was. You aren't gonna believe this:

Through questionable interrogation methods of a suspect captured in Nevada after one of the gang's heists, a Judge Robert Parker in Topeka, Kansas was said to be the true brains of the gang and gave orders to Brinkman who subsequently gave directions and orders to his "Professionals". Judge Parker was arrested in Topeka by Allan Pinkerton himself."

"Is that what they call an iron, amigo – a judge being a crook?"

"Not an iron you dunce, an irony. An iron is something you iron your…oh forget it. Here's more:

After the raid, it was made known that the marshal of Abilene, Marshal Richards took orders from Brinkman and was a no good scoundrel. He is on the run as well.

Lastly, Luke Barnes implicated a one Lillian Langtree, a.k.a. Diamond Lil as a possible thief and murder suspect for killing a person when she was associated with another gang. Rumor has it that she fled west, possibly to San Francisco, California. Pinkerton stated that more evidence was needed to be obtained before an arrest could be made.

Lillian Langtree – ole Diamond Lil."

"You know this Diamond Lil, amigo?"

"You bet I do. We had a thing going on up in Deadwood. She worked at a saloon in town, the Saloon #10. That's the one Hickok was killed in. It was a sleazy place. She was a whore - but classier than any whore I ever met. She had plans to buy the #10. That is until she shot and killed an unarmed vagrant who aggravated her to no end. She knew she was in deep trouble at the time so she packed up and left town - but not before she emptied the saloon's safe. That ole Diamond Lil was no good – classy, but no good."

Dakota paused for a few seconds, stared into the flaming campfire and said as if he was talking to himself,

"So she went to San Francisco, eh? We may have to pay her a visit and let things cool off some around these parts."

Then he woke up out of that momentary stupor and his eyes moved back toward the newspaper. He began reading again,

"Luke Barnes has plans to marry Kathleen Brinkman and settle down in Hays City where he has committed to expanding the local church and becoming a permanent minister of St. Patrick's.

After the gang was captured and some killed, Allan Pinkerton met with President Arthur and told him that he feared that there was a larger criminal

network at play here and that this capture was just the beginning. He did not have any further information on the subject and he made it clear that it was just conjecture on his part.

I don't know about any criminal network but I do know one thing."

"What's that amigo?"

Dakota stood up and started pacing back and forth cogitating about his revenge. He stopped, looked at the paper one more time, then crumpled it up and threw it into the fire.

"I'll tell you what. We're gonna form our own gang. That's right, our own gang. It will be made up of the best pistoleros in the country. We may even break some of the old gang members out of jail in Abilene. But before we break those guys out, we'll hit some of the biggest banks in the country with our new gang. We'll show the Pinkertons they can't mess with Dakota Wilson. Then when we have all the money we need, we're goin' back to Hays City and kill that yellow belly Pinkerton skunk Rusty Blake, or whatever his name is."

"And maybe Kathleen too?" Pecos asked as he unsheathed his 12 inch blade and rubbed his thumb down the side of the razor sharp edge.

"Yes Pecos, and maybe Kathleen too," Dakota said as he pulled his pistol and twirled the cylinder checking to see if it was fully loaded. Then he aimed his pistol at the flaming campfire with a demonic look on his face and said,

"Bang, you're dead Rusty Blake. Bang, you're dead Miss Kathleen."

Pecos looked at Dakota and grinned, nodding his head in agreement.

They were silent for a few minutes letting it all sink in. Then Dakota said,

"Let's get some shut-eye."

They spread out their bedrolls, removed the saddles from their horses for the purpose of using them as pillows, and threw a few more branches on the fire. Then they laid down.

It was tough to doze off – they had too much on their minds. They were both upset that they broke a Pinkerton agent out of jail thinking he would be a great addition to their gang. Rusty had not only broken up the gang, he ruined Dakota's and Pecos's opportunity to get rich beyond their "wildest dreams" as Jerod Brinkman once promised.

As they laid there with their eyes open and listening to the bone chilling serenades of coyotes all around them, Dakota said in a soft tone as if he was just mumbling to himself, but still loud enough for Pecos to hear,

"We were so close."

"So close to what, amigo?"

"So close to being richer than an east coast railroad president."

Just then they both heard a growl. It sounded like an overgrown barn cat. They heard the growl several times – it was fairly close. Then they heard a bloodcurdling scream.

"What's that?" Pecos whispered.

"It sounds like a cougar. I think it's mating season in these parts. We had a bunch of them up in the Dakota Territory. They're as mean as can be during mating season."

"I never saw a cougar – don't know anything about them," Pecos said.

"They are the biggest cats in North America. They're about eight feet long from the tip of their nose to the tip of their tail. A cougar can leap as high as 15 feet in the air and as far as 40 feet straight away. They have teeth the size of railroad spikes and jaws that can clamp down on your head as hard as a gator in the Louisiana swamps. Cougars eat large animals like deer and elk and sometimes humans if they get hungry enough – you know like during mating season. I heard tales that they especially have a craving for Mexicans – no really – there's been more Mexicans devoured alive by cougars than any other species on this land. You people must have a certain agreeable flavor about you that cougars find quite appealing."

"Ay, Dios mio."

"They say they hunt alone and when they find a worthy victim, they attack from behind, pouncing on their prey and breaking their neck by biting it at the base of the skull with those long canine teeth.

Oh it won't eat you all at one time, Pecos – no sir. You don't need to worry about that. After killing you, it will bury you and leave you, and then come back and feed on you when it gets hungry again…Sleep well now my friend," Dakota said as he grinned and closed his eyes.

Just then they heard another growl. Pecos skinned his two pistols and gripped them tightly laying them crossways on his chest. With his eyes wide open and slowly looking to his left and then slowly to his right, he whispered to himself.

"Ay, chihuahua!"

CHAPTER TWO:

The Trail to El Paso

Judge Isaac Parker
Fort Smith, Arkansas

There are several fugitives whom we believe are traveling south from Kansas, possibly through your jurisdiction. They are murderers and thieves. I will be in your area in four days. I would like to meet with you and discuss your pursuit of them. I understand you employ many marshals. I am short of men at this time and the ones I have are pursuing other criminals. Let me know what is possible.

Allan Pinkerton
Chicago, Illinois

Allan Pinkerton
Chicago, Illinois

I am at your service Mr. Pinkerton. I will be happy to hunt down those dogs and hang them, after a fair trial of course. I will meet with you as soon as you arrive in town, if I'm not in court. Otherwise I will meet with you after my trials.

Judge Isaac Parker
Fort Smith, Arkansas

The race was on. Pinkerton's health was failing, and he had a great desire to catch the remaining members of Jerod Brinkman's gang before they caused any more havoc west of the Mississippi. He knew that down the road apiece he would have to pursue this Diamond Lil, the cunning saloon and game hall high class floozy, who Rusty Blake gave up after the capture of the Brinkman gang. But for now, the Diamond Lil pursuit could wait. There really wasn't enough hard evidence yet to convict her of a crime. There was only speculation from Rusty which did warrant serious consideration – but not just yet.

Pinkerton was not aware that Dakota and Pecos were the perpetrators of the Medicine Lodge bank robbery and killing. He read about the incident in a gazette but at this point the case was being handled by the local law enforcement.

While Pinkerton was preparing to catch a train west to Fort Smith, Dakota and Pecos were breaking camp, saddling up and riding south to El Paso by way of New Mexico Territory to stay clear of the Texas Rangers. That was Dakota's idea. Besides it was more of a direct path to their destination and shaved off a few extra days versus riding south through Texas and then west to El Paso. From what Pecos remembered about El Paso, it was a lawless town - a good place to begin picking up a few new gang members.

The ride from Cimarron County to El Paso was a good 500 mile trek – some desert terrain, some mountainous regions, some rocky paths, and some barren lands. By no means was it an easy trip.

They traveled by day and slept at night. They robbed a few trading posts along the way and even killed an old-timer – the owner of the Black Water Trading Post near the first Euro-American settlement of Aqua Negra Chiquita, "Little Black River" in English, which would later become known as Santa Rosa, New Mexico Territory.

The old-timer was known as Apache Jack. He was a half-breed who refused to trade a horse with Pecos. Pecos's horse had gone lame from traveling the rough terrain. Apache Jack denied Pecos a trade – a good horse for a lamer - even though his corral was chock full of saddle-broken calicos. His refusal caused him to experience the wrath of a James Black double edged blade at the hands of Pecos.

Apache Jack was still breathing when Pecos pulled out the steel from Apache Jack's gut, and saddled up his new calico. However, the half-breed bled out before anyone else arrived. It was becoming increasingly obvious to Dakota that the more Pecos killed, the easier it became to do the despicable deed. But once again, there was no one around to witness the murder.

Pecos had one habit that surprised Dakota. Like many from the south side of the Rio Grande, Pecos was superstitious – maybe more than most. He felt that his luck or good fortune – "Buena fortuna" he would call it - came from the contents he carried in a small pouch that he kept in his left front pocket. He explained it to Dakota one night on the trail while they were sipping on some mescal, sitting around the crackling campfire south of the trading post where Pecos murdered for that calico he stole.

"One of these days you are gonna get both of us killed or hung if you keep up your reckless killing spree," Dakota said.

"Maybe you, not me amigo."

"How's that? You aren't invincible my Mexican friend. You will bleed red just like the rest of us when you get shot. If you get hung instead, I guarantee you that your neck will snap just like any other criminal when that trapdoor opens and you plunge to your demise in front of a crowd of good riddance whiskey guzzlers celebrating your departure from the human race and into the pits of hell."

"Me no think so amigo. You see, many years ago, I visited an uncle near Mexico City. I was a young chico – maybe doce."

"Doce?"

"Si, doce, you know, twelve years old. He took me to an open market. They called it el mercado de brujeria, 'the witchcraft market'."

"Witchcraft? You don't believe in that nonsense do you?"

"It is not nonsense. Mexicans come to this market many times during their lives to buy charms, potions, and herbs. These things bring Mexicans good luck."

Pecos reached into his pocket and pulled out a small pouch and held it up for Dakota to see.

"This is my good luck pouch."

"What's in your mystical pouch?" Dakota asked as he began laughing. "Voodoo magic?"

Pecos pulled out his blade and pointed it at Dakota. While staring directly into Dakota's eyes with the look of pure evil that appeared to arise right from the soul of Lucifer himself, he said,

"Don't laugh at me gringo. Don't ever laugh at me."

Dakota was taken aback. He had never seen Pecos in such a revealing defensive mode. Pecos proved on this night that he could turn on a friend quicker than a cottonmouth pit viper could sink its fangs into an unsuspecting muskrat.

"I can see you are a man of conviction, Pecos. What's in your pouch?"

"It's a combination of coyote hair, snake skin, dried gray wolf blood, pieces of dried sagehen heart, and special herbs. This mi amigo is what brings me luck. This is why I will live long. This is why I am not afraid of anyone."

Pecos sheathed his blade, then grinned and said,

"I don't know if it protects me against mating cougars though."

During the afternoon of the next day, Pecos got a quick glimpse of someone following them. His instincts had previously told him that a rider was on their tail for a few days but he actually never spotted anyone – that's why he didn't say anything about it – it was just a feeling he had. However, the feeling was that the tail was getting closer; but the hombre dogging them was keeping his distance, trying to stay out of sight.

If it was the law, he probably would have tried to overtake the two fugitives by now – at least that's what Pecos thought. He told Dakota to stay alert – just in case.

The sun was setting, so it was time to make camp. They were getting stiff in the saddle anyway. Traveling on rocky terrain will do that to a fella. You never seem to get used to it - your knees hurt, your hip joints pain, and your back gets sore and tender from your tailbone to the base of your skull. That's just how it was; there was no getting around it.

The two dismounted and began collecting wood for a fire. It gets pretty cool at night in the higher elevations of New Mexico Territory. When the fire was blazing sufficiently, Dakota removed the iron skillet from the gunnysack he still carried from Medicine Lodge and told Pecos to fetch the grub from his sack. Dakota began cooking up some strip steak and whistle berries. That's saddle tramp talk for bacon and beans.

"What are we gonna do about that dogger, Dakota?"

"We wait, but we prepare, and we stay alert."

The night was dark. There was no light from the moon because of the heavy cloud cover. Thunder was clapping in the distance after streaks of lightning flashed across the western sky.

Dakota thought it was best to build a large fire but stay in the shadows in case they had uninvited company come in on this dark night. Both kept their pistols skinned and spun their cylinders on occasion – nerves of steel were softening some – getting a little edgy too. It's one thing to square off face to face with a stranger down the middle of Main Street. It's another thing to literally be in the dark not knowing from which direction a polecat would approach from, or when.

"Drop them – now!" The stranger yelled.

It was like one second he wasn't there and then the next second, he was. It was no wonder – he was an Indian – an escapee from a reservation in the Indian Territory. He was from the central east portion, the Muscogee area, between the Cherokee Nation and the Choctaw Nation.

"I've been following you since you left 'No Man's Land'. I'm on the run from the cavalry and from the law; figure you are too. Am I right?"

"You are right amigo."

"Well then, pick up your weapons and holster them; I'm on your side. Can I have a cup of that coffee?"

"Si, you want some frijoles and sowbelly? Still some left."

The Indian nodded yes, so Pecos prepared a plate. Dakota poured him a cup of coffee, jitter juice as he would sometimes call it; that's what the caffeine did to him when he drank too much at night.

The Indian sat down and began scooping up the food like he hadn't eaten in two moons. Pecos and Dakota just stared at him and then looked at each other and smiled. This stranger was just plum hungry. That's all there was to it.

"I've been living on rattle snakes and prairie dogs the last several weeks. Good to have something different for a change."

The Indian held up a piece of half eaten sowbelly and said,

"Good food."

"Much obliged," Dakota replied. "Now, before we decide to catch some shut-eye, we'd like to know a little about the stranger we're gonna bunk with tonight - like, what's your name? Where are you from? What are you doin' out here in the middle of nowhere? And what tribe are you from? Are you Apache, Comanche, or something else? We aren't goin' anywhere so have at it and take your time if you want to."

The Indian didn't say anything until he was finished eating. In the meantime, Dakota poured himself a cup of that black as coal jitter juice while Pecos threw some more pine branches and dried wood on the fire; the mountain temperature was dropping fast. The pine crackled, popped, and sparked like someone just tossed a handful of Chinatown firecrackers on the blazing campfire.

When the Indian finished eating, he walked over to his horse, took off the blanket, laid it on the ground next to the campfire, and sat on it. He first stared into the fire for a few seconds and then began talking.

"I am a Muscogee, also known as a Creek. My name is Menewa. In English it means 'Great Warrior'. I earned that name in the old days – before reservation life. I have left the reservation like so many of my brothers before me. My father and mother died there. White-eyes took our guns, promised us food and clothing, all we needed. White-eyes lied to us. Food was scarce, clothing was little. Winters were hard. The land that was given to us to farm was not fit to grow maize. Many from my tribe died. My tribe is from the southeast. We moved to what they called the Indian Territory because of the white-eye chief called Andrew Jackson."

In fact, in 1829 President Andrew Jackson addressed a group of Creek Indians. This is what he told them:

Friends and Brothers – By permission of the Great Spirit above, and the voice of the people, I have been made President of the United States, and now speak to you as your Father and friend, and request you to listen. Your warriors have known me long. You know I love my white and red children, and always speak with a straight, and not with a forked tongue; that I have always told you the truth ... Where you now are, you and my white children are too near to each other to live in harmony and peace. Your game is destroyed, and many of your people will not work and till the earth. Beyond the great River Mississippi, where a part of your nation has gone, your Father has provided a country large enough for all of you, and he advises you to remove to it. There your white brothers will not trouble you; they will have no claim to the land, and you can live upon it you and all your children, as long as the grass grows or the water runs, in peace and plenty. It will be yours forever. For the improvements in the country where you now live, and for all the stock which you cannot take with you, your Father will pay you a fair price ...

President Jackson signed the Indian Removal Act into law on June 30, 1830 and most of the Creeks relocated in 1834 to the Indian Territory (later to become Oklahoma) during what was known as the time of the Trail of Tears.

"I have been out of the reservation before," Menewa said. "I rode as an outlaw, side-by-side with my Cherokee friend Sha-con-gah. White-eyes called him Blue Duck."

"Blue Duck?" Dakota questioned.

"Yes, you know of him?"

"I heard of him," Dakota said.

"Every outlaw west of the Mississippi and north of the Rio Grande has heard of Blue Duck. I'd say his wanted posters are in every town in Texas, the Indian Territory, New Mexico Territory, and Arkansas," Pecos said.

"Yes, Judge Isaac Parker has lawmen out searching for him and me both – more so him. We were robbers and thieves in the 70's. He hooked up with a woman thief named Belle Shirley."

"Never heard of her - heard of a Belle Starr," Dakota said.

"They are one and the same. Blue Duck and Belle Shirley were like warrior and squaw. But then she married Sam Starr and became known as Belle Starr. Me and Blue Duck joined Belle and Sam's gang. We rode with the gang for five, maybe six years. Blue Duck killed without reason. I was not like Blue Duck. I need reason to kill. We split up after so many killings without reason."

Dakota looked at Pecos after that "killing without reason" statement. Pecos looked at Dakota at the same time and grinned.

"We are forming another gang," Pecos said. "We are lookin' for good men who will help us become rich. Are you interested?"

"I will ride with you," Menewa replied.

"Good, well let's call it a night. We have a long ride ahead of us tomorrow," Dakota said.

After two more hard days on the trail, they spotted what appeared to be a small ranch down in the valley apiece just beyond some tall ponderosa timber. They could see it easy enough from the path on the ridge they were traveling along. There was a cabin, a corral with six horses, about twenty-five head of longhorns drinking from a creek that ran in front of the cabin, and a small barn about 100 feet from the bungalow. It was about dinner time and the smoke from the wood burning stove carried the aroma of something mighty-nice cooking up for supper.

"You know, I haven't had a good home cooked meal in weeks," Pecos said.

"That makes two of us," Dakota replied.

They both looked at Menewa and he nodded in the affirmative meaning he could go for a square as well.

"Well then, let's ride down there slowly and then storm the place before the food is gone," Dakota said. "Let's stay in the pines as long as possible."

The three squeezed their horses with the sides of their legs to a slow walk and began descending down the mountainside all the time keeping a keen eye out for spotters. In this part of the country, strangers could be shot on sight if they traveled off the beaten trail onto someone's property. It generally meant they were up to no good.

When they reached the edge of the pine rows, they stopped and scanned the place from left to right before they crossed the 100 foot clearing and then the creek. The creek was deeper than normal on this day - about two feet deep. Heavy rains from two days prior caused it – over 1,000 acres of watershed always created a swift flowing, swollen stream after a heavy rain. That's why the cabin was built away from the creek, and on a slight elevation.

The coast was clear; they figured everyone in the cabin must be chowing down. So with their six-shooters skinned, they dismounted and quietly walked their horses over to the corral and tied their steeds to the buck fence. It was not unusual to find buck fence corrals in these parts. The ground was too hard and rocky to sink posts, so buck fencing was the one of choice and necessity. Luckily there were plenty of pines around for fencing material.

The unknown factor was who and how many people were in the cabin; and of course, were they dangerous – caution was a wise thing at this point – carelessness could get you killed.

"What do we do now?" Pecos asked, just above a whisper.

"I guess we bust in and eat," Dakota said.

With their pistols pointing forward, they quietly walked over to the cabin. There was one step to walk up and a four foot porch to cross. Dakota led the way. As he walked toward the door, the porch wood planks squeaked loudly.

"Dang!" Dakota yelled. He knew he had no other choice now but to move fast. He put his left shoulder to the door, pushed it open, looked at the people sitting at the table, and said,

"Don't move," as he pointed his gun from person to person.

When he came out of the moment, he was shocked but relieved to see that the inhabitants of this small cabin looked helpless. It was a young family of four who were scared out of their wits. There was a feeble looking young man, the head of the household; a thin young good looking woman, most likely in her mid-twenties; and their two young daughters who were under five years old.

The look of shock and fear was written all over their faces. No one said a word at first as the helpless family just quietly stared at the intruders. Then Dakota said,

"Relax folks, no one's gonna get hurt. All we want is a good meal this evening and then a nice breakfast tomorrow morning before we head out and be on our way."

While Dakota was talking, Pecos was glancing around the cabin looking for firearms. He nodded to Menewa to fetch the double barrel shotgun that was racked above the front window. Then Pecos looked back at the young woman with lust in his eyes. She was fair-skinned with long flowing strawberry blonde hair.

She could see and easily interpret the evil passionate look in Pecos's eyes. It was worrisome – she feared the worst.

"You are a very pretty woman, senora. Your husband is a very lucky man," Pecos said.

"Relax Pecos, we're here to just get some grub in us," Dakota remarked.

The two small girls were scared speechless. The older one began crying. The young mother stood up, walked over to the girls, grabbed both by their hands and walked them over to two chairs near the fireplace and told them to sit and be still – and not to worry, as she stooped over and used her thumb to wipe away the tears running down the cheeks of the one sobbing.

"Now stay sitting here and don't move or talk," she whispered. "Everything is going to be all right."

Dakota looked at the man of the house and asked,

"What's your name?"

"I'm Jonathan Mueller. This is my wife Anna. We are immigrants from Germany. You don't need those guns. We'll feed you tonight and tomorrow."

"What are your daughters' names?" Pecos asked.

The man looked at Pecos for a few seconds and said,

"That's not important."

Anna saw the look on Pecos's face and didn't want any trouble so she walked over to the girls and looked at Pecos and said,

"The older one here is Adela, and this one is Carolyne. What are your names?"

"It's best you not know," Dakota said. "Just leave it at that."

Anna walked nervously over to the table and removed her family's plates and utensils except for her husband's. There was still food on the plates since they had just sat down to the table, said grace, and only been eating for just a few minutes before the three outlaws busted in.

She then set the table for the three uninvited guests, filled some bowls with vittles and meat from the pots on the wood burning stove, and asked the three to sit down. They did but the tension in the room remained high. Dakota tried to keep the peace and relax the family but Pecos, well, he just looked unpredictable. Menewa said nothing the whole time.

It was already becoming dark outside and Anna's objective was to get them out of the house as soon as possible after they ate. While they were chowing down, Anna said,

"Our cabin is small. You can sleep in the barn tonight. I will give you extra blankets to stay warm. There's hay in the loft that you can use for bedding to be comfortable."

"I don't think so Anna, mi amiga. I think we sleep in this warm house tonight. I think maybe you keep me plenty warm," Pecos said with an evil grin on his face.

Anna looked at Jonathan for comfort and safety, but the feeble young man was more frightened than he wanted to admit. He was helpless. He only had one arm. He lost his right arm in a logging accident the year before. He was self-conscious about it and felt that he was only half a man. Anna did most of the chores around the ranch since the accident.

Pecos knew that if his urges came to an uncontrollable level, there was no one standing in his way. At least that's what he thought. Dakota would not have any of it. In fact, Dakota told Pecos and Menewa that they were sleeping in the barn as Anna suggested. They made a thorough search of the cabin to make sure there were no more firearms left in the dwelling. They found one other weapon, a Prescott single-action six-shot Navy revolver in a .38 caliber rimfire. Jonathan had picked it up at an auction in Springfield, Missouri.

Some said it belonged to Davis Tutt, the man who Wild Bill Hickok gunned down in a duel on July 21, 1865, in the streets of Springfield, Missouri. The street fight was due to several disagreements about unpaid gambling debts, and fondness for the same woman.

But the auctioneer was a flimflam man and a tinhorn. So the intriguing story most likely was a ruse in an attempt to swindle more money from a greenhorn for an overused target pistol. Jonathan fell for the story and parted with $150 for a $30 six-shooter.

The night was long for this young terrified family; but morning came, breakfast was served, and the three outlaws were on their way with no harm done to the Mueller family. Jonathan learned a valuable lesson though. He needed to snap out of his "feeling sorry for himself" mood and learn how to draw and shoot with his good arm to protect his family against future uninvited strangers. Anna suggested they find a good guard dog to warn the family of trespassers. They both agreed this frightening incident would not change their plans to raise their family on their small dream ranch in a remote New Mexico Territory valley. On that day, Anna informed Jonathan she was three months along. He smiled, hugged her the best he could and said,

"Praise and thank the Good Lord for our blessings and safety."

While the three outlaws continued their ride south to El Paso to pick up more gang members, Pinkerton had arrived in Fort Smith, Arkansas to meet with Judge Isaac Parker, the hanging judge.

His train arrived at 9:00 a.m. He was carrying warrants for the arrests of Dakota Wilson, Pecos Fransisco, and Marshal Richards, the crooked lawman - Brinkman's puppet. The three outlaws had hightailed out of Abilene, when Pinkerton was hot on the trail of the Brinkman gang. Pinkerton had plans to meet with Judge Isaac Parker, have dinner with him that evening, and then catch a train back to Chicago.

After he got off the train, Allan Pinkerton walked over to the Shady Oak Hotel and got a room for one night. It was a brand new hotel – fancy on the inside for these parts. When Pinkerton signed in, the hotel clerk turned the logbook around and looked at the name.

"Allan Pinkerton? Say, are you the Allan Pinkerton of the Pinkerton Detective Agency?"

"That's right."

"Heard you never caught up to the James – Younger Gang. Heard they killed a lot of your men in those days. Heard…"

"Heard this place is a fleabag, but I will take a room anyway," Pinkerton said. "And I'll take it now."

The skinny little weasel behind the counter backed off real quick when he saw the fiery anger spewing from Pinkerton's eyes. The hotel clerk mentioning Pinkerton's failure to catch the James – Younger gang was like pouring sour mash Tennessee whiskey on an open wound.

"Here's your key Mr. Pinkerton. You are in room 210. It's upstairs and then down the hall to the right. It's a pleasure to have you staying here sir."

Pinkerton grabbed the key without saying a word, picked up his overnight bag and went up to his room. He had plans to seek out Judge Isaac Parker right away. When he entered his room, he threw his bag on the bed and then headed down the stairs and over to the courthouse. He knew that's where he would find the judge this time of day.

The courthouse was not difficult to locate. All he had to do was to look for Parker's infamous gallows. It was one of a kind – a killing machine. It had a beam long enough to accommodate eight convicted criminals swinging by their necks - all at one time. When that 16 foot trapdoor opened after Parker's nod from his second story office window, all eight desperados would meet their maker and judgment day when their necks snapped from the sudden plunge and abrupt stop. It was a morbid scene for some, and a picnic outing for others. It all depended on your point of view.

Pinkerton walked into the courtroom. Parker's court was in session. Two brothers were on trial. They were picked up in the Indian Territory by one of Parker's many marshals. It seemed that the two were part of a four man gang who rustled cattle and killed three drovers out of Texas who were driving cattle to the railhead in Dodge City, Kansas.

When Pinkerton walked in, Parker looked up at him and nodded. He recognized Pinkerton from a previous description and a picture he once saw of Pinkerton and Abraham Lincoln together on a Civil War battlefield. Pinkerton worked for Lincoln during the days of the Civil War.

Pinkerton nodded back to the judge and then sat down in the last row of benches. The twelve man jury had just completed deliberations. Everyone watched while the twelve paraded into the courtroom, walked in front of their chairs, and then sat down.

"Gentlemen of the jury, have you reached a verdict?"

The lead jurist stood up and said,

"Yes, we have your honor. We the jury find the defendants Billy Lane and Sam Lane guilty on one count of cattle rustling and guilty on three counts of first degree murder."

"Thank you for your hard work, jury. Would the defendants please rise? Billy Lane and Sam Lane, you two are despicable examples of the human race. Outlaws like you have no place in a civil society. For your crimes of cattle rustling and first degree murder, I sentence you both to death by hanging. The sentence will be carried out Saturday at noon with the other six who were sentenced to death earlier this week. Court dismissed," Parker said as he banged his gavel on the block.

As people were leaving the courtroom, Parker waved Pinkerton to come up front. Pinkerton made his way toward the front down the middle aisle as the rest of the crowd was exiting in the opposite direction.

"Allan Pinkerton, I presume," the judge said as he extended out his hand for a handshake.

"That's correct judge. It's a privilege to finally meet you. I heard a lot about you."

"Let's go into my chamber in back and talk. I only have about 30 minutes before the next trial begins."

When they sat down, Judge Parker behind his desk and Pinkerton in front, Parker said,

"I understand you want me to track down a few criminals. Are they of the hanging nature?"

"I'll let the jury decide that," Pinkerton said.

"You know what I mean, Pinkerton. Did they commit a capital crime?"

"Well let me explain what I have here. I have warrants for the arrest of a Dakota Wilson, a Pecos Fransisco, and a crooked marshal named Ben Richards. Dakota and Pecos were members of the Brinkman gang who were known as the 'Professionals'. You probably read or heard about that gang. And I'm sure you heard who was calling the shots for Brinkman."

"I did. I wasn't shocked to hear that it was my cousin, the Judge Parker up in Topeka. I wasn't surprised because he would always get himself in trouble when he was young. I was more astonished to hear that he was assigned as a judge up in the state of Kansas a few years ago. Whoever made that appointment was either crooked himself, received payment for the appointment, or was too ignorant to know any better. Anyway, go ahead."

"All right. Dakota and Pecos are wanted on numerous counts: robbing a Federal mint, breaking into and destroying government property in terms of Federal prisons, breaking criminals out of jail, and several counts of murder. Marshal Richards was a puppet for Brinkman so his warrant is issued as an accomplice to both robbery and murder. Now as I stated in my wire, I don't have the manpower to pursue these criminals so I would like to pass these warrants over to you and have several of your marshals hunt them down. We believe they are traveling within your jurisdiction."

"Even if they go beyond my jurisdiction, my marshals know it's OK to continue the pursuit, although I would vehemently deny that they ever heard that from me," the judge said.

"Of course," Pinkerton remarked.

"I have a marshal and two deputies in town here waiting for these warrants. They are ready to ride at a moment's notice. Their names are: Marshal John Short, and Deputy Marshals Bobby Green and Tom O'Hara. Two of them rode together in the Civil War. I don't know what side they were on. Hell, I don't really care. I don't know where they picked up the other guy from either. I needed men, and they wanted work. So I swore them in. It's as simple as that. This will be their first job. We tested out their shooting skills. All of them are quite skillful with both pistols and rifles."

"Which ones rode in the Civil War together?"

"Heck, I don't remember anymore. It doesn't really matter, now does it?"

"I guess not but not knowing their backgrounds, how do you know you can trust these guys?"

"I don't. If they turn on me, I'll hunt 'em down and hang 'em. I'll send my best marshal after them, Bass Reeves."

"I heard of him, he's a black man isn't he?"

"That's right. He was a slave until the 13th Amendment was signed by President Lincoln. But don't let the color of his skin fool you. Like I said, he's the best marshal I have.

Where are you staying?"

"Over at the Shady Oak," Pinkerton replied.

"OK, I'll have someone round them up and send them over to meet with you. My next trial is coming up in a few minutes. What do you say we meet for dinner tonight around six at the Fort Smith Steakhouse on Main Street for a steak and a few beers? It's not far from your hotel. I'd like to hear about some of your escapades around the Missouri/Kansas border back in the 70's."

"That sounds like a good plan. I will be there."

Pinkerton went back to his room and waited for the three lawmen to show. Judge Parker had another capital crime case to hear. The defendant was a half breed, part Cherokee and part Mexican. He was being tried for killing a homesteader's wife. He was brought in from the Indian Territory by Marshal Reeves.

It took about an hour but the new marshal and his two deputies finally arrived at Pinkerton's room. Pinkerton gave them the warrants and descriptions of Dakota, Pecos and Richards and told them they were probably headed into Texas. The three lawmen saddled up and headed south.

Later that evening Pinkerton and Parker met for dinner as planned. After they placed their steak order and ordered two mugs of beer produced in a local brewery just outside of town, Judge Parker pointed to three men sitting at a table eating dinner on the other side of the room.

"Do you know who those three men are?" Judge Parker asked.

"Have no clue," Pinkerton said.

"Those three are Scott Johnson, Thomas O'Brien, and Jesse Caldwell. They introduced themselves to me earlier today. They're pretty famous people. They're known as the *Three for Hire*."

"Yes, I have heard of them. What are they doing here in Fort Smith?"

"They're just passing through. They're on a mission for the President of the United States."

Just then the waitress brought the judge and Pinkerton their beers and distracted them by tossing around some trivial small talk. In the meantime the *Three for Hire* left the payment for their meals on the table and walked out the side door. When the waitress walked away from Pinkerton and the judge, Pinkerton picked up his mug, and while taking a sip, he looked over to the *Three for Hire's* table, but they were gone. He was disappointed - he wanted to meet them.

During dinner, Pinkerton told Parker about how he took out Brinkman's gang. He told him that he informed the President of the United States that he thought there was a major criminal network working the land – in fact, he was sure of it.

Dakota and Pecos were leaving a trail of fear on their way to El Paso. Word was now out in every major town west of the Mississippi that two murdering thieves were on the loose. Sketches of them were on wanted posters hanging in every law office and post office throughout Kansas, Arkansas, the Indian Territory, and Texas.

Pinkerton had read about the killing and bank robbery in Medicine Lodge. He also later read about a young ranch family who was held hostage for two days by two drifters matching the description of Dakota and Pecos. The article also stated that an Indian was riding with the two desperados. Nothing was known about him.

Judge Parker had a system worked out with newer marshals. They were to wire him every three days of their whereabouts. If Parker had any information on the lowlife who his lawmen were tracking, he would wire that information to his marshals. Six days out, after hearing from Marshal Short, Parker wired him back the news of the hostage taking in the New Mexico Territory, and his speculation of the outlaws' destination.

Parker figured the criminals, who his men were after, were involved in the hostage affair. Looking at the large map hanging on the wall in his office, he traced the movement of the two outlaws: Abilene to Medicine Lodge, and Medicine Lodge, Kansas to a remote town in eastern New Mexico Territory. His wild guess was they were heading to the lawless town of El Paso, Texas. That's where many desperados went when running from the law. In fact, it was a dangerous place for lawmen to be. He also added in his communication that they picked up an Indian on the trail. There was no information about his identity.

Since the three lawmen were already halfway through the Indian Territory, they planned to ride to the Texas Panhandle and turn south at a ranching community which was known as Amarillo. Then they would travel through Old Lubbock near Yellow House Canyon, and Odessa (founded in 1881 as a water stop and cattle-shipping point on the Texas and Pacific Railway). From there they would head west to El Paso, a small town along the Rio Grande.

After that last telegram, Judge Parker did not hear from his three lawmen for weeks. He had no clue as to why – but he was willing to give them the benefit of the doubt – at least for now. As far as he knew, the three lawmen were on their way to El Paso.

Up to the time of the Civil War, El Paso was mainly populated by Mexicans. But when the War ended in 1865, people began spreading out, looking for new farmland, and new cattle grazing pastures; or just some place different to take off their boots and hang their hats. Anglo Texans began moving into the area, and they soon became the majority.

El Paso was situated along the Rio Grande, just a stone's throw from the Mexican border. It was incorporated in 1873. The population began booming with the arrival of the railroads: the Southern Pacific; the Atchison, Topeka and Santa Fe; and the Texas and Pacific. The small town was growing fast. It became a melting pot of nationalities: Anglo-Americans, recent European immigrants, old Hispanic settlers, and Mexicans who were crossing the river to find work and greener pastures.

The mixture of nationalities, the rapid population growth, the railroads, the saloons, brothels and gambling houses, and the location of the town, all contributed to El Paso becoming violent and lawless. It earned its reputation as the "Six-Shooter Capital" of the West.

After a few weeks on the trail, Dakota, Pecos, and Menewa finally arrived in El Paso. Pecos was familiar with the area because he had been there before. Buildings were pretty much scattered around with very little organization. Main Street was buzzing with a lot of small saloons – nothing fancy – just drinking holes.

When they were riding through town to the hotel, they spotted the marshal's office. It was temporarily boarded up though. Dakota, Pecos, and Menewa rode up to the Railroad Stop Hotel, dismounted, hitched their horses to the rail and walked up the six wooden steps to the front door. They weren't surprised to see three soiled doves at the door to greet them.

"Not now ladies, we just got off the trail. Maybe after a bath and a shave," Dakota said.

The three signed in using their real names – didn't see any reason not to – not in this town – not under the current circumstances. It appeared this town was wide open since the marshal's office was closed down.

"Senor, why is the marshal's office boarded up?" Pecos asked the hotel clerk.

"The marshal was shot in the back of his neck with a double barrel shotgun loaded with buckshot while playing poker in the Alamo Saloon – dang near blew off his head. The scuttlebutt was that it was the killing machine by the name of Deacon Miller who gunned him down. That's what was said right after the shooting.

The poor cuss didn't have a chance. Oh he wasn't much of a lawman anyway. All he did all day long was to sit in that smelly saloon down the street, playing poker or faro, and drinking rye – couldn't hold his liquor to save his soul. It seems he got on the wrong side of the Deacon one day. Whatever he did or said, the Deacon didn't take kindly to it. Matter of fact, the Deacon didn't take kindly to much of anything anyone did or said.

Some say he's the devil himself, that Beelzebub character you read about in the Good Book, you know, the Bible. Some say a slithering snake crawled right out of the pits of hell and took on a human form," the clerk said slowly while leaning forward as he looked straight into the eyes of Pecos - almost like a preacher behind a podium preaching fire and brimstone on a Sunday morning in the Appalachians.

Then the clerk looked to the left and then to the right. Pecos did the same as did the Indian. Pecos and Menewa did it as a reaction to an action. The clerk did it for effect.

"Some say he can pick up a handful of rattlers and hold them right up to his face and the snakes won't bite him or even so much as to hiss at him because, some say he's not only one of them, he's their leader."

The clerk momentarily had Pecos in a trance – like a voodoo spell. After wiping the sweat from his brow, ole Pecos pulled out his lucky pouch and began squeezing it as he quietly said under his breath, "Ay, chihuahua."

Dakota looked at Pecos and said,

"Come on Pecos, snap out of it."

Then he looked back at the hotel clerk and said,

"Give us our room keys preacher man."

"Here you go. Your three rooms are together: 214, 215, and 216. They're upstairs. You'll find them easy enough. And Pecos, I haven't seen him lately but some say the Deacon is still in town. He hides in the shadows – so watch your back."

The clerk actually believed all of those frightening stories about Deacon Jim Miller, and he could see that Pecos was a believer now as well.

"By the way friend, where can three saddle bums pick up a good square tonight?" Dakota asked the clerk.

"No place has better food than right across the street. It's called, 'Mollie's'. She fries up a tasty beef steak."

Dakota looked at Pecos and Menewa and said,

"Well then, let's meet in a couple of hours over at Mollie's, say six o'clock. I'm gonna find a place to get a shave and a bath before then."

"There's a bath in back of the barbershop. They have hot water, and regular soap, or that sweet smellin' soap. It's from France," the clerk said.

"I'll use the regular soap. I'm not lookin' to smell like no saloon whore," Dakota replied.

"I think I will take a walk around town," Menewa remarked. "I'll take our horses to the livery stable."

"Wait, let me give you a few bucks," Dakota said as he reached into his pocket, pulled out a wad, flipped through it and handed a few greenbacks to Menewa. Dakota then looked at Pecos and asked,

"What about you Pecos? What's your plan?"

"I'll be in my room, maybe with one of those pretty senoritas."

Dakota got his bath and shave and then went back to his room for a short snooze. After he was resting for about thirty minutes, the hotel clerk began frantically banging on his door. Dakota jumped out of bed, still groggy from his nap, reached for his pistol that was holstered and hanging on his bedpost and yelled,

"Who's there?"

"It's the hotel clerk, open up, quickly!"

Dakota rushed over to the door, turned the key and opened it.

"What's the problem?"

"It's your Indian friend! They're hanging him!"

"What?"

"They're hanging him down by the livery stable. He got into a fight with a guy in the saloon. He didn't start it, but he finished it – stabbed the guy three times and killed him. That's what someone just told me. You better hurry up if you want to save your friend."

Dakota quickly knocked on Pecos's door. He knew Pecos was with a fallen angel. So he yelled from the hallway,

"Get up, get dressed, and grab your hogleg – do it now! They're hanging Menewa down by the livery stable! I'm headed down there now!"

Dakota ran down the stairs, out the door, down the front steps and toward the livery stable. But when he was halfway down the street, a group of about ten men were walking back up the street. They were headed back to the saloon.

Most were all liquored-up, a couple still holding half empty bottles of whiskey, and they were all laughing. Dakota stopped dead in his tracks when he looked toward the livery stable and saw Menewa swinging from a rope tied around the board protruding out from the top of the loft door. Menewa was already dead.

"Dang!" Dakota said as he took off his hat and hit his leg with it in disgust.

"Dagnabbit! What kind of town is this?" Dakota shouted out loud.

"It's a lawless town, mi amigo," Pecos said as he walked up behind Dakota.

They both stood there and stared at the poor Creek, swinging in the wind. Then Dakota said, "I'll cut him down, go see if you can find an undertaker."

Dakota walked down to the stable, climbed up the ladder inside to the hayloft, and cut Menewa down. Menewa's lifeless body hit the ground hard. Dakota then climbed back down and drug Menewa's body into the stable, and waited for Pecos to come back with the undertaker.

"I reckon he's a friend of yours," the stable hand said.

"That's right," Dakota responded.

"Well if it's any consolation, I heard he killed that other guy in self-defense. Unfortunately that other guy was kinfolk to a bunch of those drunks who hung him. Was he Apache?"

"No, he was a Creek."

"Don't know nothin' about Creeks," the stable hand said.

"Well neither do I."

Pecos and the undertaker rode up in a wagon. Dakota paid him the burial fees and that was the end of that.

"What are we gonna do about this?" Pecos asked.

"Nothing. I'm not lookin' for trouble with that hanging mob. We hardly knew the Creek anyway. Let's go get one of those beef loin chops over at Mollie's and forget about this. We have other things to worry about."

One of the other things to worry about, which Dakota referred to, was being tracked down by the law. At this point they figured they were still being chased by Pinkerton and his law dogs, as Pecos would call them. They had no idea that the hanging judge was now involved and sent out three of his lawmen to track them down and drag them in for their fair trial and then their hanging. If they knew that, there is no way they would have planned to spend the next two weeks in El Paso signing up new gang members. When that project was completed, they intended to make a trip to San Francisco to visit an old friend of Dakota's, the ever so classy, Diamond Lil.

Before they began recruiting, they thought it was savvy to just hang around town, mingle with some drifters in several of the not so swanky saloons, to get a read on possibilities before putting sidewinders like themselves on the payroll. They weren't interested in overenthusiastic elbow-benders, or bloviaters - the kind who talked more than they listened. That went for bloviating with their six-shooting hoglegs too before rational cogitation was applied first – a loose rein was not a welcome saddle pardner. They weren't looking for any button bucks either. No sir, they needed men who were middle-aged, steady thinkers, and straight shooters. All of those prerequisites meant that they needed to take their time and do the job right.

However, on their sixth day in town, an unexpected turn of events befell on them in the form of hard cold steel pressed to their craniums.

It was just past midnight. The streets were cleared. The Texas night was steaming hot and uncomfortably humid – typical of Texas river towns. So it was a sure bet that every room in the hotel had its windows propped wide open.

Marshal John Short, and his deputies Bobby Green and Tom O'Hara just rode into town. They had made temporary night camp one mile outside of town until they figured the town's night-lifers had called it a day. They hitched their horses in front of the Railroad Stop Hotel and slowly made their way to the front counter. There was no one in sight. The guest book was closed, but it was sitting right there – in plain sight.

Marshal Short opened the book to the current page and saw the room numbers where Dakota and Pecos were staying. He noticed that the name "Menewa" was crossed out but that didn't mean anything to him. After he found the names he was searching for, he closed the book, turned around, and said to his deputies as he skinned his six-shooter and twirled and eyed the cylinder,

"Their doors are probably locked, I doubt if there are any extra keys around here so we'll climb up on the balcony porch and crawl through their windows. I'll take Dakota in room 214, you two take Pecos in room 215. Remember, we need them alive. Make sure you're as quiet as a cat. We don't want any gunplay."

They looked at a piece of paper on the counter that had a layout of the rooms and determined where the two outlaws were located. Dakota and Pecos were sleeping – out like a light. They spent half the night over at one of the saloons in town drinking cheap liquor and as a result, had problems finding the keyholes to lock their doors when the time came for them to bunk down. But they did, and they were both stretched out in minutes and sawing wood.

The three lawmen had no problems climbing into their windows and sticking the barrels of their revolvers against the drunken cheekbones of the two outlaws. Both Dakota and Pecos were startled and reached for their pistols, but the lawmen had already confiscated them.

The deputies walked Pecos over to Dakota's room and knocked on the door.

"Open your door," the marshal said to Dakota as he held the gun on him.

While Dakota stumbled over to the door to let Pecos and the two deputies in, the marshal lit the lantern.

Then the marshal ordered the two outlaws to sit on the bed. The three lawmen then lined up shoulder to shoulder facing the two with their guns pointed directly at the heads of Dakota and Pecos. The two outlaws were close enough to the pistols to see the bullets in the cylinders. No matter how tough of an hombre you are, a loaded gun pointed at your head, close enough to smell the black powder residue in the barrel, is an ominous situation for anyone.

"What's the meaning of this?" Dakota asked. "And who are you guys?"

"I'm Marshal Short and these are my two deputies, Green and O'Hara. We're lawmen for Isaac Parker out of Fort Smith – you know – the hanging judge."

Dakota and Pecos looked at each other. They just came to their senses. They realized their carefree and criminal lifestyle had just come to an abrupt ending. But then the marshal holstered his pistol and so did his deputies and all three began laughing.

"What's so dang blasted funny?" Dakota asked.

"You are Dakota and Pecos, right?" The marshal asked.

"Obviously you know who we are," Dakota replied.

"You belonged to the Brinkman gang, did you not?" The marshal asked.

"It's obvious you know that too," Pecos said.

"Well, so do we. Only it's not the same Brinkman. We belong to the gang led by his brother, Cole Brinkman. We tracked you down to bring you into the fold – back into the organization – you know, the network."

"The network? What are you talkin' about?" Dakota asked. "Wait a minute. I read that Pinkerton's theory was that there was a criminal network working the West and Midwest. You mean to tell me he was right – there really is a network?"

"That's right my friend. You were part of it just like we are - except for one thing - your boss was not quite as canny as ours. Your boss got himself killed along with most of his gang members, and the ones who weren't killed are now in jail and waiting for trial. If they go to trial, they're gonna be hung. We're not gonna let that happen. They're too valuable to the organization. We have plans to break them out of jail and bring them back into the fold. You don't need to know any other particulars right now except that Mr. Brinkman is gonna make us rich beyond our wildest dreams."

Dakota looked at Pecos and said, "Where have we heard that before?"

Then Dakota looked back at the marshal and said,

"Say, how does Judge Isaac Parker play into all of this? Is he one of us too?"

The three began laughing. "No, we hornswoggled the sap and took his money – and we used him to find you two," O'Hara said.

"That's right. In fact, I have a free grubstake for you two compliments of the judge," Short said.

Short reached into his pocket and pulled out a wad of greenbacks and counted them out. "Here's $500 for each of you, compliments of Judge Isaac Parker." The marshal handed $500 to each, and Dakota and Pecos grinned from ear to ear.

"What now mis amigos?" Pecos asked.

"There are a couple of things. First, the organization has a code. If there's a traitor in our midst, the code is to kill him. You had a traitor in your organization. We know all about him. He was your safecracker. You knew him as Rusty Blake; his real name is Luke Barnes. He's currently living in Hays City, Kansas. He's the town preacher now. The organization wants you two to kill him. But we will tell you when. Understood?"

"Yeah, I got ya. It will be our pleasure. I can guarantee you the preacher will be hearing ole Gabe's horn the minute we lay eyes on him. What else?" Dakota asked.

"We want you to meet at our hideout in about three to four months. It's outside of Pueblo, Colorado. When you get to Pueblo, hang out – don't look for us – we'll find you. We're planning a pretty big job in about five months. You're gonna be part of it. That gives us time to break your old gang members out of jail and bring them in as well. In the meantime, lay low and keep dodging the law."

"We have plans to take a trip to San Francisco and look up an old friend," Dakota said.

"Who's your old friend?" Short asked.

"You wouldn't know her."

"Try me."

"She's known as Diamond Lil. Her real name is Lillian Langtree. She's as crooked as an Osage fence post. Do you know her?"

"No – don't know her personally – heard of her though.

Green, I want you to hang with Dakota and Pecos. O'Hara, you come with me. We'll head back to Pueblo," Marshal Short said.

And so Short and O'Hara rode out of town. They made camp on the outskirts of El Paso before they headed back to Pueblo.

Pueblo, Colorado is located on the confluence of the Arkansas River and Fountain Creek (a tributary of the Arkansas River) and just over 100 miles south of Denver. It doesn't get much snow there in the winter because the area is considered a semi-dry desert land. Although Pueblo was once a lawless town, things have changed drastically and now it is an agricultural town of sorts. Law and order prevail.

Like his felonious brother, Jerod Brinkman, Cole Brinkman was a prominent businessman. He was tall at 6'1", well built, well groomed, sported a goatee, and was considered quite handsome by the ladies. Brinkman concealed his criminal activities in plain sight but he also concealed his identity. He used an alias. He was gentle as a lamb on the outside, but as mean as a venomous spitting cobra on the inside, and as aggressive as a Louisiana swamp cottonmouth when it came to seeking out wealth and power.

Like his younger brother Jerod, he had no problem killing anyone who got in the way of his excessive greed. The question which would eventually be asked in good time was, how many more brothers were there in the Brinkman's snake pit to wreak death, horror, and destruction throughout the new frontier?

CHAPTER THREE:

Diamond Lil's Crystal Palace

"Here's your draft for $50,000, Mr. Brennen. I deposited the money this morning in a special account over at the First National Bank of San Francisco. Your client, the owner of the building, can cash the draft at any time."

"Thank you, Miss Langtree, and here are your keys from the owner. I was surprised he came down so much on his price – but he did, and now you can begin to build your dream. I'm anxious to see how you turn that empty warehouse into a fancy gaming and dance hall saloon. Have you decided on a name for it yet?"

"Yes I have, Mr. Brennen. I'm calling it, Diamond Lil's Crystal Palace. Has sort of a nice ring to it doesn't it?"

"It sure does."

Good ole Diamond Lil – a classy lady larger than life. Diamond Lil was determined to get back into the saloon and dance hall business upon her arrival in San Francisco, which was immediately after she point-blank and cold-bloodedly shot and killed her manager, Tommy Schaefer and threw his lifeless body into the Smoky Hill River. Oh if that river could talk.

She had plenty of money to do whatever she wanted. She heisted a half a million bucks from the Smoky Hill River Gang's loot before their demise, which she single-handedly set up herself back in Ellsworth, Kansas.

Lil always had high aspirations. She was a classy lady – classier than most – and her establishment would mirror and compliment her stylish looks. Her institution would be one of a kind. Oh, you could find some of those fancy saloon and gaming houses in Dodge City, all right; that's for sure. And then there was the Oriental in Tombstone where Wyatt dealt faro and which was boasted as the fanciest saloon west of the Mississippi. But Diamond Lil wasn't about to settle for second best – no sir – she had plans to build an establishment like no other – the best in the west. And the best in the west would be right in the heart of the growing metropolis known as San Francisco.

San Francisco: the City by the Bay, the City that Knows How, the Paris of the West.

It all started on January 24, 1848 when a foreman named James W. Marshall, who was working for John Sutter, found an interesting piece of shiny metal at a lumber mill on the American River. Marshall took it to Sutter and they privately had it tested. They tried to keep their results a secret but it was not to be.

Word got to Samuel Brannan, a San Francisco newspaper publisher and local merchant, by March of the same year. Being a sharp businessman, he quickly set up a store to sell prospecting tools and supplies. Then he strode through the streets of San Francisco holding high a glass jar of gold while shouting at the top of his voice, loud and often, "Gold! Gold! Gold from the American River!" The shouts were heard across the country and beyond the depths of the great blue oceans.

On August 19th, in the two-cent Saturday morning edition of the *New York Herald*, on page one in column two, which was under the subject title, "Affairs in Our New Territory", it read:

"I am credibly informed that a quantity of gold worth in value, $30 was picked up lately in the bed of a stream in the Sacramento."

This was the first announcement in the East of the discovery of gold in California. Four months later, on December 5, 1848, President James Polk addressed Congress and confirmed the discovery of gold in California. Soon the birth of the forty-niners manifested itself with a great migration to the Golden State. San Francisco became a hub for a growing population and commerce. The population grew from about 1,000 in 1848 to 25,000 in 1850.

They first came from the closest scarcely populated frontier lands of the West, then from Mexico, Chile, Peru, and other South American countries. Then they arrived from China, Italy, and Spain and docked their ships in the San Francisco Harbor. They came from everywhere to find their fortunes and endeavor to become rich beyond their wildest dreams. They came by land and by sea, over mountains and through rough waters. Many made it, but some didn't. The ones that did not, well, they died from accidents, and from diseases like cholera, fever, dysentery, and the likes.

They thought they could just pick up their fortunes right off the ground and place them in a bucket. At first it was almost that easy - they panned, and panned successfully. But then when the easy pickings were gone, it became tougher. The only way to gather gold then was to mine it. You needed both money and labor to do that. Mining companies sprung up all around California. The population grew and grew and many went to work for those companies.

In the years following the great migration into the Bay City, crime ran rampant – the social climate was disgraceful and chaotic at best. Political corruption was the norm. This uncontrolled environment gave birth to vigilante committees in 1851 and again in 1856 which cleaned up the city and undesirable elements with lynchings, kidnappings and forced government resignations.

Eventually law and order was established – at least somewhat. San Francisco had a red-light district during this time period which became known as the Barbary Coast. It was a center and hotbed for prostitution, saloons, gambling, and shanghaiing.

Benjamin Estelle Lloyd wrote about this den of iniquity in his printed work entitled, *Lights and Shades of San Francisco,* (Publisher: Printed by A.L. Bancroft, 1876, ©1875.) In it he wrote:

"The Barbary Coast is the haunt of the low and the vile of every kind. The petty thief, the house burglar, the tramp, the whoremonger, lewd women, cutthroats, murderers, all are found here. Dance-halls and concert-saloons, where blear-eyed men and faded women drink vile liquor, smoke offensive tobacco, engage in vulgar conduct, sing obscene songs and say and do everything to heap upon themselves more degradation, are numerous. Low gambling houses, thronged with riot-loving rowdies, in all stages of intoxication, are there. Opium dens, where heathen Chinese and God-forsaken men and women are sprawled in miscellaneous confusion, disgustingly drowsy or completely overcome, are there. Licentiousness, debauchery, pollution, loathsome disease, insanity from dissipation, misery, poverty, wealth, profanity, blasphemy, and death, are there. And Hell, yawning to receive the putrid mass, is there also."

Eventually though, things began to change. From the 1860's to the 1880's the city began to clean up and expand in all directions, creating many new business districts and neighborhoods. It transformed into a major metropolis, a city of wealth, commerce, banking and entertainment. San Francisco became aptly known as the "Paris of the West".

Diamond Lil purchased a warehouse just on the outskirts of the Barbary Coast. She had looked at the site for quite a while before she bought it. What she liked about it was the location and especially the fact that it was large and it was empty. It was the cost that kept her from grabbing it immediately. She had this great vision of what she wanted the interior of her Crystal Palace to be – so elaborate and ornate, that it would be the talk of San Francisco and the entire country. It would be host to the likes of business elite, politicians, and wealthy entrepreneurs. It would be a gaming house, a saloon, and dance hall all in one.

Her wish list added up to big bucks. Being a pragmatic person of sorts, she figured for every dollar shaved off the asking price for the warehouse, it would be an extra dollar she could use to fancy-up her establishment. She eventually persuaded the owner to take the price down from $65,000 to $50,000. It was a little more than just sweet talking that enabled her to negotiate a $15,000 price decrease. "Whatever it takes", she told the owner over a bottle of champagne. The contract was signed early the next morning, and that was that. Diamond Lil got her building.

Diamond Lil knew she needed a partner who could take care of himself and her as well, and to help coordinate and manage her business. So she sent word to a longtime acquaintance and partner in past crimes - a gunman, ex-saloon owner, and business entrepreneur, Bret Stone.

Stone was working as a gaming house bouncer in Deadwood at the time he received the telegram from Lil. She promised him a good salary and a good time. Stone dropped what he was doing in Deadwood and immediately boarded a train to San Francisco.

In the meantime, Lil worked with an architect and an interior designer to layout her Crystal Palace. She had worked in many dance halls and gaming houses in her day so she had a reasonable idea of what she wanted. Before she even met with the two people who would help her design her establishment, she drew a rough sketch of the Palace. But her design was quite rudimentary at best compared to what her fastidious architect and interior designer had in mind. Both of these individuals were bona fide professionals who learned their crafts in France, and came to America, specifically the Bay Area, to take full advantage of the robust expansion and financial rewards available in their fields of endeavor. Diamond Lil was fortunate to discover these men of extraordinary talents.

After breakfast together at a quaint little café about three blocks away from Lil's to be Crystal Palace, the three hurriedly walked over to the warehouse to begin discussions on the interior layout. It was cloudy, misty and quite chilly on that morning. The warehouse was cold and damp as well - it had been vacant for about fifteen months with no heat or fresh air. There was a slight leak in the roof on the south corner and a musty odor coming from that direction. But that was the least of Diamond Lil's worries. Her biggest challenge was to transform this empty building into an extravagant palace.

Steven, the interior designer, and Robert, the architect, both had prior entry into the building and collaborated on their ideas previous to this first joint meeting with Lil. So they were there today to begin sharing some of their preliminary thoughts with Lil.

As they stood in the middle of this 15,625 square foot empty building, Lillian said,

"Well gentlemen, here we are. I hired you to do your magic. You know what I want, so who wants to begin?"

"I will," the architect said.

"Well then Robert, have at it honey."

"Yes ma'am. I must tell you Lil, I am really excited about the potential of this project. Just look at it. This building is a perfect square, 125 feet by 125 feet. It's large enough to give us a lot to work with. We can get as creative as we want and, of course, as luxurious as you want.

First, I'm happy to say that the building is structurally sound; that's good news. No repairs are needed here, except for that slight leak in the roof. I love the fact that there is a partial second floor which will accommodate three offices and adequate living quarters for two people, you plus one other of your choice. You won't have to spend money building an upstairs area.

Now, let's start with the simple stuff first then move on to the larger things. Look back toward the front. We'll leave the entrance on the street side and put two banks of double doors in the front. They can be used for both entering and leaving the Palace.

Now picture this. When you walk into the front doors and look straight ahead toward the back of the building, you'll see the entertainment stage at the other end in all its glory."

With enthusiasm in his voice, he said,

"Here's the way I see it, Miss Lillian. The stage will be elevated five feet off the floor so everyone in the Palace can see it without any obstructions. In front of the stage will be the orchestra.

Can't you just see those can-can girls kicking up their legs and the patrons yelling in jubilation with every kick?"

Lil smiled as she was getting her own kick out of watching Robert display an abundance of passion for his submissions.

"Well honey, I'm doing more than just having can-can girls kicking up their legs, pulling up their ruffled skirts, flashing their black stockings and drawers, and then doing cartwheels across the stage. I'm putting on all sorts of productions that will run almost every hour we're open for business, like: solo singers, chorus singers, and male acts, you know, acrobats, comics, and magicians - those types of performances and they'll be nonstop. We'll show the world of entertainment how it's done. That's what I'm talking about honey. Now you can continue, my dear," Lillian said.

Even after Lil's slightly amusing corrective interruption, Robert would demonstrate he was really in his element. He became so enthusiastic and animated you would have thought he was designing his own Crystal Palace. He passionately gestured with every suggestion he offered.

"OK Lil, this is great. You have more than enough room to make the stage as large as you want, but here's how I see it. The stage should be fifty-five feet long, centered between both walls, and rounded on the ends in front for a stylist European look. That will leave thirty-five feet on both sides of the stage. There will be stairways on both ends of the stage for the can-can girls to walk down and mingle with the crowd after their performances, or sing while they are walking between the tables. You get the idea, I'm sure. The stairways will start straight out to the sides and then curve toward the front.

There will be a large red velvet curtain which will hide the backstage. Steven will talk about that in a few minutes. The main stage will be fifteen feet in depth. That's about what we do in Europe. Behind the curtain there will be twelve feet of space, I'm talking depth again, from the curtain to the back wall. We'll section off dressing rooms for the girls, and a small one for the men. We'll also save space for a costume room."

"Will twelve feet be enough space for a backstage?" Lillian asked.

"Oh yes ma'am, twelve feet depth is plenty because the backstage will be the whole width of the building, one hundred twenty-five feet wide.

Do you concur with everything I have covered so far, Miss Lillian?" Robert asked.

"I do, and I love everything honey. What's next?"

"The bar is next. This will be another focal point in your Palace. You do not want to spare any expense here. In relation to the entrance, the bar will be on the right side of the building. I see the bar being fifty feet in length. We'll center it between the front of the building and the front of the stage. That means there will be twenty-four feet of free space on both ends."

Robert brought an album book which contained pictures of saloon bars designed and built by an eastern, master woodworker who he friended and used several times on other projects. They weren't just ordinary type bars found in a trail's end railhead town saloon in Kansas. No sir, they were the most ornate and artistic wooden structures one could ever imagine. The master craftsman not only built the long bars, but the decorative structures behind them as well, inserting banks of mirrors with wooden arched tops, and shelves across the bottom, three feet high in front of the six foot tall mirrors, to hold hundreds of bottles of liquor, wine, and champagne. You could pick your species of seasoned wood: oak, walnut, maple, or mahogany. He had access to it all. And if you had a preference for a color of stain, he could produce that color with no problem - although dark was in vogue at the present.

Lil took her time paging through the book of pictures. Then it hit her like a bolt of lightning.

"This one, this one right here is the one I want," Lil said.

"Let's see," Robert said as he reached over and removed the book from Lillian's hands.

"I should have known. You certainly have class ma'am. This one is the most elaborate and most expensive one in the book. It was built in a ritzy establishment in Williamsburg County, South Carolina. I've seen it myself. It's a beauty! The cost of building this whole unit is about $6,500."

"I can handle that. It's definitely the one I want. I want it in that same color and wood shown here."

"All right then, mahogany it is. I'll have the carpenter ship in the materials. I'll take care of everything. He'll build it and stain it right here on site. By the way, I'm planning it to be a stand-up bar with a bronze foot rail. You can add stools any time if you want."

"Sounds good to me, what's next honey?" Lil asked.

"I believe we need to talk about the gaming area now."

"That's good, but we need to speed things up a bit. I have an appointment with the mayor and my lawyer this afternoon regarding the same topic. That sweet little mayor promised to issue me a special permit to allow in-house gambling. The plan is to sign the papers this afternoon that will make all forms of gambling legal in the Crystal Palace for the next ten years. He was a pushover. All I had to do was to show some charm, a little skin, wink, give him a dirty little smile, and I got everything I asked for."

"That sounds encouraging, but borders on being a bit naughty. However, whatever it takes," Steven, the interior designer remarked as he cleared his throat – a voluntary alternative to…hmmm. Then Robert continued,

"Well OK then, I drew up the gaming area on the left side of the building, opposite the bar, right over here. Obviously you can choose the gaming of your choice but here is what I recommend based on my experiences and the room available: two dice tables, two roulette tables, two blackjack tables, three faro tables, several poker tables, and two billiard tables. All of these things will fit with ease in the space allowed. Can you think of anything else you want in this area?"

"Yes, I am going to need a banking area to 'give-out and cash-in' chips and exchange money."

"I have that all figured out. That will go on the gaming side up towards the stage."

"Against the wall?"

"That's right Miss Lillian, against the wall. We'll have enough room for three cashiers and a safe there."

"Make sure you order a safe that can't be cracked, honey."

"Miss Lillian, I assure you, the safes I order cannot be cracked."

"Don't bet on it…I knew this guy in Ellsworth…never mind."

"OK then, the last thing I have is the seating in the center of the room. I believe the bank of tables in the middle should be a group of tables that seat 8's, 6's, 4's, and a few 2's. In that way we can efficiently accommodate many different group sizes. How do you feel about that, Miss Lillian?"

"Darling, I like everything you've covered so far. I think that takes care of the layout, doesn't it?"

"Yes ma'am. We'll go upstairs when Steven gets done with his suggestions."

"OK Steven, you're up sweetie. Throw your magic my way."

"Yes ma'am. Well, are you familiar with the Nob Hill Mansions? By the way, that nob is not spelled like a doorknob. It's spelled, n...o...b."

"Well thanks for clearing that up, darling. I was wondering what a doorknob had to do with a mansion. Yes, I saw them, but I don't know much about them except, they are the dang biggest homes I have ever seen, if they are indeed homes."

"Oh they are indeed, Miss Lillian, and I had some involvement in designing the interior in one of them which I believe could have some application to what we do here. Do I have time to give you a bit of history of those four mansions sitting on top of Nob Hill?"

"Honey, whoever lives in those mansions could 'give me and get me' a lot of business. So yes, Steven, I have the time."

"OK then, the word nob means a person of wealth or high social status. So the term Nob Hill gets its name from the people who built the mansions there on the hill located on California, Powell, Pine and Mason Streets. Before the 1850's that location was called California Hill after the street's name and because of the elevation there. The view of the city, the bay, and surroundings from the Hill are marvelous. The location was renamed Nob Hill after the wealthy Big Four built their mansions there. Do you know who the Big Four are, Miss Lillian?"

"No I don't. Who are they?"

"They are the ones who built the west wing of the Transcontinental Railroad. They are Huntington, Stanford, Hopkins, and Crocker. They owned the Central Pacific Railroad and bought the Southern Pacific Railroad Company as well. They are four of the richest men in the country and their mansions reflected their wealth and status and from on top of the Hill, they could look down on the little people I suppose – but that's conjecture on my part," Steven said. Then he continued,

"Leland Stanford built the first palace in 1874. I was the interior designer for him and I can use some of those applications here. His home cost two million dollars to build.

Mark Hopkins built the second mansion. The story goes that Mr. Hopkins was a simple man with simple tastes and he told his wife Mary, 'I have all the money in the world. You can build a combination of Buckingham Palace and the Petit Trianon as long as you are happy'. The mansion was started in 1875 and cost one and a half million dollars. It took three years to build. Mr. Hopkins actually died before it was completed. It's the gothic style with that somber gray-black color. I haven't been in that mansion but I hear the interior is decorated with rare woods and frescoes."

"What's a fresco?" Lillian asked.

"Oh, it's something I will be proposing to do here. A fresco is a painting done quickly in watercolor on wet plaster on a wall or a ceiling, so that the colors penetrate the plaster and become fixed as it dries."

"Are you going to suggest we plaster these walls?"

"Oh yes ma'am. That's a must. Getting back to the Hopkins mansion, here is a side note that has no relevance to anything other than it is quite amusing. When Mr. Hopkins passed away, Mrs. Hopkins fell in love with her interior decorator, my friend, Edward Searles. Edward was a bit of a con artist, a swindler of sorts. I was told he earned favor with Mrs. Hopkins because he told her that he was a medium, when he found out she was a spiritualist. It was a fabrication on his part – a devious one I must add. Anyway, that's how the story goes.

And now to the next mansion. Huntington did not build his dwelling. It was actually built by David Colton who was the chief legal counsel for the railroad. It was constructed before the Hopkins and Crocker mansions. Huntington bought it later but I don't know all the facts about that one.

The story that is comical to me is the last mansion built by one of the Big Four, the Charles Crocker mansion. It is famous for its hideous looks and so called 'spite fence'. The story goes like this. Crocker wanted his huge mansion to be situated on an entire city block. But a neighbor named Nicholas Yung presented a problem. Yung was, and I guess still is, an undertaker by trade. That had nothing to do with anything – the fact that he was an undertaker that is. Yung's property and house had a great view of the city and the bay. Crocker needed Yung's property to have access to the entire city block. Crocker offered Yung $5,000 for his property. Yung knew Crocker was worth millions so he asked for $7,000. Well Crocker, being a stubborn cuss decided to ignore the request and instead built a forty foot wall that towered the undertaker's house on three sides cutting off airflow, light and worst of all I suppose, the views. Now here's where it gets good.

Yung retaliated by putting a giant coffin with a skull and crossbones on his roof facing the Crocker mansion."

"My word, is that the truth?"

"Yes ma'am, every bit of it."

Lil laughed and said, "I like that undertaker. That sounds like something I would do."

"Well I don't know about that, Miss Lil."

"I do. Anyway, give me your suggestions, Steven."

"Yes ma'am. I designed the interior of the Stanford mansion and we can use some of those ideas in your Palace."

Steven went on to offer all of his deluxe concepts and designs which were fitting for Diamond Lil's Crystal Palace, things like: a large crystal chandelier hanging in the center of the room with smaller chandeliers scattered throughout, beautiful frescoes on the walls and the plastered ceiling, luxurious Victorian style sofas flanked by small marble top end tables, and three marble fireplaces. The carpet would be very stylish with ornate patterns of red rosettes and gold geometric designs. The windows would be covered with velvet drapery with fringe on the ends and tassels to boot. The stage curtain would also be made of velvet, luxurious looking red velvet, matching the drapery on the windows. Large potted green palm trees would be scattered throughout in addition to other green potted plants.

The Palace would have the latest inventions and amenities: electricity and indoor plumbing. The outside marquee would be in lights - "Diamond Lil's Crystal Palace, Gaming and Entertainment". All of this was covered by Steven, and all of it was authorized by Diamond Lil. This was exactly the extravagant house of entertainment she envisioned.

They ended the meeting upstairs discussing both her and her manager's living quarters plus the three business offices.

When they went back downstairs, Lillian asked,

"Well, when do we get started?"

"We'll draw up the plans, line up the craftsmen and materials, and then give you an estimate of the cost. If you agree with everything, we should be able to begin the work immediately – I'd say in just a few weeks," Steven replied.

"I have another question. Once the project is started, how long do you think it will take to complete it, Steven?"

"With the exterior structure already in place and we are just talking about constructing the interior, I believe you can set your grand opening for six months after we begin work. How does that sound to you, Miss Lillian?"

"Honey, that sounds just marvelous."

When Steven and Robert left the building, Lillian hung around for a while. She fantasized about her luxurious Crystal Palace Grand Opening: the crowds, the entertainment, and the income. She was always about having the biggest and the best, but that wasn't all. She wanted fame, money, and extreme wealth – a wealth which would allow her to buy all the diamond jewelry she wanted – she loved diamonds – lots of diamonds. Her greed was so great that she would allow nothing or no one to get in the way of her aspirations.

Diamond Lil could sweet talk you with "honey" all day long, but sting you hard with lead from her hidden derringer at a moment's notice. That was ole Diamond Lil all right; she could switch from nice to wicked at the drop of a twenty dollar gold piece – and although it was only known by a few, she got away with murder more than once in her lifetime.

While she was standing where the orchestra would be located, looking toward the stage area, she heard the front door creak as it opened. The building was dark. All she could see was a large silhouette.

"Can I help you?" She yelled.

"Well I guess you can. You sent for me."

"Bret, Bret Stone, is that you, you big thug?"

"The one and only, Miss Lillian, at your service, all the way from Deadwood."

"Well come on over here and give me some sugar, darling. It's great to see you."

Bret walked over to Diamond Lil, smiling from ear to ear; they hugged, and pecked each other on the cheeks. They had been away from each other too long to show any more intimacy than that for the time being. However, with Diamond Lil, that could change at a moment's notice. Albeit, she was always the one who made that decision. Yes sir, she was in charge of everything.

Small talk ensued and they agreed to meet later for dinner and discuss the business proposition at hand. On that evening Lil offered Bret the managerial position and a modest salary for now, but 20% of the house's take as well, starting the day of the Grand Opening. Lillian also offered him free room and board, the other living quarters on the second floor of her Palace.

Bret accepted the deal because Lillian convinced him that the great monetary potential of the Crystal Palace would make him a wealthy man in less than one year. She also told Bret that he would be responsible to manage the construction of the interior. She did not want anything to do with that herself. Her job would be the fun stuff: scheduling and hiring weekly acts, interviewing and employing pretty young ladies for her can-can shows, along with other important things relating to entertainment. When the time came, Bret would hire the personnel to run the gaming tables.

This was a business match made in heaven; well maybe a wee bit, no, a whole bunch south of heaven. They both had criminal pasts and could never find the path – the path of the straight and narrow that is.

As time went on, work on the Crystal Palace began and was progressing well. It was just prior to the Grand Opening though that Lillian received a newspaper article in the mail. She had no idea who sent it. It was a mystery. It was the same article that Dakota read to Pecos back in "No Man's Land". She was shocked to read that Rusty Blake was really Luke Barnes working for Allan Pinkerton. She really liked Rusty. He was a gentleman compared to the other members of the Smoky Hill River Gang. But she thought he was killed in Hays City with the other gang members. She had no idea he was broken out of jail and joined another gang, the so-called "Professionals".

She also was surprised to learn that Dakota was a member of the "Professionals". Her relationship with Dakota went all the way back to Deadwood. Lil and Dakota actually had a thing for each other. Unfortunately, Bret had a thing for Lil as well. The town of Deadwood was not big enough for both. Dakota figured she wasn't worth getting killed over, so he left Deadwood and headed south.

Reading this newspaper article dampened Lillian's spirits before the Grand Opening, and well it should have since she saw her name in the article. She thought she was home free since everyone in the Smoky Hill River Gang was killed. But everyone wasn't killed. Rusty was still alive, and he was a Pinkerton agent. The question was, how much did he really know about Diamond Lil's involvement in the demise of the gang, the money she stole, and her role in the killing of her manager back in Kansas? Reading this newspaper article made Lil sick to her stomach. But she had to put this information aside because it was now coming close to the Grand Opening of her Palace. It was only a few days away.

Special invitations were sent out for an Open House Party scheduled the night before the Grand Opening. She planned a first class affair. One hundred city dignitaries and wealthy businessmen and their spouses were invited and attended; they all showed up wearing their best attire. There was no gambling on this Friday evening, but she had an open bar, elaborate hors d'oeuvres, pastries, and delicious chocolates. The entertainment was delightful: the orchestra played and there was a performance by her showgirls, a comic, and some male acrobats. The guests were allowed to walk on the stage and go backstage after the last performance of the night, and even tour all of the rooms upstairs. They saw it all. It was laid out just like it was planned, in all of its luxurious glamour.

Diamond Lil was in all of her glory. She looked fabulous. Like always, she was dressed to kill wearing a beautiful long green evening gown that complimented her tall slender physique. Her reddish hair was put up in her favorite style, swept up in an elaborate coiffure. She sparkled with diamonds: diamond earrings, necklace, bracelet, and even a small diamond tiara. She looked like the queen of San Francisco. And that walk, oh that slow walk, swinging from side to side – she could turn heads a hundred feet away.

The Open House Party went on without a hitch. It was a perfect evening. Diamond Lil met individually with several guests that night in her office - some who she asked favors of for her business, and others who asked favors of her. A couple of those meetings lasted much longer than the others. While Lil was meeting with people, Bret and some of the stunning can-can girls took care of the guests.

After her meetings, Diamond Lil came back downstairs. She wasn't beaming with a joyful look like before. Bret noticed the change.

Bret walked over to her and asked,

"Are you OK Lil?"

She paused, thought about it for a few seconds as if she were in a different world, and then she said,

"Oh, I'm sorry Bret. Yes, I'm all right. I'm just getting worn down. There's been a lot of stress the last few weeks and I guess it's finally working on me."

"Lil, why don't you grab a glass of wine and do some mingling. There's only about thirty minutes left before we close down."

"I'll do just that, Bret."

Bret knew something was up – he knew her too well – he could read her like a pocket watch. He knew it wasn't the Palace stressing her out. It was something else, something that began gnawing on her the minute she came downstairs from those meetings. But he thought it was best to leave it be for now.

The Grand Opening of Diamond Lil's Crystal Palace was on Saturday, the day after the Open House.

"EXTRA! EXTRA! READ ALL ABOUT IT!" was the shouting from newspaper boys all around town as they swung their San Francisco Saturday morning newspapers over their heads.

"DIAMOND LIL'S CRYSTAL PALACE OPENS TODAY!" they yelled as they continued to twirl their newspapers high in the air with one hand, while holding several newspapers with the other. People were snatching up the morning edition like forty-niners grabbing picks and shovels when they heard the shouts of "gold" echoing through the streets of San Francisco.

What a day it was! The excitement of the Grand Opening was building like the old Los Angeles County Vaquero Rodeo was coming to town. The anticipation was boundless. The ribbon cutting was planned for 2:00 p.m. People began lining up at noon to be the first ones in, some to get good seats for the stage shows, others to get a chair at the gambling tables. Horses and buggies were parked up and down adjoining city blocks.

The ribbon cutting ceremony brought out many dignitaries: the governor, the mayor, the chief of police, and other politicians. They all stood side by side with Diamond Lil and Bret Stone. Newspaper columnists poured in from around the country. They came to witness this great event and were anxious to send their stories back to their home offices.

And then at exactly 2:00 p.m. facing a bank of tripod box cameras with a big smile, and holding an oversized scissors in her hand, Diamond Lil cut the ribbon among loud deafening cheers that could be heard ten San Francisco city blocks away, some say even all the way to Sacramento.

Bret walked over to the doors and propped them wide open while the gorgeous Diamond Lil and her beautiful chorus girls, decked out in colorful can-can dresses, stood in a reception line greeting the guests as they entered. Some patrons went right for the bar, others to the center tables, and yet others to the gaming.

The orchestra was made up of a typical symphony style ensemble with woodwinds, brass, percussion and strings (violins, violas, cellos and a double bass). They were playing beautiful classical Strauss waltzes when the crowd entered the Palace. The first one was recognized by many of the high society patrons. It was the G'schichten aus dem Wienerwald, Op. 325, Tales from the Vienna Woods (1868).

The Palace was packed on this day – shoulder to shoulder. The entertainment that Diamond Lil scheduled was fantastic, and opening day was an immense success. The crowds continued to be huge during the successive days and weeks to follow, it never let up. One afternoon on the fifth week of business, while Lil was up in her office going over the finances with her bookkeeper, Bret came upstairs and said,

"One of our old friends just walked in with a Mexican and a saddle tramp. He wants to see you."

"Who is it?"

"Dakota Wilson from Deadwood."

"Dakota Wilson? Why I haven't seen that ole reprobate in years. Of course, I'll see him darling. Send him up. Tell the Mexican and that saddle tramp to belly up to the bar. Their first two drinks are on the house."

Bret went back downstairs and reluctantly sent Dakota upstairs. He walked the other two men over to the bar and told the barkeep to give them anything they wanted. "The first two are on the house. Anything after that, they pay."

"Give us a bottle and two glasses, Senor," Pecos said.

"A bottle of what?" The barkeep responded with a frown on his face and turning his head some. The two saddle bums badly needed a bath and a shave. They were quite rank and the folks around them showed repulsion at their presence in this fancy establishment.

"Whiskey, the best you have," Pecos said.

The barkeep turned around, grabbed a bottle of Tennessee sour mash, and then placed it and two glasses on the bar. Then as he backed away rubbing his nose he said,

"There's a bathhouse down the street. Hope you visit it soon."

"We intend to as soon as we leave here," Bobby Green said.

Pecos grabbed the bottle and Green took the two glasses and they walked over to one of the tables that sat two.

After pouring the drinks, Green lifted up his glass and said, "Here's to our new gang." Pecos picked up his, tapped Green's glass, and it was down the hatch.

"Say Pecos, what do you think those two are talking about upstairs?"

"I have no idea amigo. But you know, those two once had flames in their hearts for each other up in Deadwood. That's what Dakota said."

"How did this Diamond Lil get all the money to open up a place like this?"

"Don't know," Pecos said. "Since we're in a fancy joint amigo, I'll call it, probably soiled dove activities. You know what I mean, gringo?" Pecos said as he laughed and poured another glass full of sour mash.

"I know what you mean, Pecos," Green responded.

Meanwhile upstairs, Diamond Lil and Dakota were getting acquainted again. Lil refused to hug her old friend until he discovered a barber and a bar of soap. The sequence did not make a difference. It was the results that did.

"What brings you to San Francisco, old friend?"

"You."

"Me? Why me? Say, you aren't still running from the law are you? Actually, you don't need to answer that. I read a newspaper article a while back. I read you got mixed up with a gang they called the 'Professionals'. I read you escaped and you have the law lookin' for you."

"Heard the law might be lookin' for you too," Dakota said.

"They don't have anything on me," Lil growled back.

"Maybe not," Dakota responded.

"Sit down. I'll pour us a drink for old times' sake."

Lil walked over to a small table and poured two snifters of brandy. She turned around and handed one to Dakota, sat down next to him at the round table, and said as she lifted her glass,

"Here's to old times in Deadwood."

Dakota knocked his glass against Lil's and took several sips while looking around at the fancy furnishings in the room. Lil did not take a drink but put hers on the table.

"Are you impressed with this joint, Dakota?"

"Yeah, I'm very impressed. Where did you get the money to do all of this, or shouldn't I ask?"

"Oh, you can ask all right honey. I just don't think I want to tell you."

"I didn't think you would," Dakota said.

Lillian then took her first drink and said while still holding the brandy snifter in her hand,

"I read where we have a mutual friend."

"Who's that?" Dakota asked.

"A person by the name of Rusty Blake."

"How did you know him?"

"I knew that little weasel in Ellsworth. He was a gang member of the Smoky Hill River Gang. He and the gang hung around my joint in Ellsworth. I had nothing to do with that gang. They just hung around my joint," Lil said as she lied straight up.

"I guess you read he was a Pinkerton agent and took down my gang."

"I saw that."

"Well the code of the gang was to kill anyone who became a traitor. Pecos and I aim to kill Rusty sometime in the future. Don't know when, but it's gonna happen all right."

"Oh, hell Dakota, he's a preacher now in Hays City. Why don't you let him be? Your gang is broken up anyway."

"Can't - he has to pay the price. Like I said, it's the code, code of our new gang too."

"Dakota honey, you're gonna get yourself killed some day if you keep hanging out with the wrong crowd."

"Lil, you made it rich. I'm goin' to make it too, only in a different way than you. You're legal. I have other plans. I know you'll keep this to yourself. I have joined another gang. The ramrod is a brother of the boss of my last gang. They had a network of sorts goin' on. My new boss is supposed to be much smarter. He's gonna make me rich. You have all the money you need. Someday, I'll have all the money I need."

"Honey, I'll never have all the money I need." Lil then stood up and walked around the table looking like she was cogitating about something.

"What are you thinkin' Lil?"

"Well, there's this guy that's been hangin' around this place shooting off his mouth about gold, a lot of gold, more gold than what's needed to run a country."

"Do you know this fella?"

"Honey, anytime someone mentions gold, you better believe I'm gonna get well acquainted. Say Dakota, you gonna be in town a while?"

"A few days at best before we head to Colorado."

"Well, stay out of trouble, and be back here in a couple of days. I might have a job for you and your new gang, if what this guy says is legitimate. I'll get it out of him for sure. Now honey, go downstairs and take your buddies and yourself to a bathhouse down in Chinatown. It won't cost you much there. Besides, those little Oriental gals will be glad to help you bathe and do whatever else you ask," Lil said as she winked and stood up to open the door.

As Dakota was walking out, he turned around to give Lil a hug. She pushed him away and said, "Darling, I smelled polecats better than you. We'll talk hugs after you put a couple bars of soap to good use. Send word where you bums are staying so I can get ahold of you when I get more information."

"Say, what's Bret Stone doing here?"

"I called for him, that's what."

"You know he's twelve inches lower than a snake."

"Yeah, well, that makes two of you."

Dakota snickered and then walked downstairs. Bret was at the bottom of the stairs looking up at him as Dakota came down.

"Good to see ya again, Bret," Dakota said halfheartedly.

"Wish I could say the same, Dakota," Bret replied.

Dakota looked around the crowded room.

"Your cronies are over there," Bret said as he pointed to the other side of the room toward the billiard tables.

Dakota stopped to look up at the can-can girls doing their cartwheels across the stage. Then he walked over to Pecos and Green and said,

"Come on boys, we're headed to Chinatown and then I'll fill you in on what could be a lucrative proposition."

"Chinatown? What's over in Chinatown?" Pecos asked.

"Soap and Oriental chiquitas, mi amigo."

"Ay, chihuahua!"

During the next two days, Diamond Lil met briefly with the gentleman who would claim he knew where a great amount of hidden treasures were located, as he put it. But he needed to talk to someone who could hire a group of people to acquire it, a fancy word for steal. She told him she could set up a meeting with a few individuals who had access to the right kind of people to get the job done.

Lil found out where Dakota was staying. She then sent word to him to be at the Palace in three days, on Thursday evening at seven o'clock, to meet with the mysterious gentleman. Instead of setting aside a table for them downstairs in the Palace where the risk was inevitable that their conversation would be picked up by anyone nearby, Lil decided that it was best to have the meeting upstairs in the parlor of her own quarters. That also ensured that she could hear every word that was spoken among the group.

On that evening Dakota, Pecos, and Green arrived first. Diamond Lil took them up to her parlor and gave them a snifter of brandy. She told Bret to send Mr. Harrington up when he arrived. Lillian had introduced Harrington to Bret Stone previously but would not tell Bret anything about him, only that they were working on a business proposition. She told Bret she would inform him of the doings when the time was right. Bret did not care for this one bit especially since his old rival Dakota and his two saddle partners were involved.

Harrington was late for the meeting and Dakota began thinking that this whole thing was too good to be true. However, at about 7:35 p.m., there was a knock on Diamond Lil's door; she answered it. It was Harrington but he appeared to be a bit inebriated, and you could smell liquor on him five feet away. This is when Dakota stood up and said, "Let's go boys. This guy's drunk."

Green and Pecos stood up but Diamond Lil grabbed Dakota's arm and said, "Wait, hear him out. What do you have to lose?"

Dakota pulled his arm out of Lillian's grasp, thought about it for a few seconds, and then said,

"All right, we'll stay. But as soon as this guy slurs three words in a row, we're out of here."

"Fair enough," Lil said. "Now let's calm down and I'll introduce everyone. Gentlemen, this is Ben Harrington. Ben Harrington, meet Dakota Wilson, Pecos Fransisco, and Bobby Green."

They all nodded at each other, but no one shook hands. Lil then asked Harrington to sit down at the large round table with the others.

"Can I get you a drin… Wait, scratch that…Can I get you a glass of water, Mr. Harrington?"

"No thank you. I'm fine."

"Well then, Mr. Harrington, why don't you begin," Diamond Lil said.

All eyes shifted to Harrington. Dakota and Pecos were skeptics about this whole thing. Past experiences taught them that if it sounded too good to be true, it probably was. But Green, well, he was anxious to hear what Harrington had to say.

"The only reason I am here is because Lil told me I can trust you, Dakota. She said since I can trust you, I can also trust your friends. I'm just a messenger mind you."

Harrington looked toward the door to make sure it was completely closed. He then peered into the eyes of everyone in the room, leaned forward, and began talking at a volume just above a whisper.

"I have a boss. He shall remain nameless for now. My boss knows things – things other people don't know or ever will. If he publicly divulges his knowledge of these things, he will be assassinated in days. He is in hiding now because he quit an underground organization, a secret society, one that is hoarding riches and treasures beyond comprehension. Since he knows the movements of these treasures, he is being hunted like a dog."

"Movement?" Green inquired.

"Yes the movement. Those treasures never stay in the same location for very long. But there is a system, a system only high ranking insiders know."

"A system for what, amigo?" Pecos asked.

"A system to determine the destination of the next move. The system is known only by the highest of ranks in the secret organization. My boss was a high ranking member of that secret society. He knows the pattern of movements."

"This sounds like a bunch of donkey dung to me: secret societies, treasures beyond our wildest imagination, treasures being periodically moved, and your boss in hiding fearing an assassination from a secret society. What kind of fools do you take us for?" Dakota asked.

"Well if you aren't interested, then I'll leave," Harrington replied.

"Now hold on there, I'm interested," Green said.

"So am I boys," Diamond Lil added.

"Dakota, maybe I can convince you if I told you this," Harrington added, "my boss knows everything about you."

"Is that so? Like what?"

Harrington proceeded in spending the next five minutes listing Dakota's past criminal activities. Dakota was stunned and sat there like a bison staring directly down the barrel of a .50 caliber Hawken muzzle-loading rifle waiting for a lead projectile to hit him right between the eyeballs. Then Harrington looked at Green and did the exact same thing.

"Shall I continue with Pecos and Lillian?"

"You made your point, Harrington," Dakota said, "now what?"

"Stay in town. I'll be in contact with Lillian in a few days and we'll set up another meeting. This was a get acquainted meeting. The next one will be an instructional meeting," Harrington said.

He then stood up, looked at everyone in the room, nodded and said, "Gentlemen and Miss Lillian, until next time."

Lillian stood up and said, "Come on Mr. Harrington, I'll see you out. You three help yourself to some brandy. I'll be back up shortly."

Lillian walked Harrington all the way to the front door. Stone nodded to Harrington as he and Lillian walked by. Stone tried to pick up some of their conversation. He overheard a few sentences but not enough to make any sense to him.

When Diamond Lil went back upstairs to be with the three desperados who were now looking like partners in crime, she asked a thoughtful but simple question,

"Well, what do you think boys?"

"I don't know what to think," Dakota replied. "Do you think this guy is for real? What do you think Green? Should we put our faith in him?"

"I don't put my faith in any man. There's just one thing I trust and that's my .45," Green said as he unholstered his six-shooter and aimed it at the bottle of brandy on the other side of the room.

"Put that thing away and don't you ever take it out of your holster again while you're in this establishment. That goes for all of you. Now let me ask the question again. What do you think about this Harrington fella and do you think he's on the up-and-up?" Diamond Lil asked.

"Miss Lillian, I don't know but I think we should wait before we make a decision. Sometimes on mi padre's ranchero in Old Mexico, we would think every snake was a rattler. But when we waited to get a better look, some turned out to be rat snakes that ate rattlers. I say we wait, hear more, see more, and then make a decision," Pecos suggested.

"I agree with Pecos," Green said, "how about you Dakota?"

Dakota had just rolled a cigarette, put it between his lips and was reaching for a match when the question was asked by Green. Diamond Lil quickly walked over to Dakota, snatched the cigarette out of his mouth just when he was ready to strike a match and said, "There is no smoking in my parlor, honey. Now answer the question. What do you think we ought to do?"

"I say we wait and see what he brings to the next meeting. What do we have to lose?"

"Why don't you bum around Frisco for a few days. I suggest you stay away from the Barbary Coast though. If you get shanghaied, I'm not sending a posse lookin' for you little darlings. I'll let you know when I hear something back from Harrington."

Meanwhile, Judge Isaac Parker knew now that the three lawmen he sent out looking for Dakota and Pecos, as a result of Pinkerton's request, were either killed or had vamoosed with Parker's advanced expense money. He sent a telegram to Pinkerton that read,

Allan Pinkerton
Chicago, Illinois

Bad news my friend. Looks like the three lawmen sent after your fugitives have vanished. Have not heard from them in weeks. Currently have my marshals tied up on the trail of other criminals. Can't say when I can free up men to track down your criminals and my three lawmen. Keeping you informed.

Judge Isaac Parker
Fort Smith, Arkansas

Pinkerton received the telegram and responded immediately.

Judge Isaac Parker
Fort Smith, Arkansas

Disappointed on all accounts. If I can free up men before I hear back from you, I will do so. I'll stay in touch as well. I am determined to bring Dakota Wilson, Pecos Fransisco, and the crooked marshal to justice. I can assure you that justice will be served one way or the other.

Allan Pinkerton
Chicago, Illinois

While waiting for the next meeting with Harrington, Green thought it would be wise that they send off a wire to the pretending Marshal John Short - Short's hypocrisy ended when he discarded his badge into a creek as he and his fake deputy Tom O'Hara approached their hideout in Pueblo. O'Hara's badge found the bottom of the creek as well.

On the next day after lunch, Green did just that. He sent a telegram to inform Short that he, Dakota, and Pecos were staying in San Francisco for a while. He told Short that something came up that might have lucrative possibilities for the gang. He would know more in a few days. Short relayed the message to the gang leader, Cole Brinkman.

Brinkman didn't think much about the news. He was quite disturbed that the new gang members were making decisions and acting on their own. He was a control artist – a dominating, authoritative control artist just like his brother Jerod. There was another trait Cole and his brother Jerod shared as well – greed – a greed that dominated every decision and every move they made. It was ingrained in their very souls. They lived with it, slept with it, and killed for it.

After Green, Pecos and Dakota walked out of the telegraph office, Pecos said,

"Amigos, let's go down to the Barbary Coast and have a few drinks. We have nothin' better to do."

"Heard it's a putrid place," Green said.

"I'm a putrid person I'm told," Pecos remarked.

"Well then, let's go have a drink with all the other putrids," Green replied.

"You know Dakota, I like this guy. He makes mi rias," Pecos said.

"Rias?" Dakota asked.

"Si, you know, laugh."

They all chuckled, walked down the small flight of stairs to their horses, grabbed their reins, then some mane, saddled up, and trotted down to the ramshackle deplorable Barbary Coast.

Most establishments around San Francisco were asking patrons to leave their sidearms at the front door with their doormen – not at the Barbary Coast however. No sir, this was still a dangerous place. Any type of weapon check-in would be a futile effort. These visiting thugs carried concealed small caliber pistols or Arkansas toothpicks in their boots, up their sleeves, in their pants pockets, and everywhere else imaginable. The red-light district women did the same. Necessity dictated that they do so for their own survival. This part of town was still a risky place to hang a hat for a drink or two.

The three entered the Rum Barrel Saloon. The place looked ordinary from the outside, but it was a shipwreck on the inside. It was dark, smoky, and musty. There were nautical paraphernalia hanging on the walls and dangling from the ceiling. Oil lamps were burning whale blubber oil giving off a strange odor – one not familiar to the three, but to the sailors scattered around, well, it was just one of the foul stenches they became accustomed to.

"Get that table over in the corner," Green told Dakota and Pecos, "I'll fetch us a bottle from the bar."

Green walked up to the crowded bar and waited his turn. The barkeep made his way over to Green and asked,

"What's your poison today mate?"

"What's your specialty here, barkeep?" Green asked.

"Didn't you notice the name of this fine establishment on the window before you walked in?" The barkeep asked. "Rum, fellow – rum is what you wanna order when you visit the Rum Barrel Saloon. Oh we have some fine whiskeys we made in the back room last week all right. Most say they're better than that Tennessee rotgut you find further east – not sayin' it is – not sayin' it ain't – just sayin' what most is sayin'."

"Well then, give me a bottle of that fine rum and three glasses."

"That'll be five dollars, friend."

Green reached into his pocket, pulled out a five dollar gold piece, tossed it on the bar, picked up the bottle and three glasses and strolled over to Dakota and Pecos. The barkeep picked up the coin, tested it between his teeth, and then placed it in his cash drawer and shouted, "Who's next?"

After Green poured the drinks, they toasted to "getting rich quick". They didn't say much at first while they were glancing about the dingy saloon watching some of the carryings-on around the place with the fallen angels table-hopping seeking out early afternoon customers. But then Dakota asked the other two,

"What do you guys think about that Harrington fella?"

"I don't have much of an opinion yet. I don't know whether the guy is telling us a story or is telling us the truth. Right now, I'm ready to just show patience, and just keep listening," Green said.

"What about you Pecos? You seem to have an instinct for these things. What's your opinion?" Dakota asked.

Before Pecos could answer, a table-hopper came over and sat herself flat down right in Green's lap, threw her arms around his neck, and gave him a big hug after she kissed him on the cheek. Green stood up with her in his arms and dropped her on the floor. She screamed. A bouncer came over and grabbed Green's shoulder from behind. Green pulled his pistol, turned around, and shoved it into the neck of the bouncer and said,

"Back off, now. I came in here for bottle and I still have some left. Now I aim to finish this bottle without any harassment from you or your trashy ladies in this establishment. Do I make myself clear?"

The barkeep, who was the owner of this sleazy place, came over and said, "Go ahead, finish your bottle and when you do, leave here and don't come back."

The barkeep reached down for the girl's arm and helped her up off the floor. When he, the table-hopper and the bouncer walked away, Green holstered his pistol.

"You seemed a might bit aggravated, Green," Dakota said. "What was that all about?"

"I don't like being interrupted when I'm talkin' business. That's all," Green replied.

"Amigo, me thinks that was muy impressive. I'm glad I'm with you, and not against you," Pecos said as he gave Green a south of the border smirk.

Green smiled and said, "Yes sir, we're gonna make a good team." He picked up the bottle and filled up the glasses. Then he said,

"Ever since the War, I have a short fuse. I guess that War changed a lot of us, and not for the better I reckon."

"What side were you on?" Dakota asked.

"Lincoln's side. I didn't last long. I was wounded on the first day at the Battle of Gettysburg - caught a .50 caliber lead ball in my left arm on Seminary Ridge. Actually it ripped a big chunk of flesh off of it. I was lucky it didn't hit a bone. Even with that, I almost bled out on the battlefield before I was fixed up by the sawbones before sundown."

"They say Gettysburg was a turning point in the War," Dakota remarked.

"It was one. That's for sure. It stopped Lee's advancement to the north. Anyway, that's what they say. I heard that battle involved the largest number of casualties on both sides; they say numbers like 23,000 on the North and 23,000 to 28,000 on the Rebel's side.

After the first day of battle and when night fell, you could hear the eerie moanings from soldiers on the battlefield who were wounded and left for dead. Those sounds haunt me to this very day. Those poor cusses weren't as fortunate as me. Every once in a while you would hear a lone gunshot during the night. We surmised it was someone takin' his own life – the suffering I guess was unbearable. It's a horrible thing when you have to take your own life because the pain is so great. I guess that's what you do when it seems all hope has run out and you feel helpless lying there during a long lonely night on the battlefield with the stench of death all around you. Were you in the War Dakota?"

"No, I was fighting the Sioux on my pa's ranch up in the Dakotas."

They all picked up their glasses and put a couple more gulps down the hatch. Then Dakota asked Green,

"Have you been in Brinkman's gang a long time?"

"Long enough. I got myself in a heap of trouble down San Antonio way… well, I don't care to get into that now. It's a long story," Green said. "Say, let's get out of this dump. I'll meet you back at the hotel for dinner. I need to go buy me a new pair of boots at the saddlery."

"While you're doing that, I'm gonna head over to the livery stable and trade my sorrel in for another one. That old mare seems to be on the verge of goin' lame. I need to trade it in while she still has value and before she's too far gone. Do you wanna tag along Pecos?" Dakota asked.

"No, I'll just hang in here a while and drink a few more rounds. Maybe after five more drinks some of these lap senoritas will start lookin' good to me."

"Suit yourself," Dakota said.

A few days went by before Diamond Lil sent someone out looking for Green, Dakota, and Pecos. A message was left at their hotel to meet at the Crystal Palace on Monday evening at 7:00.

The three showed up on time. Once again Harrington was about thirty minutes late. Green was getting annoyed at his tardiness.

"This guy is never on time. How the heck can we trust him with anything he tells us?" Green asked.

It was a rhetorical question and Dakota was just about to offer a response when there was a knock on the door. Diamond Lil walked over and opened it. This time Harrington did not smell like he'd been out on a drinking binge all night. On the contrary, he was well dressed and groomed, and had the appearance of a wealthy businessman. All four were impressed. If his new professional look was meant for him to be taken more seriously, it worked.

Diamond Lil offered him a brandy. While the others had already accepted theirs beforehand, Harrington turned down the offer.

"Gentlemen, again I must tell you that I am only the messenger. What I briefly discuss with you tonight comes from the initiator of the message, my boss. During our last meeting I informed you that this meeting would be an instructional meeting. That will in fact be the case here tonight.

As I said before, my boss knows of the location of a great amount of gold, silver, and jewels. He needs the help of an organization or gang he can trust to help him acquire that treasure. Whoever successfully assists in the acquisition of that treasure will share in the wealth. My boss will not divulge what he knows to just anyone.

He is a fugitive like you gentlemen. However, not from the law, but from a secret society which shall remain nameless at this time. Being a fugitive from this secret society means sure death by assassination if his location is discovered. The very fact that I know of his whereabouts also puts me in great danger. The fact that I have shared this with you, even though I have shared very little, means your lives are now in danger."

"Well thank you for that," Dakota said.

"Since our lives are now in danger, could you please tell us a little more than just San Francisco gibberish?" Green asked.

Dakota chuckled as did Pecos. Harrington looked at Green but with a grave look on his face. Green read that look accurately. This was no laughing matter to Harrington.

"Here are your instructions. My boss will only divulge his information in the presence of your boss. When your boss comes to San Francisco, he is to make contact with me through Lillian. At that time, a meeting will be set up with him and two of his choosing, and plans will be made. All of this must happen, or there is no deal. Understood?"

"Well, for your information, our boss will remain nameless until we decide it's time to make his name known to your boss," Green said.

"As I told you and demonstrated before, we know more about you and your gang than you think. Your boss's name is already known to us," Harrington said. "That is all I will say about that at this time."

"Somehow I believe you," Green remarked.

"Good, one last thing, a double cross by anyone in your gang would be foolish, and catastrophic. This I will assure you."

CHAPTER FOUR:

The Warning

"The town hall meeting will now come to order," the city council chairman said as he struck the wood block with his gavel.

This was the monthly town hall meeting held on the first Saturday of each month in Hays City, Kansas, which was known for having the very first Boot Hill Cemetery in the Old West. Back in the early cow town days, Hays City was visited by some of the meanest and cruelest saddle tramps west of the Mississippi. They came up from Texas on cattle drives bringing their herds of maverick longhorns to the railhead. Others were just passing through looking for a card game, a saloon to guzzle down cheap backroom made whiskey, or a brothel to spend an hour or two with a soiled dove.

During those rough years there were several notable figures who lived in Hays City: George Armstrong Custer and his wife Elizabeth, William F. Cody (a.k.a. Buffalo Bill), Martha Jane Canary (a.k.a. Calamity Jane), and even James Butler Hickok who became known as "Wild Bill Hickok". Hickok served as sheriff in 1869 for only a brief time.

That was Hays City less than a decade ago. But now the town was civilized. Legitimate businesses were opening their doors, and land on the outskirts was purchased by homesteaders who raised crops and families. The cow town era of the past had long been gone but not yet forgotten.

"Thank you for attending this month's meeting. We have so much to discuss this afternoon. So, for the first order of business I would like to introduce to you our new deputy marshal, Jake Lucas. Stand up Jake. Let's give him a big Hays City round of applause."

The crowd clapped their hands while Deputy Lucas stood up and acknowledged the warm welcome.

"Jake comes to us from the small town of West Plains, Missouri where he spent time as a deputy sheriff for Howell County. He's not married so all of you young ladies out there, here's another eligible bachelor for you."

The crowd laughed and then the chairman said, "Deputy Marshal, would you like to say a few words?"

"Yes I would; thank you sir. I grew up in the northeast part of this state and then left during the Civil War. After the War, I lived in St. Louis for a while and then moved to West Plains. I wanted to come back home to live in Kansas again. I heard so much about your great city I figured this is where I wanted to make my home. I came here looking for a law enforcement job and I was lucky that your marshal hired me. It's an honor to serve this fine community as one of your law enforcement officers. I will do everything in my power to help you keep your fine city a safe place to live - thank you very much."

The crowd applauded. The deputy nodded his head as he looked around the room, acknowledged the applause, and then sat down. Even though he was tall and well built, he seemed rather shy for a lawman. But he wore two fancy pearl handled six-shooters - not the type of iron a greenhorn would be packing.

"The next order of business is to make you aware that the Mercantile Bank has received their new safe. It's a beauty. Mr. Franks said there is no need for you to be hiding your savings under your mattresses any longer. Do you want to make any comments, Mr. Franks?"

"Thank you Mr. Chairman, only this. Folks, you can bring your money in now where it will be secure. We will be open two additional hours next Saturday to accommodate your needs. This safe was shipped in from New York and even dynamite won't open this vault. That's all I have sir. Thank you."

"Thank you, Mr. Franks. Next on the agenda is Reverend Luke Barnes. He wants to talk about the recent fire which destroyed his church last Tuesday. Thankfully he got out in time before he met his maker. Reverend Barnes, would you like to talk from your place or come up to the front?"

Luke stood up and said,

"I'll come up there, thank you."

Luke walked up to the front of the hall and stepped up on the small stage that was elevated about one foot off the floor. There was no podium, just three chairs: two at a small table, and the third one on the other side of the stage. Luke did not use notes; he spoke from his heart.

"My dear fellow citizens, as you know we had a devastating fire at out church last week. We lost everything. There is speculation about how it started, but that's not why I am here. I'll leave that up to the law. I'm here to ask for your help. A community as large as ours cannot survive without a place of worship where fine folks like you can go to give thanks to the Lord for all of your blessings and also ask for His forgiveness.

We need a place of worship where we as a congregation can pray for each other; whether it be for Mrs. Bains who has been sick in bed now for four days with the fever, or little Johnny Sullivan who was thrown from his horse two days ago and broke his collarbone. We all have something going on in our lives that need prayers, prayers from our community going up to the heavens. We know the power of prayer. We have seen it all around us.

In Matthew 7:7-8 we read, 'Ask and it shall be given to you; seek and you shall find; knock and it shall be opened to you. For every one who asks receives, and he who seeks finds, and to him who knocks it shall be opened.'

In James 5:16, we learned, 'The earnest prayer of a righteous person has great power and wonderful results.'

And there is more good news. In Psalm 37:4 we learn, 'Delight yourself in the Lord, and He will tend to the desires of your heart.'

Now, it's going to take money, lots of money to rebuild our church. Today I am asking for contributions from the community - contributions from businesses, families, and individuals as well. But what I need in one week are pledges. The reason we need pledges is so we know exactly where we stand with our finances.

We will meet for service in this hall every Sunday until our new church is ready. Please bring your pledges tomorrow. As for businesses, I will be visiting with each of you in the next several days for your pledges. I am asking everyone to please be as generous as you can.

And let me add this. Folks, even if you don't participate in our services, I am still asking for your help. You will be making Hays City a good place to live, one of high moral standards which are required for a community to survive in these times.

The bank has set up a special account for the church. So you can take your donations over to the bank at any time. However, I am requesting that you begin making your donations in the next two weeks so we can begin ordering the building materials. But again, I still need your pledges. Thank you my friends and may the Good Lord bless you in all things you do."

The crowd gave Reverend Barnes a nice round of applause as he went back to his seat. Reverend Barnes acknowledged the applause by nodding to the crowd and saying thank you several times.

There were a few other things discussed so the meeting went on for another hour or so. When it came to an end, the new deputy marshal walked over to Luke Barnes and introduced himself.

"Reverend Barnes, can I have a few words with you in private?"

"Sure you can deputy. We can stay in the hall here or we can walk outside."

"Let's stay in here. I'm Deputy Marshal Jake Lucas. You can call me Jake," he said as he extended his hand for a handshake.

"Well it's a pleasure to meet you. I'm Luke Barnes. Most people call me Reverend Barnes. I'd be honored if you just call me Luke. Say, it's almost dinner time. My wife Kathleen always makes more than what the two of us can eat at one sitting. Why don't you join us for dinner."

"Are you sure it's no trouble?"

"Of course, I'm sure. Come on, let's go now, and we'll talk at dinner. Kathleen will enjoy meeting you."

The two strolled down Main Street on the boarded walkway to Luke's home. Luke and Kathleen bought the cute little bungalow next to their church. But the beautiful white church with the towering tall steeple was now reduced into a pile of rubble and black cinders. The only thing recognizable was the steeple bell which was charred and lying there mostly covered in ashes.

Before the two walked into the house, they stood there momentarily and looked at what had been the town's church. Jake noticed the downhearted look on Luke's face.

"I'm sorry for your misfortune, Luke. I know it must be very hard on you."

"Thanks Jake, it is. However, I have faith in the Lord that he will eventually provide us the means to rebuild. We'll just keep praying until our prayers are answered. Come on, let's go inside."

When they walked into the house, the aroma of supper on the wood burning stove filled the entire house.

"Wow that smells great," Jake said.

Kathleen heard a voice she did not recognize so she walked into the parlor to see who it was.

"Kathleen, we have a guest for dinner. I want you to meet the new deputy marshal. This is Jake Lucas."

"Nice to meet you, Deputy Lucas."

"Oh, you can call me Jake, ma'am. It's a pleasure to meet you too."

"Thank you Jake, you can call me Kathleen."

Kathleen looked into Jake's eyes for just a few seconds and then asked, "Have we met before? You look very familiar to me."

"You know, I thought the same thing Kathleen," the Preacher said.

"Not unless you spent time in West Plains, Missouri."

"I guess not. I don't even know where West Plains is," Kathleen responded.

Kathleen set the table for three and they sat down, said grace, and began passing around the beef stew and cornbread.

"Nothing fancy tonight, Jake. If I knew you were coming for supper, I would have made a beef roast or fried a couple of steaks."

"This is great, Kathleen. I haven't had a home cooked meal in months."

The conversation during supper was just small talk. But when the dishes were picked up, the table cleared, and coffee and dessert served, the conversation became more serious.

"Luke, if you don't mind me asking, I was told by the marshal that you received a threatening telegram a few weeks ago."

"That's right, I did. The telegram said that somebody would be gunning for me. It shook me up for a while. We were at our church social, eating lunch outside with our congregation. I made the mistake of telling the telegraph operator to read the telegram out loud. Well, everybody sitting around heard the threat. It sort of put a damper on the luncheon. I tried to brush it off, but it wasn't real easy to do."

"Do you know who sent the message?"

"No, but somebody was warning me. This I'm sure, because the message said, 'They are gunning for you, preacher'."

"Why would a preacher have enemies?" Jake asked.

"It's a long story. It may be hard for you to believe but I was a Pinkerton agent at one time. I belonged to the Smoky Hill River Gang out of Ellsworth for a while – I was an undercover agent. Circumstances were such that the gang was wiped out here in Hays City. The gang planned to rob the bank. The townspeople knew we were coming and set up a trap. I thought I knew who informed the town of the robbery. I shared that information with Allan Pinkerton. They are on her trail."

"Her?"

"That's right. Anyway before I blew my cover, I was broken out of jail by another gang. Can you believe that? This other gang needed a safecracker and I was their man. Being a good undercover man, I decided to go along thinking I could maybe bring another gang to justice. But this second gang was more dangerous than the first. They were killers and it was led by a man named Jerod Brinkman, who was very intelligent but evil to the core.

He put together a gang of professionals with the intention of knocking over the Carson City Mint. We successfully did it. Up to then I had trouble reaching Pinkerton to let him know what the gang's plans were. But I finally found a way and we took down the gang in Abilene - most of them at least.

Unfortunately, three guys got a clean getaway."

"Yes, I know: Dakota, Pecos and the town marshal in Abilene," Jake said.

"How do you know that?"

"I read about it. Also read your alias was Rusty."

"That's right. I believe it is Dakota and Pecos who are gunning for me. The gang I belonged to had a code. Traitors were to be killed. I was a traitor to them so I believe they will be coming to Hays City to kill me. I guess I always knew that. I also found out that Pinkerton's theory is correct."

"What's that?" The deputy asked.

"There is a crime network working. Jerod Brinkman was just one arm. Brinkman has two more brothers. I wouldn't be surprised if Dakota and Pecos join up with either one of them. That puts my life, as well as Kathleen's, in grave danger I fear."

"That's why I'm here," Jake said.

"What do you mean?" Luke asked.

"I'm an undercover Pinkerton agent, too."

"What?" Luke responded.

"That's right. Mr. Pinkerton heard about the threat to you and sent me to protect you and kill or capture whoever was chosen to do the deed. We think that whoever set the fire to your church while you were in it, wanted to send a message that they mean business."

"What are we going to do, Luke?" Kathleen asked. "This whole thing seems to be much more serious than we thought."

"We're going to rebuild our church and live our lives like we planned. I am not going to live my life looking over my shoulder all day, every day. That's not living – that's not a life."

"That's what we want you to do – I mean, live a normal life – the best you can under these circumstances. This should help ease your mind a bit. There's another undercover agent in town. He'll remain nameless for now," Jake said. "We both will be watching over you. But if you see anyone or anything suspicious, don't hesitate to let me know. Don't plan on sending any telegrams to Pinkerton or anyone on the subject we talked about here this evening. A wise policy is to trust no one."

Jake took one last sip from his cup of coffee and then stood up.

"Well, I need to be going now. Thank you for the nice meal, ma'am," Jake said as he nodded to Kathleen and walked toward the door. He picked up his hat off the coat rack as Luke opened the door. They both walked outside together.

"Watch your back, Luke. These Brinkman gang members are as evil as Satan himself. They could show up at any time. I know Kathleen can handle a gun."

"Yes she can."

"That's good. That's real good. I know she's the one who put a slug into Jerod Brinkman. Jerod's kinfolk won't take too kindly to that. They'll be lookin' to doing you both in. I'm not trying to frighten you. I'm telling you, that's just how it is."

Luke went back into the house. Kathleen was standing just inside the door and heard every word Jake had said.

"What are we going to do Luke? We can't live every day wondering if we're going to be shot in the back walking down Main Street or even in our own home. Maybe we should leave this place, head farther west or even go east, find another town where no one knows us."

"It doesn't make sense to move to another town, Kathleen. They'll find us anywhere we go. You know that."

Luke walked out to the kitchen, Kathleen followed. He reached for a mug in the cabinet, and then poured himself a cup of coffee. Kathleen watched and knew Luke was thinking about something. She watched and waited and remained silent. Then Luke took a sip and turned around and asked,

"I have a question for you, Kathleen. Did you ever met Jerod Brinkman's brothers when you were growing up? I mean, could you recognize them if you saw them?"

"No, even if I could, they probably wouldn't do the dirty work themselves."

"You're probably right there," Luke said. "I know what Dakota and Pecos look like. I think those are the two we need to watch out for. I know they have a firm resolve to kill me. It was the code, the code of the 'Professionals'."

"Luke, I knew you were through with this but I think you ought to be carrying a gun with you when you leave the house," Kathleen said.

"I don't think so honey. I don't think it would look appropriate for a preacher packing a six-shooter," Luke said as he chuckled a tad.

"Luke, this is not a laughing matter, I don't know what I'd do if something would happen to you. If you don't want to pack your six-shooter, carry my derringer in your pocket. No one needs to know."

"Kathleen, listen to me. I'm not ever picking up a gun again. I have seen enough killing in my lifetime and certainly am not going to be the one to send somebody to their eternal resting place, no matter who it is. I'm trusting in the Lord to take care of us, and I believe He will. I believe the Good Lord held my hand through all my other perils, and for a reason. The reason is to minister to the good folks of Hays City – and that's what I intend to concentrate on. Now, what we both need to do is to put our efforts toward getting our church rebuilt."

Luke and his congregation prayed that the folks and businesses would come through: pledge, and then donate the money required to build a new church. Luke was not disappointed. When he added up the pledges and saw that the funds would be sufficient, he took a short-term loan from the bank and began ordering building materials.

As the days and weeks went by, good progress was made on the construction of the church. Most building materials were shipped in by rail. Luke worked with an architect but gave many recommendations himself.

While Preacher Barnes's church was being constructed, his previous gang members and now adversaries, or potential assassins, were deep into deciding whether or not this Harrington character in San Francisco had a legitimate lucrative deal, or if this whole thing was a sham.

Oh it was there all right; at least that's what Harrington said - millions of dollars in gold, available to the willing, precarious for the adventurous, but rewarding for the risk-taker.

After Harrington's second meeting with Dakota, Pecos, Green, and Diamond Lil, Green fired off another wire to John Short. He told Short about the potential for a huge business adventure; this was code for a big heist. In the telegram Green wrote Short he would be sending a letter through the mail to explain details - it would be safer that way.

Things would soon be moving fast. Brinkman would have to decide in short order whether to accept the potentially perilous challenge, or to let it ride. Then there was the question, could he pull it off? Odds were favorable that he could. This Brinkman was much smarter – more clever than his two brothers, especially Jerod who was gunned down by his own adopted daughter, Kathleen Brinkman, during Pinkerton's raid on Jerod Brinkman's hideout in Abilene, Kansas. The raid was after the Carson City heist.

Cole Brinkman needed to hear the facts, and then once he did, make his calculated decision.

Green, Pecos, and Dakota stayed in San Francisco because they had hoped to be part of the meeting themselves with Harrington's boss.

When Short received the letter a few days later, he rushed it to Cole Brinkman.

Cole, like his brother Jerod, lived a double life. He was a well-respected lawyer and lived in town. He also was the leader of a gang and had a small hideout outside of town. However, there were three differences between Cole Brinkman and his brother Jerod. The first one was Cole never went out to his gang's hideout; secondly, he did not reveal his identity to anyone in his gang except for one person, John Short; lastly, Cole Brinkman had an alias only known to John Short. It was Attorney Robert Burns.

Cole always told his brother Jerod not to trust anyone, even his gang members. Jerod Brinkman did not heed the warning - Rusty was responsible for Jerod's demise. Cole's plan was to never make the same mistake as Jerod. And as for now, neither Cole Brinkman nor his alias was officially wanted by the law.

Cole read the letter over and over again. He thought about it for days - millions of dollars in gold belonging to a secret society, a society that had assassins searching out the very person who knew where the gold was located, and the person he would have to rely on to lead him to the treasure.

Brinkman had plans to have his thugs break out the survivors of his brother's gang, Johnny Dane, Kenny Burkley, and Doctor Eddie Hawkens for another big heist, but he decided to put everything on hold until he made up his mind about the San Francisco opportunity. There wasn't a trial set yet for those three. Their lawyers were still putting together defenses.

It was greed, a hunger for excessive wealth, a lust for great fortunes, which made Cole decide that he would meet with the shadowy man in California and hear what he had to say. But he would not go as Cole Brinkman, rather as a surrogate, his alias, Attorney Robert Burns. His hopes were that he could convince the mysterious man to divulge the secrets of the hidden treasures to his alias without giving up his true identity.

Cole had John Short send a telegram back to Green to inform Green that Short and one other person would be taking a train to San Francisco in a few days. He stated that Brinkman himself would not be attending the meeting; it was paramount to the success of Brinkman's organization that his identity be kept a secret. Instead, Brinkman was sending his trusted lawyer, Robert Burns.

Short wrote that he would keep Green posted when the two left Pueblo. Also, Short made it clear that Dakota and Pecos would not be allowed to meet with the secretive California gentleman. They were too new to the organization to be trusted yet. Green decided to let Short give that piece of information to Dakota and Pecos himself.

Short left the other pretend deputy, Tom O'Hara, in charge of the gang members who stayed in Pueblo. O'Hara, though a close friend of Short, was not aware of Cole Brinkman's identity or his alias. In addition, Cole had Short send a gang member named Colorado Jackson, a gunman, to Hays City on a mission – to seek out an individual and put three slugs into him. He also instructed the assassin what to do with the body.

Five days later, and after placing a sign on his window that read, "Gone on vacation, will be back in two weeks", Attorney

Robert Burns, along with John Short, caught the train to San Francisco. But they didn't travel side by side. It was important that they put on the appearance that they were not acquainted, not only as the train pulled out from the depot, but on the entire trip to San Francisco as well. They took no chances because they did not know the identity of the other passengers on the train.

Meanwhile in Hays City, a dead man was found at sunup one morning on the front porch of Preacher Barnes's house. Deputy Jake told the preacher in private that it was the other Pinkerton agent in town, the other agent responsible to protect him.

CHAPTER FIVE:

The Secret Society Revealed

"Is the train from Colorado on time?"

"Yes sir, it appears that it is," the depot manager said. "It should be rolling in here in about..." The depot manager pulled out his pocket watch, flipped open the lid, looked at it for about five seconds and said, "Should be here in about fifteen minutes."

Green walked over to Dakota and Pecos and said,

"They'll be here in fifteen minutes."

"Hey Green, mi amigo, do you know this Attorney Robert Burns, John Short is bringing with him?"

"I know of him, but I never met him before and didn't know he had anything to do with the gang until I received word from Short that he was coming instead of Brinkman. I'm not sure if that will suit Harrington's boss or not. You heard the same thing I did. They wanted Brinkman."

Dakota, Pecos, and Green sat in the depot waiting for the arrival of the Central Pacific. The depot was crowded with people – some waiting to catch this train to Sacramento, others waiting for friends, relatives or business associates to arrive.

And there it was, right on time, ole engine 99, blasting its shrieking whistle through the brisk San Francisco air, and belching off a cloud of thick black smoke which left a one half mile long stream trailing behind it. The recognizable clickety-clack of the steel wheels against connected steel rails became louder and louder signaling that the 11:15 was quickly approaching the depot.

At the first sounds of the oncoming iron horse, the sitting crowd stood up in unison and hastily squeezed through the depot doors like the rapids of the Colorado River rushing through the corridors of the Rocky Mountain Range. The crowd quickly filled up the wooden walkway and watched the train as it approached. Then the locomotive came to a screeching halt and blew the excessive steam through the wheels signaling to the conductor that the passengers could now step off – the train had come to a complete stop.

Green stood in front of Dakota and Pecos, his eyes shifting back and forth between the six passenger cars, searching for Short and Attorney Burns among the passengers stepping off the train. It took a while but Green finally spotted Short stepping down from the fourth car back. A well-dressed gentleman followed behind him. The walkway was now packed with people, double the size because of the large number of passengers exiting the train cars and the large number of greeters already on the waiting platform. It wasn't easy to look over the heads and through the crowd for the one you were searching for.

"There they are," Green said.

"Where?" Dakota asked.

"Come on, follow me."

Dakota and Pecos followed Green as he led the way. They walked down two cars, maneuvering themselves in and around the mass of people.

Green walked up and shook hands with Short. Short then greeted Dakota and Pecos with handshakes as well.

"Well gentlemen, I want you to meet Mr. Brinkman's lawyer. This is Attorney Robert Burns. Robert, these are the gentlemen I told you about: Bobby Green, Dakota Wilson, and Pecos Fransisco," Short said.

Attorney Burns set his luggage down. He seemed friendly enough to the three all right. He had a smile on his face, and he offered a firm handshake. But Burns (a.k.a. Cole Brinkman) was working on obtaining a first impression of his new gang members, especially Pecos who had baggage – killer baggage, and unpredictable "fly off the handle" baggage.

"Well Green, what's the plan?" Short asked.

"Here's what I thought we would do. First we'll travel over to the hotel where we are all staying. We booked a reservation for you. You can sign in, take your luggage to your rooms, change clothes if you like, and then we'll meet for lunch in the hotel's restaurant. They have a nice luncheon menu. After that, I thought we would all travel over to Diamond Lil's Crystal Palace to talk and set up a meeting with that Harrington person I told you about."

"Sounds good Green, what's our means of transportation?" Short asked.

"I leased a carriage for you and Mr. Burns. We three are riding horses. Come on, I'll show you to the carriage, then you can follow us to the hotel."

The hotel wasn't far from the train depot. It took them only ten minutes to get there. The two signed in, went up to their rooms, and then came down looking for Green, Dakota, and Pecos in the crowded restaurant – it was right at noon.

Green spotted the two and waved them over to their table. When they sat down, Burns picked up his menu and asked how the food was at this restaurant.

Dakota replied that the food was excellent. But while everyone was looking over their menus, Pecos stared at Mr. Burns for a minute or so. Even though Burns didn't walk, or even closely resemble his brother Jerod Brinkman in the way he was built, Pecos saw something in his eyes, and heard something in his voice, that made him think maybe this gringo Burns was not who he said he was. But he kept his feelings to himself, at least for now.

There was no business discussed at the table during lunch, even though the urge was there by everyone. The place was too crowded and their conversation would have been heard too easily – they all understood that.

When they finished their meals, Burns politely picked up the bill. They then went up to Green's room for a short meeting. That's when Green told Short and Burns everything he knew up to that point about the treasure and the risks involved. Burns was doubtful about everything he heard, yet the potential treasure trove tipped the scales more to his greed side than his skeptical side.

After their short meeting, they all rode over to the Crystal Palace to meet with Diamond Lil. You couldn't carry a pistol in her establishment. Instead you had to drop it off in the coat check room at the front of the building. They didn't follow the rules before, but today they did.

The four were surprised when Attorney Burns checked in a Smith & Wesson Model 3 "Schofield" revolver with a pearl handle. He removed it from a shoulder holster underneath his suit coat. However, he was not about to relinquish the second pistol he had hidden in the inside pocket of his suit coat, a Colt New Line Pocket Model Revolver, .22 caliber, nickel plated, with walnut grips manufactured in 1876. Truth be known though, the other four had hidden second pistols as well, with one of them concealing an Arkansas toothpick in his boot, ole Pecos.

Diamond Lil was standing at the bar talking to a customer when she glanced over at the front door and saw the five gentlemen enter. Actually only one was dressed the part of a gentleman. That was of course Attorney Burns.

Diamond Lil signaled with her head and eyes for them to go upstairs. She waited about five minutes. When the orchestra began playing and the dance hall girls came out on stage, that's when she went up as well.

The boys already had brandy poured for themselves. Burns politely waited until Diamond Lil offered him a choice between brandy or straight up Kentucky bourbon. He took the bourbon.

"Here you go sir. I'm Diamond Lil. I take it you are Brinkman's lawyer, Mr. Burns."

"Thank you ma'am. That's right ma'am. I'm Robert Burns. Mr. Brinkman couldn't make it here today…"

"Cut the crap Burns. I know why he's not here. Let's get one thing straight. We are all in this together. Oh that's right guys, Harrington and his boss agreed that I should get equal shares of your take. If you don't agree, then we'll find other means to confiscate the loot. Got that gentlemen?"

For whatever reason, Lil began talking tougher during this get together. She thought it was about time she let this group know where she stood on this matter.

The four guys looked over at Burns as if waiting for some type of affirmation on Diamond Lil's demand.

"Today I speak for Mr. Brinkman. I can assure you that your share will be the same as everyone else's. After all, you're the one who brought us all together," Attorney Burns said.

"Dang right… Good, now that we have that out of the way, when do you want to meet with Mr. Harrington?"

"The sooner the better," Burns said.

"I can have him over here within the hour. Is that soon enough?"

"Yes, go ahead, send for him."

"I'll do it right now. In the meantime you can walk around downstairs and enjoy the Palace. We have drinking, gambling and some great shows today. Although I would suggest you stay sober for our next meeting."

Diamond Lil wrote a note, put it in an envelope, sealed it, and wrote Harrington's name on it. She then gave it to an errand boy and sent him over to the hotel where she knew Harrington was staying.

Harrington opened the envelope and read it.

Harrington. They are here and wish to meet with you now. Brinkman did not come. He sent his lawyer instead…Lillian.

This letter infuriated Harrington because he knew his boss would be more than upset not being able to personally meet with Brinkman. Since Harrington was just a messenger, he decided to go ahead and meet with the group of desperados.

Within the hour he was walking through the front door of Diamond Lil's Crystal Palace. The five men were scattered throughout the Palace. Harrington saw Diamond Lil standing at the bar flirting with a couple of customers. He approached her and she signaled him to go upstairs. She then called Green over and told him to gather the other four and go upstairs, one by one - "Don't make a scene," she said. Lil then followed Harrington.

There were no drinks offered. This meeting was too serious to allow alcohol to make the mind dull, or give someone foolish verbal courage which could kill the deal before it even began. The costs were too high for any type of mistakes like that.

Diamond Lil did the introduction of Harrington to Attorney Burns. Harrington and Burns were the two best dressed men in the room. They both had the appearance of professional businessmen. The others resembled clean-cut tough looking cowboys, gun hands of sorts, but without their pistols strapped to their sides. Diamond Lil was all fluffed up like normal, pretty as a peacock. Everyone sat around the large round table in the room except for Diamond Lil and Harrington. He appeared a bit nervous or unsettled. Diamond Lil stood there like a spectator guarding the door so no one would walk in on the meeting.

"Mr. Burns, why are you here instead of Mr. Brinkman?" Harrington asked. "I believe you were told that this deal would not move forward unless Brinkman himself showed up."

"Mr. Harrington, there is something you must know about Mr. Brinkman. He's a shrewd and very successful man in everything he does. He is successful in his ways because he remains incognito. That's the way he has always worked his deals. That's the way it has always been, and that's the way it will continue to be.

Look, what I know is that you have a proposition to offer that can reap large monetary rewards. I also understand that this mission could be quite lethal without the best planning and the best team to go in and get the job done. I guarantee Mr. Brinkman and his team are the ones who can make this project a success. Now, where do we go from here?" Burns asked.

"I'll go back and talk to my boss. I'll tell him the circumstances. That's all I can do."

"Where is this mysterious boss of yours?" Burns asked.

"I'm sorry, but I cannot tell you that. If he agrees to meet with you instead of Brinkman, then you will meet with him soon."

"Soon meaning what? Days, weeks? I have other business to attend to back home. How soon are you talking about?" Burns asked.

"Just a few days, that's all. Also, I must tell you that my boss is well versed in the secret society he belonged to. He knows how they gathered this great amount of wealth and what they plan on using it for. He is a very detailed individual, very educated, and if he accepts your team as the ones to participate, he will be informing you of everything, I mean everything. His meeting with you could take a few days. I will go to him right after this meeting.

However, there is one last thing you must know about my boss," Harrington said.

"What's that?" Burns asked.

"My boss at one time held a position with the secret society, which fit him perfectly. He was one of their trained assassins – they say the most callous. He's hard, hard as rocks. One might even call him pure evil - born and bred in the pits of hell. He has no morals - seems like he never did. He was known to torture people before he killed them. They say he got great pleasure in both. This is one man you do not want to double-cross. When he defected from the secret society, three assassins left with him. Four trained assassins immediately went searching for them; they dogged the defectors all the way to the west coast. Those four doggers met their demise near my boss's hacienda. Their body parts were scattered all around the countryside. Just thought you needed to know that before you meet him," Harrington said.

Quiet filled the room. That appalling story gave everyone pause.

Two days went by before they heard from Harrington again. But when they did, he brought back good news. The mysterious boss agreed to meet with three individuals, Attorney Burns, John Short, and Bobby Green. It was Short who informed Dakota and Pecos that they were not welcome in the meeting. Pecos was visually perturbed at the news. Dakota understood and accepted the directive, at least for now. However, Burns insisted that Dakota and Pecos ride on their horses alongside for his own protection. Burns's money belt was virtually bulging at the seams. He was never without it. That's why he wanted protection.

Harrington leased a four seated carriage for Burns, Short, Green, and himself. The destination was a large hacienda at Half Moon Bay, which was straight south from San Francisco. It was a long 22 mile trek and would take most of the day since they had to rest and water the horses a few times along the hardened dirt path.

The trail was well traveled so they hoped for a safe journey - free from marauders and such. Oh there was always the risk of stagecoach robberies along the route all right, if you were traveling by that means of transportation. The Wells Fargo Stage constantly feared holdups from the infamous double barrel shotgun toting Black Bart, although his hits up to now were north of San Francisco.

Half Moon Bay was a beautiful place in San Mateo County, along the shores of the blue Pacific Ocean. On a calm day inland you could hear the sounds of the waves pounding the sandy Pacific shorelines in a rhythmic pattern, and the constant unique barking of sea lions, especially during mating season in May.

Half Moon Bay began as a pastoral agricultural area which was mainly utilized for grazing cattle, horses, and oxen owned by the Spanish Mission San Francisco de Asis. The small settlement was established in June of 1776 and named for St. Francis of Assisi, the founder of the Franciscan Order. The Spanish mission eventually became secularized in the 1830's.

It was around the year 1840 when the community began to develop as the first bona fide town in the county. The settlement was first known as San Benito but the name was later changed to Spanishtown. It attracted a thriving fishing industry and continued as an important coastal agricultural area. It was an ethnically diverse community, settled by: Portuguese, Scots, Canadians, Chinese, English, Germans, Irish, Mexicans, Italians, and Pacific Islanders.

During the California Gold Rush of 1849, the town began to expand. Two good roads were established between San Francisco and Spanishtown and the area became a resort and entertainment district. Some of the old mission properties were sold and leased for saloons and gaming houses. Even racetracks were constructed. In 1874 Spanishtown was officially renamed Half Moon Bay.

Harrington did not give specific directions for their exact destination. He only stated that it was on the north side of Half Moon Bay, and it was an established hacienda that had existed for many years. He told them it was owned by a wealthy gentleman of Portuguese ancestry, who of course was his boss – who remained anonymous up to now.

The gang of five and their guide, Mr. Harrington, left San Francisco at sunup after grabbing an early hearty breakfast at the hotel. Pecos and Dakota were not only armed with their pistols but both had rifles stashed in scabbards. The others were armed as well but with sidearms and, of course, their concealed weapons. Green's horse was tethered to the back of the carriage.

Dakota and Pecos interpreted their responsibilities accurately. They were the sentries along the trail - the first ones to meet danger head on if circumstances necessitated such. At times they rode along each side of the carriage and at other times, Pecos took the point and Dakota took the drag. They kept their eyes peeled at all times. Pecos and Dakota were notorious gunmen, fast on the draw and as accurate as James Butler Hickok (ole Wild Bill) at great distances, so Burns felt relatively safe traveling with them by his side.

At about 4:00 in the afternoon, the six men came upon old adobe walls which surrounded a huge Spanish mansion. They stopped in front of the large thick double wooden doors – they were too large to be called gates. There were two armed sentries, in what appeared to be guardhouses protruding above the wall, positioned on each side of the entrance. Burns perceived them as two of the defecting assassins Harrington spoke of. The place had the appearance of a fortress – a greatly secured fortress.

Harrington waved to one of the sentries who in turn signaled to a person on the ground, and within a few seconds, the large doors began to slowly open toward the inside. Harrington grabbed his buggy whip and lightly touched the hindquarters of his Belgians to move them forward and ride through the entrance. Dakota and Pecos followed, meticulously observing everything in sight. At this point, no one knew the perils which might lie ahead. Exercising caution at this stage seemed to be rather prudent.

As the men entered the courtyard of the hacienda, the bulky doors were quickly closed and three sentries secured them shut with a large cross-beam just a few inches thinner than a railroad tie.

Dakota and Pecos quickly looked back and both felt trapped with no way out at this point.

No one came out of the house to greet them. As Dakota and Pecos dismounted, the others climbed out of the carriage. They all left their belongings in place except for Dakota and Pecos – they pulled their rifles out of their scabbards – a matter of habit.

Then they all walked up to the front door. Harrington knocked on it. They could hear four bolts slide, one right after the other, and then the door opened. Welcoming the six with a smile and a nod was an elderly gentleman, about seventy-five one would guess, maybe older. He looked distinguished enough – graying hair and goatee – well groomed. He appeared to be the house butler, a servant.

Harrington took charge at this point and asked the five men to sit in the parlor while he fetched the owner, the one claimed by Burns to be the "mysterious man". While they were waiting, the servant offered each a snifter of brandy. They all accepted without hesitation. Instead of sitting down though, they walked around the parlor eyeing all of the Spanish artifacts that were on display. The room resembled a Portuguese or Spanish museum with displays of: several armored conquistador suits, lances, old war muskets, silverware, swords, art, bronzes, and more. It was quite a sight to behold. But what caught their eyes more than anything were the medieval torture devices in one of the corners of the room.

Harrington then walked out from a large study and said,

"Pardon me gentlemen, but I would like to introduce to you Mr. Carlos Bautista."

Everyone quickly turned their attention toward Mr. Bautista, anxious to get a quick look at the mysterious man who had been a high ranking officer and a ruthless assassin in a secret society, and the one who allegedly knew the whereabouts of the secret society's hidden treasures, a wealth valued at well over 100 million dollars.

His appearance was not what Burns expected: he was tall, slender, very educated looking, neatly dressed with a tight vest, and sporting a long gray mustache. He bore a resemblance to a quintessential fencing instructor from Spain because of his appearance, dress, and the fact that he entered the room holding a fencing sword at his side. However he hung it on the wall next to the double doors after he made his entrance and before walking over to his guests.

Harrington first introduced Mr. Bautista to Attorney Burns.

"Ah, so you are Attorney Burns."

"That's right, sir."

"You are the attorney for Cole Brinkman, yes?"

"That's right."

"I am sorry that your Mr. Brinkman did not think enough about the opportunity that this project has to offer to come to this very important meeting himself. However, I do understand his position, after it was explained to me by Mr. Harrington.

Mr. Burns, are you an educated man?"

"Excuse me sir?"

"Are you educated? Do you have a higher education?"

"I am an attorney and yes, I have a higher education. Why is that important?"

"It's important because I'm not just going to inform you where the treasure trove is, oh no. I'm going to give you the history of these treasures, where they came from, what they were used for in previous centuries up until now, and what the current intentions are regarding the use of these treasures by this secret society. Once you know these things, you will understand the lethal danger that is inherent in an attempt to confiscate any amount of this wealth. But that being said, please introduce me to these other gentlemen. Mr. Harrington gave me their names. Now I would like to put faces to those names."

"All right, this is Mr. Short, Mr. Green, Dakota Wilson, and Pecos Fransisco," Burns said. "I was told by Mr. Harrington that only three of us could attend your meeting. Mr. Short, Mr. Green and I will be attending. Dakota and Pecos will not."

"I saw that you were admiring some of my medieval torture artifacts," Bautista said.

"We were looking at them; not sure you can say we were admiring them," Burns replied.

"Well let me show you a few. Right behind you on that table is what's known as a 'head crusher'."

Everyone turned around as Bautista walked over to it and put his hand on the handle that screwed the crusher down. It wasn't a large device – maybe about twenty inches tall – but it was very effective.

"Have you seen or ever used one of these before?" Bautista asked.

Everyone obviously said no.

"No? That's too bad. They are very effective you know. You see, with the head placed under this upper cup right here and the chin placed above this bottom bar… well wait a minute, would one of you like to demonstrate it by placing your head in it? I promise I won't do you harm."

Bautista paused and looked at each one. There were no takers.

"No? Then I will continue. Once the head is in position, the top screw of this beautifully effective device is slowly turned, compressing the skull tightly. First the teeth are destroyed, shattering and splintering into the jaw – I can assure you that is very painful. Then the eyes are squeezed from the sockets – this little receptacle on the side here is used to catch them. Lastly the skull is fractured and the contents of the head are forced out. At this point the pain ceases after the person screams for the last time just before the crushing."

"Ay, chihuahua!" Pecos said as everyone else cringed at the word, "crushing".

Bautista smiled slightly as he pointed out several more evil torture devices giving just shorter explanations: the cat's paw or Spanish tickler made of steel and used to rip and tear flesh away from the bone from any part of the body; the knee splitter which disabled a person for life; the Judas chair and Spanish donkey which were extremely painful to sit on; and the crocodile shears which destroyed a person's manhood.

"I think we've seen enough," Burns said.

"Very well then, my servant will show you to your rooms upstairs. You can take your drinks with you if you wish. By the way, plan on being here at least three days. You are my guests."

Mr. Bautista then walked over to his fencing sword hanging on the wall, removed it, turned around pointing it straight down, and said,

"One might say you are my prisoners as well since you will not be allowed to leave the outside walls until this meeting is over and we have an agreement. But then again, I don't consider you prisoners, my friends. That's why I allowed you to keep your weapons. However, make no mistake, if anyone plans to leave here before it is permitted, it will be his demise. That is not a threat, gentlemen, that is a fact.

Now, you can freshen up and rest in your rooms, dinner will be served in two hours in the main dining room. One last thing, none of my servants know the true reason why you are here. That's how I would like to keep it. Therefore, I would ask you not to communicate with them. They have been given similar instructions. If any of you are caught or it is reported that you were seen talking to anyone other than Mr. Harrington or myself, that would be very unfortunate. These are my rules. I hope you understand."

"We do," Burns said.

After they were shown to their rooms, Short snuck over to Burns's room and quietly knocked on the door. Burns unholstered his pistol, cocked the hammer, and held it in his right hand as he slowly cracked the door with his left hand to see who it was.

"Come on in," Burns said.

Short walked in. Before Burns closed the door he looked in the hall to the right and then to the left. There was no one in sight so he quietly closed the door.

"What do you think?" Short asked.

"This guy is dangerous; I know that for a fact. But I intend to hold judgment until I hear all the specifics. This Bautista has a lot of explaining and convincing to do before we commit our resources to this project. In the meantime, I'm going to enjoy the rest, the good food, and fancy drinking. At the end of the three days, we'll make our decision. If we buy into his story and the whereabouts of those treasures, we'll begin making plans right here."

There was no holding back on dinner that night. A whole pig was roasted on a spit over hot timbers in the courtyard and slices of juicy pork were served at the meal with an assortment of boiled and creamed vegetables. The subtle sweetness and lightness of the pork called for the buttery, fruity flavor of a wonderful California chardonnay.

Mr. Bautista kept a wide assortment of wines in his cellar from the oldest premium winery in Sonoma. It was the Buena Vista Winery which was founded in 1857 by "Count" Agoston Haraszthy: a farmer, innovator and vintner, author, cunning businessman, and a zealous promoter of his great wines. These wines were considered the best California had to offer at that time.

Mr. Bautista refused to discuss business at the dinner table. Instead, the discourse was about the area known as Half Moon Bay and how it came into existence. He cunningly veered away from most of his past which was as much a mystery as the secrets of the secret society with which he was well acquainted.

This was the time of year when the days were long and nightfall came late. So there was plenty of time left after dinner for recreational activity in the courtyard. Mr. Bautista had a shooting range set up for pistol and rifle target shooting. He thought it would be wise to test the skills of the men he intended to partner with to steal the hidden treasures. After all, to pull off such a magnificent feat, it would require marksmanship skills far above the average westerner. Dakota, Pecos, Green, and Short were all willing to demonstrate their shooting skills with their six-shooters.

Bautista supplied the ammunition for the exhibition. Burns did not participate but stood with Bautista on the sidelines wanting to observe the demonstration himself. Harrington stood with them.

A servant placed ten various hand fruits on a rail. Then he took five large steps away from the rail and drew a line. The distance was about fifteen feet. Bautista asked the four to line up shoulder to shoulder just behind the line and face the targets; from left to right were Short, Green, Dakota, and Pecos.

"Gentlemen, when I shout out your name, draw and shoot just two targets, only two. I am anxious to observe your quickness and accuracy. Are you ready?" Mr. Bautista asked.

They all nodded in the affirmative.

"Then make ready!" he shouted.

"Dakota!"

Dakota drew faster than lightning and picked off the two on the right.

"Pecos!"

With skill equaling Dakota's, Pecos splattered two oranges on the left.

"Green!"

Green drew his pistol, a tad bit slower than the other two desperados but his aim was perfect, shattering two apples and sending multiple pieces through the air.

Short did not wait for his name to be called but skinned his six-shooter as fast as any of them and picked off two pieces of fruit of the four remaining targets.

They all began laughing and carrying on about their marksmanship skills until a rifle shot from one of the guard towers rang out and picked off one of the two remaining pieces of fruit while a rifle shot from the other guard tower picked off the last piece of fruit.

The men ducked when they heard the shots. They looked toward the towers and then where the targets were set up. It was obvious to all that those sharpshooters up in the guard towers were assassins showing off their skills. Bautista set up that demonstration to prove a point.

"Very impressive," Bautista said. "Set them up again, Jose."

He did and the target shooting began once more - this time the men in the guard towers refrained from the exhibition. Bautista asked Burns to sit on the porch and have a drink and smoke a cigar with him while the four blasted away and used up the free ammunition. Harrington stood and watched the shootings from a hitching rail nearby.

While enjoying the shooting match and sipping brandy, the two gentlemen on the porch endeavored to get a perspective of the other but interestingly enough, neither one wanted to discuss their background which made the conversation quite dull and inconsequential.

Bautista told Burns to have his men ready for breakfast at 7:00. He said the meeting with Burns, Green and Short would start promptly at 8:00 tomorrow morning in his study. When Bautista was about to excuse himself, Burns pulled a surprise request.

"Mr. Bautista, I want you to reconsider your demand to only allow three people in your meeting. I trust all four of these men to the fullest. I want them to hear your story. I value their opinions as I will be the one communicating to my boss the feasibility and veracity of your claims. Please understand, I mean no offense sir."

"None taken Burns.

Do you make those kinds of decisions for your boss?" Bautista asked.

"I have that authority."

"Well then, if it's OK with you, it's OK with me. However, let me be blunt. Anyone, and I mean anyone, who hears my story and plans a double cross, will pay – and I'm not talking in monetary terms."

Bautista smiled slightly then turned around and walked to his study. He did not give Burns time to respond. Burns stared into the air at the smoke he blew from his cigar. His authoritative pride was verbally slapped down, and he didn't like it one bit. However, as Attorney Burns, he had to turn the other cheek and back off.

Bautista spent the next couple of hours with Harrington in the study and made last minute preparations for the presentation to Brinkman's gang. Bautista was determined to be detailed in such a fashion that he would convince the gang to accept the job and partner with him on this perilous, but extremely lucrative adventure. That is, of course, if they could actually pull off the biggest treasure heist in history.

When the next day finally arrived, and breakfast and coffee were consumed, Mr. Bautista invited the five men and Harrington into his large study. The room was large but simple, yet it had the appearance of a library of knowledge blanketing the west wall; there were twenty feet of shelving full of an assortment of leather bound books of all sizes - neatly placed - from the floor to the fifteen foot high ceiling. A ladder system on a rail was installed to give access to the books above a person's normal reach.

The morning was cool with the winds blowing out of the west coming off the Pacific Ocean. The servants had built a fire in the large masonry fireplace at first light, so the wood was flaming and crackling; the warmth was felt a good distance into the room already.

There were two six-foot round tables in the middle of the room, situated about five feet apart from each other. The chairs were placed away from the tables and lined up against the east wall. There was a rolled up map on each table which Bautista would eventually use as props; a Bible, which seemed to be out of place, was on one of the tables, as well.

On the south wall behind a bulky mahogany desk was a large map of North America highlighting the states, the territories, and Mexico. This room was decorated with just a few Spanish artifacts, not as many as the main hacienda room.

Everything seemed quite normal except for the object on a 2' x 4' table, five feet in front of the fireplace. It appeared to be a model of an ancient structure one might find in the Middle East. It got everyone's attention when they entered the room.

A servant brought a fresh pot of coffee and six cups into the study. He placed them on a small marble top table near the entrance.

"Gentlemen, if you wish to grab a cup of coffee before I begin, Jose will do the honors for you."

Harrington, Pecos, Dakota, Green, and Short walked over to the table and held up a cup to be filled – Burns did not. Then they walked over to Bautista who was standing next to the rectangular table near the fireplace. Bautista was holding the Bible in one hand and a double edge knife in the other which he would use as a pointer. Burns saw a look in Bautista's eyes that he deemed impressive. He accurately read an inner passion that was about to reveal itself to the group.

"Gentlemen, let's get started," Bautista said. "My premise, the foundation of my assertion, is a fact and a simple truth. I know this because I was part of it; I lived it as an assassin and a chief officer of a clandestine society until I defected. This secret society is more powerful than man has ever known. That is a fact. What makes it so powerful is that there has been a great amalgamation of many prominent secret societies in the world, all agreeing to one specific goal.

That's how I wish to begin this meeting; but that will be my closing conclusion as well as I lay out the facts for you, one by one, and finally relinquish the name of the new secret society and the whereabouts of their great wealth - their accumulated treasures.

I am standing here next to a model. The actual structure no longer exists; but there is another structure in its place. This is a model of what was known as Solomon's Temple. In its place today is what is known as the Dome of the Rock – at least it is believed to be at the exact location of the original Temple. Solomon's Temple was located in the heart of the holy city of Jerusalem. If you aren't familiar with the Old Testament, Solomon was a spectacularly wealthy and a wise king of Israel. He was the son of King David, the previous king of Israel. King David established Jerusalem as the Capital of Israel around 1003 BC. His reign as king was 1010-970 BC. Solomon's reign as king was around 970 to 931 BC.

According to the Bible, during Solomon's reign, Israel enjoyed great commercial prosperity, with extensive traffic being carried on by land with Tyre, Egypt, and Arabia, and by sea with Tarshish, Ophir, and South India. This was a time of great wealth, prosperity and power for the tribes of Israel."

Bautista paused and opened the Bible to 1 Kings 9:10. He read that it took 20 years during Solomon's reign to build both the Temple and the king's palace. But the Temple itself took right at 7 years. At this point he made it clear that he wasn't a Bible reading person for the sake of being sanctimonious. He was just interested in the relevant history.

Then he referred to 1 Kings 9:11.

"This verse explains where Solomon acquired some of his material used to build the Temple and palace. It reads, 'Hiram, King of Tyre, supplying Solomon with all the cedar wood, fir wood and gold he wished – King Solomon gave Hiram twenty cities in the land of Galilee in return'."

"What's the point?" Green asked.

The other men looked at Green and then back at Bautista for an answer. Bautista smiled and said,

"Patience my good man, I am getting to the point. The Temple was built of precious things like gold, silver, copper and ivory too. It was dedicated to Yahweh, the God of Israel, and it was said to house some of the greatest treasures ever known to mankind, items like the Menorah, the Table of Showbread, and the treasure of all treasures, the Ark of the Covenant."

"What are those things, Senor?" Pecos asked. "And why are they so important?"

Bautista looked at Pecos. His eyes moved from the Mexican's boots to the top of his head. Then he asked,

"How tall are you, Pecos?"

"Not tall, maybe 5'5" or 5'6", I don't know. I know this though; I can draw quicker than a man 6'2" tall, Senor. Why you ask me this, mi amigo?"

"Because the Menorah was about as tall as you at 5'4", and it was made of pure gold."

"Pure gold? Ay, chihuahua! Are we going to steal this thing?"

"Not likely, Pecos – but there will be gold - lots of gold. I can assure you of that. Anyway, the Menorah resembled a candelabra but it is described in the Bible as an ancient Hebrew lampstand used in the portable sanctuary established by Moses in the wilderness and then 300 years later in the Temple. Candles didn't exist back then. It was actually an oil lamp – they used fresh olive oil of the purest quality to burn daily. The Bible states that God himself revealed the design for the Menorah to Moses and describes the construction of the Menorah in Exodus 25:31-40," Bautista said as he held up the Bible.

"The Table of Showbread was not pure gold but a small table made of acacia wood and overlaid with pure gold. It had significance with Moses and in the Temple as well, and information about it can be found in Exodus 25:23-30."

Bautista paused a minute to walk over to the fireplace and stoke the logs. Then he walked back beside the model and with great vigor he said,

"The real treasure that was stored in Solomon's Temple was the Ark of the Covenant which housed the actual tablets that God gave Moses on the mount. The Ark of the Covenant also contained Aaron's rod and a pot of manna. The design of the Ark can be found in Exodus 25:10-22. I won't get into that now."

"Who is this Aaron fella?" Short asked.

Dakota jumped into the conversation and said,

"I can tell you. My ma used to read the Bible to us when we were youngins. That's how we spent many cold winter evenings in the Dakota Territory. I can remember with the light and warmth from the fireplace, she led us in prayer asking for protection from the Sioux. Then she would read excerpts from various parts of the Bible – she called it the Good Book. I think it was the King James Version.

She would sit in her rocking chair and me and my brother would sit in front of her with our backs to the fireplace. Pa would sit at the table smoking his pipe. He didn't show much interest in the Bible. His mind was always on the possibility of Indians breaking down the door, swarming our cabin, and scalping all of us. He always kept his double barrel 10 gauge shotgun nearby. Anyway, I never forgot the parts about Aaron's rod because as a kid, it frightened me. I was afraid of snakes."

Everyone was now captivated by Dakota's story – everyone except for Burns. This Bible stuff was boring him to death. He just wanted to know about the treasures - that's really all he cared about.

If Bautista was impressed that Dakota knew this part of the Bible, he sure didn't show it. However, Dakota felt an inner pride that he could relate this particular Bible story to the group. For just a few minutes it seemed like there was a softer side to this hardened criminal.

"You see, Aaron was the brother of Moses. According to my ma, and I guess the Bible, God performed many miracles through that rod: it turned into a snake in Pharaoh's court, it turned the water of the Nile into blood, and summoned the plagues of the frogs and gnats."

Dakota paused, looked down, shrugged his shoulders, and said almost in an embarrassing fashion,

"That's about all I remember."

"Ay, chihuahua!... snakes, blood, frogs, and gnats?" Pecos questioned as his eyes almost popped out of his head at the very sound of those things. It sounded like voodoo stuff or witchcraft to him. So he put his hand into his pocket and began rubbing his Mexican mystical pouch which was full of a magic potion of strange dried animal offcuts, and special herbs which he claimed brought him good luck.

"Seems like you know your Bible, Dakota," Bautista said. "Aaron's rod played an important part in God's plan to lead the Israelites out of Egypt and into the Promised Land."

Then the passion on Bautista's face, and in his voice, shown through like a man who just discovered the last clue to the Lost Dutchman's Gold Mine in the Superstition Mountains, near Apache Junction, east of Phoenix, Arizona Territory.

"The Ark has been sought after by many. The legend is that it contains supernatural powers, and any army possessing it could completely destroy its enemies. That gentlemen, made it worth going after – made it worth going to war for.

Solomon's treasures were said to be enormous, and consisting of not only what I just mentioned, but jewels, thousands of sacred objects, and cases and cases of gold and silver coins.

They say Solomon's gold came from his gold mines in Mount Ophir located in Malaysia. He sent his empty ships there, and they came back loaded with trunks and barrels of gold. But no one really knows exactly where those mines were located.

Now, Israel over the many centuries had been attacked by outsiders - enemies seeking land and treasures no doubt. Solomon's Temple, which was known as the first Temple, along with Jerusalem was destroyed in 586 BC by an individual known as Nebuchadnezzar – and a portion of the population of the Kingdom of Judah, South of the Kingdom of Israel, was taken into exile in Babylon. But in 520 BC, 50,000 Jews returned and the construction of the Second Temple began on what was known as the Temple Mount. It stood there between 516 BC and 70 AD. The Second Temple still housed the Menorah and the Table of Showbread. However, the Ark of the Covenant was nowhere to be found."

Bautista paused again and put the Bible and knife down. Then with both of his hands, in what appeared to be an anxious moment, he ran them through his hair, from the front to the back. This gesture took them all down the path of anxiety.

Then Bautista said slowly and deliberately while looking straight into the eyes of Attorney Burns,

"Here's the important part. Throughout the years of attacks on the Kingdom and specifically Jerusalem, most of Solomon's treasures were never found - at least, not yet."

Then Bautista paused and said,

"This is a good time to fill up your coffee cups if you wish. Jose just brought in a fresh pot."

"Sounds good to me," Burns said.

This time everyone participated in grabbing a cup of coffee. The room was becoming quite warm due to the large fire in the fireplace. While Bautista was talking, Jose had quietly entered a couple of times and placed more seasoned eucalyptus logs on the fire to keep the flames high. No one paid any attention to him since they were all focused on what Bautista was saying.

While Jose was pouring the coffee into the cups held out by the guests, Bautista walked over and opened the French doors to the courtyard to allow fresh air to enter. These doors were on the east side of the building, consequently the room would not get the full force of the strong breeze coming off the Pacific. However, it did allow some of the stuffy air to escape, and that was certainly welcomed.

When the coffee cups were filled, everyone walked back over to where Bautista was standing, next to the model again. They felt like they were getting close to hearing the exciting finale; but it wasn't coming quite yet. Bautista still had plans to lay the foundation of where all of the targeted treasures originated from, and what the intent was of this gigantic secret society from which he defected.

"In the next two hours I will take you through the Roman period of Jerusalem and then we'll skip up to the point which will have great interest to you and will be relevant to our cause. I'm talking about the secret society known as the Knights Templar, and Solomon's treasures later to become the Templar's treasures, which are part of the riches we intend to get our hands on."

Burns took a sip of coffee and looked at Short over the rim of his cup. Short looked back at Burns while he took a sip as well. None of them knew anything about the Knights Templar or their treasures, but it sure struck up their interest – that was a fact. It was like they were both thinking the same thing, "now we're getting somewhere".

Bautista continued,

"The Roman period in the Kingdom of Judah lasted from 63 BC to 324 AD. Of course, part of this period is when Jesus walked the earth. General Pompey captured Jerusalem for Rome in 63 BC. Christ who became the Messiah to Christians was crucified on April 25th in the year 31 AD.

There was a great revolt of the Jews against the Romans which began in 66 AD and lasted for a few years. But just before the year 70 AD, it appears that the Jews knew that Rome was sending Titus and his troops to conquer Jerusalem. So the Chief Priests hid many of their treasures and what was thought to be Solomon's treasures, in crevices and caves under the Temple Mount. They didn't have time to hide it all, but they did hide a great portion.

Titus and his army besieged and conquered the city of Jerusalem during 70 AD and destroyed the Second Temple. They eventually marched back to Rome supposedly with the Menorah and many treasures from the city. But we know that they didn't find all of Solomon's treasures. Yes, gentlemen, we know that for a fact.

From 324 to 638 AD you have the Byzantine Period – both a peaceful period and a war-like period. From 638 – 1099 AD was the early Muslim Period. Jews were allowed to come back into the city early during the Muslim Period. In 691 AD the Dome of the Rock was completed on the site of the Second Temple. It's a Muslim Mosque. But in 1010 Caliph al-Hakim ordered the destruction of all synagogues and churches and they killed many Christians and Jews and disbelievers of their faith. The Holy City now belonged to the Muslims. This is what triggered the First Crusade.

In 1096 Pope Urban II sent an army to recapture the birth place of Christianity from the Muslims. It was a bloody war – some say they were ankle deep in blood in Jerusalem. The Christian army defeated the Muslims and captured Jerusalem in 1099 and Eastern Christians were freed from Muslim rule.

People from all over Europe and the Middle East began pilgrimages to the Holy Land. But many were attacked, robbed, and murdered by thieves, bandits and Muslims who preyed upon the pilgrims. Sometimes they were slaughtered by the hundreds. The Crusaders didn't have enough manpower to protect the pilgrims.

In 1119, a French knight named Hugues de Payens approached King Baldwin II of Jerusalem with 8 other knights. He proposed creating a monastic order for protection of the pilgrims."

"Monastic? What does that mean?" Short asked.

"Well, they were like monks: they took vows of poverty, chastity, and obedience. They considered themselves soldiers for Christ. Like I said, they wanted to form an organization to protect pilgrims. However, some thought they had other motives."

"Like what?" Burns asked.

"Well, I'm getting to that. The King agreed to the request and gave them quarters in the wing of the royal palace on the Temple Mount which was above what was believed to be the site of the Temple of Solomon. From then on the knights took the name 'Poor Knights of Christ and the Temple of Solomon', or the 'Templar Knights', or the 'Knights Templar'. They were poor at first. Their symbol was two knights on a horse meaning each knight couldn't even afford his own horse.

Oh, but their impoverished state did not last long. It is told that for eight years one of their activities was to dig in the stable area under where the Temple of Solomon was located. Rumor has it they were looking for Solomon's treasures. They found some of it, actually a lot of it: stashes of gold and silver hidden in the crevices and caves that honeycombed the ground under the Temple Mount. They didn't find the Ark of the Covenant, but they found coins and jewels worth millions.

Some say there were other treasures they were searching for but probably didn't find."

"Like what?" Short asked.

"Like the legendary Lance of Longinus. The theory was that if you had this lance, you could conquer all your enemies."

"What made that so?" Burns asked.

"In Christian terms it was the spear the centurion used to pierce the side of Jesus Christ according to the gospel of John. Therefore it was thought to have great powers.

One of the other treasures which was thought that the Templars were looking for was what was known as the Holy Grail."

"What's the Holy Grail?" Short asked.

"The Holy Grail? Well it's again one of the most sought after treasures in all of history, if it truly exists. I for one believe that it does. The word grail means a cup or bowl of earth, wood, or metal. The most popular story declares that the Holy Grail was the cup that Jesus used at the Last Supper and which Joseph of Arimathea later used to collect drops of Jesus's blood at the crucifixion. The quest for the Holy Grail existed because of its powers: powers to heal all wounds, illness, and provide eternal youth. Because of these powers, it was eventually sought after just like the Ark of the Covenant.

But after the Knights Templar discovered a good amount of Solomon's treasures, there was more wealth that came their way - more wealth than one could ever imagine." Then Bautista paused for a few seconds and said,

"Pardon me a minute, gentlemen."

The room was becoming a bit chilly. So Bautista walked over to the French doors to the courtyard and closed them. Then he walked back over to the fireplace and threw some more logs onto the fire. He thought the pause right at this moment was good – it allowed the group to wonder about the "more wealth than one could ever imagine" comment. He wanted that phrase to sink in before he continued. Then he began again,

"Here's where their real wealth began to grow. The Knights Templar had a powerful backer and promoter in Bernard of Clairvaux, a leading church figure who later was canonized, Saint Bernard of Clairvaux. He was also a nephew of one of the founding knights. Bernard highly recommended the Templars and led a group of leading churchmen to officially approve and endorse the Templars. This was what the Templars needed. Now the Templars became a favorite charity throughout Christendom. The wealth began pouring in. They received money, land, businesses, and all sorts of donations.

Because of their popularity and acceptance, their ranks grew exponentially, as did their wealth. And then in 1139 AD Pope Innocent II's papal bull exempted the Templars from obedience to all local laws. This ruling by the Pope was unprecedented in that it had other great benefits. The Templars could pass without restrictions through all borders, were not required to pay any taxes, and were excused from all authority except that of the Pope."

"I guess you are eventually going somewhere with all of this," Burns remarked.

Even though Burns was growing a bit impatient, he found the information intriguing and was hoping to hear that this wealth Bautista spoke of was part of the treasures they would be seeking.

"Oh yes, I am going somewhere with all of this," Bautista said. "With the thousands of donations in every form you could think of, the Templars established an unprecedented financial network across the whole of Christendom. Many members of the organization became bankers.

With their wealth they began acquiring large tracts of land, both in the Middle East and in Europe. They bought farms and vineyards and set up people in the Order to manage them. They built massive stone cathedrals and even castles. And it didn't stop there gentlemen - oh no. They were involved in manufacturing, imports and exports. And if that wasn't enough, the next thing I'm going to tell you had important implications; they had their own fleet of ships – and it was a large fleet. Some say they were the first multinational corporation. But they were also great bankers. Their wealth allowed them to lend money. Unfortunately, all of their power and wealth created a dangerous situation.

A large percentage of the Templars were not warriors but managers of their great wealth. But those who were warriors, well, they were fierce. Most would fight to the death. After all, they were warriors for Christ, potential martyrs for Christ. The Templars were closely tied to the Crusades.

However, when the Holy Land was lost around 1244 AD to the Muslims, support for the Order faded - it faded fast in relative terms. I told you that the Order acted as a quasi-banking organization. Well, one of their borrowers was the King of France, Philip the IV. Philip had no intention of paying the Templars back, nor did he like the fact that they were so powerful. But what he did like and wanted for his own were the Templar treasures which were believed to be stored in one of their many commanderies in France, the one in Paris.

The King would not act against the Templars without the Pope's permission. I suppose two popes denied his request because they died mysteriously. Philip appointed a new pope, Pope Clement V, who wisely gave permission to Philip to move forward against the Templars.

So Philip ordered their arrest and the seizure of their assets. On a date that went down in infamy, Friday the 13th, in the month of October, in the year of 1307, hundreds or maybe thousands of King Philip's soldiers stormed all the Templar Commanderies around France, simultaneously. The Templars were overwhelmed - fought the best they could but were killed or captured in a matter of a few hours. When Philip's soldiers went to the main commandery vault to confiscate the treasures and take them back to the king, the vault was empty. The treasures were gone. There were no signs of treasures anywhere."

"Where did they go to?" Short asked.

"Great question," Bautista said. "Let's gather around this table. I'll unroll the map and show you."

They all walked over to one of the tables. Bautista rolled open the map and placed weights, flat rocks from the beach, at all four corners. Then as he pointed to places on the map, with passion in his voice and enthusiasm in his cadence, he said,

"Look here gentlemen, this is France. Here's Paris. The main treasures were located in a Templar Commandery somewhere in Paris. Over here on the west side of France is the Port of La Rochelle on the Atlantic Ocean. The Templars had a strong presence at this port, up to eighteen galleons. It was the Templars' largest base on the Atlantic Ocean. Their main fleet was there to act as intermediaries in trade between England and the Mediterranean.

Well what happened was that the Templars were tipped off about King Philip's plan, sometime before the attack, maybe the day before, maybe two days before. The head Templar, along with others, loaded up their treasures on wagons undetected, most likely in the dark of night. Then they headed fast and furious for the port. There they loaded their treasures on their ships – like I said, they had eighteen at the port. Obviously they did not use them all, maybe five to seven. The ships then went in different directions, some north to Scotland, some south to Portugal, others to North America. Gentlemen, it's the ships that went to Portugal that we are interested in at this moment," Bautista said as he pounded his index finger several times on Portugal for the sake of emphasis and interest.

Just then, Jose came into the room, pulled Bautista aside, whispered into his ear, and then left. The others watched with great interest.

"Gentlemen, Harrington and I have a visitor who we must attend to for a few minutes. Stay here and help yourselves to another cup of coffee. When we come back we'll take a lunch break."

Bautista and Harrington walked out of the study and closed the door behind them. Burns was curious who this visitor was so he quickly looked out the windows of the French doors onto the courtyard. What he saw was concerning. Since he was looking out with great interest, the others joined him.

There on the far end of the courtyard standing next to his buckboard was a Mexican wearing a serape, and a sombrero pulled down over his face. Bautista and Harrington walked out and greeted him. Then two men walked toward the wagon carrying what appeared to be a body wrapped up with gunny sacks. They tossed it into the back of the buckboard. The two men carrying the body walked away. The driver talked to Harrington and Bautista for a few more minutes on the other side of the buckboard. Burns could not see the stranger's face.

When they were finished talking, the man climbed back onto his buckboard and drove away, turning his wagon away from the house so his face could not be seen.

Green said,

"I wonder…"

"You wonder what?" Burns asked.

"I wonder if that dead body was the guy I talked to earlier this morning in the courtyard before breakfast."

"You were told not to talk to anyone, Green. You may have not only got that fella killed, but ruined everything for us," Burns said. Then the group quickly walked away from the French doors.

In the meantime, Bautista and Harrington walked back into the house and summoned the guests for lunch: pork leftovers, vegetables, and wine. During lunch, Bautista never mentioned anything about what happened in the courtyard. Instead, he carried on a discussion about what King Philip did to his Templar captives. He told them how King Philip tortured them in various horrific ways and made them falsely confess to crimes against the church and their religion.

Bautista said,

"This was Philip's false public justification for destroying the Templar Order.

However, the leader of the Order, Grand Master Jacques de Molay, who had confessed under torture like many others, retracted his confession. Geoffroi de Charney, Preceptor of Normandy, did the same. They both insisted that they were innocent of the charges and their confessions were false and came as a result of great duress – they falsely confessed in order to stop the tremendous pain they were suffering while being tortured.

This infuriated King Philip - it made him look bad in the eyes of his kingdom. So he quickly took action against the two. He declared them guilty of being relapsed heretics. Philip sentenced them to be burned alive at the stake in Paris on March 18, 1314. Jacques de Molay remained defiant until the end. He insisted that he be tied facing the Notre Dame Cathedral and be able to hold his hands in prayer. The executioner granted his request.

According to legend, he called out from the flames that both King Philip IV and Pope Clement would soon meet with him before God. The actual words he shouted out as his flesh began burning were recorded. The translation was, 'God knows who is wrong and has sinned. Soon a calamity will occur to those who have condemned us to death'.

Pope Clement died only one month later. King Philip died a horrible death in a hunting accident before the end of the year. He was mauled alive by a wild boar."

Not surprisingly, the group showed a lot of interest in the story. This King Philip guy seemed a lot like Bautista. They wondered if there was a hidden message to the story since it was told right after that courtyard incident. However, the medieval history was interesting to most. It was history they were not aware of - most weren't educated.

After lunch they walked back into the study. Bautista gathered them around the table again, the one with the map of Europe and the Middle East. He wasn't ready yet to use the map of North America that was rolled up on the other table.

"Gentlemen, again I want to turn your attention to Portugal on the map, specifically right here, the town of Tomar. It's situated in about the middle of Portugal. Tomar was born inside the walls of Convento de Cristo meaning the Convent of Christ. However, it was also a monastery. This was another Templar stronghold in the 12th century.

When the Templar Order came to an end in Europe, this particular Order survived. Its members and assets were transferred to the Order of Christ by the request of King Denis of Portugal and the decree of Pope John XXII. This happened in 1357.

Gentlemen, it is known that some of the treasures from Paris ended up behind the Templar walls in Tomar. Now, move forward to 1581, the Portuguese nobility gathered in the Convento de Cristo in Tomar and officially recognized Philip II of Spain as King of Portugal and Spain. This was known as the Iberian Union.

It was during this time period that the Order of Christ, previously the Knights Templar, secretly loaded up wagons again, headed to a port on the Atlantic and set sail with their gold, silver, and jewels to Mexico, and hid them and protected them from confiscation."

"Do you know the whereabouts of these treasures now?" Burns asked.

"Oh I most certainly do. But the treasures which I told you about are only a small fraction of the treasures we will be going after. Do you remember I mentioned that there was an amalgamation of secret societies? Well there was also an amalgamation of treasures.

That leads me to the oldest and largest secret society in the world, the Freemasons or otherwise known as the Masons. Let's look at this map of Europe again. Remember when I told you that a couple of the Templar galleons full of treasures headed north to Scotland? Well this is the route they took," Bautista said as he trailed his finger from the Port of La Rochelle on the North Atlantic Ocean to the North Sea between England, Belgium, and the Netherlands. Then he pointed to the Port of Leith and said,

"Right here at the Port of Leith in Scotland is where the Templars docked their ships. Under the dark of night, several Templars, now dressed in merchants' clothing to disguise their identity, unloaded their cargo of treasures from the galleons and loaded them into wagons they purchased that same day.

After the treasures were removed, the three ships or so headed back out to sea the next night and were purposely sunk to erase all traces of their existence. The shipmates who sank the galleons rowed back to shore in small boats and met up with the other Templars.

They secretly traveled through Edinburgh and seven miles south to Rosslyn. It was there in Rosslyn they hid the treasures in a remote area. The Templars were still a secret order and sworn to protect the treasures which we now know contained not only trunks of gold and silver coins but sacred relics as well from the First Temple, the Temple of Solomon.

The Knights Templar remained incognito knowing that the French knew that an unknown number of Templars had escaped with some of Solomon's treasures which were now Templar treasures. During the next hundred years, Masons and Templars became amalgamated as did their treasures.

When the Rosslyn Chapel was being built, the stone masons conspired with the Templars and placed many Templar symbols inside the chapel to throw off treasure seekers. You see, the Templars, who were now Freemasons, had plans to secretly move the treasures from their hidden caves once more. Word falsely wind-swept Scotland and surrounding countries that the Templars' treasures were hidden in the crypts, somewhere under the Rosslyn Chapel. But while adversary ships were headed north, east of the United Kingdom, to search out Templar treasures, galleons were headed south, west of the United Kingdom, to Ireland loaded with what was now known as Freemason's treasures.

The guardians of the treasures had traveled by land, under the guise of merchants, west from Rosslyn, Scotland, to south of Glasgow, and onward to the North Atlantic Ocean where they set sail in several purchased ships to Ireland. Now according to Masonic secret documents, the treasures remained there until the American Revolutionary War."

Bautista paused and said, "Now let's move to the other table. However, we will come back when I bring up the most dangerous secret society of all, the Illuminati and its relationship to all the other clandestine societies."

They all walked over to the other table, except for Bautista. He walked over to the marble top stand to pour himself a glass of water. In the meantime Burns, who was now displaying great interest in this history, unrolled the map himself and placed weights on all four corners to hold it flat. Bautista noticed this out of the corner of his eye as he was pouring his water; he construed it as a positive sign. Bautista walked back and thanked Burns for his help and asked the group if they wished to pour themselves a glass of water as well. No one took the offer, so Bautista continued as he pointed to locations on the map as he talked.

"Gentlemen, I have witnessed the documents myself. This Masonic treasure, worth multimillions, made its way from Ireland to the Delaware Bay in North America and up the channel to Philadelphia, Pennsylvania, where the First Continental Congress was meeting. You see, thirteen of the Founding Founders were Freemasons. It was in 1730 when the first Mason Grand Lodges were established in the United States, one being in Pennsylvania. Ben Franklin became a Freemason in 1731, and George Washington in 1752 when he was only 20 years old. I personally believe that some of the Freemason's treasures financed the American Revolutionary War."

"Dagnabbit, this is interesting stuff," Dakota said.

Bautista smiled and continued,

"Now comes the real intriguing part. The remaining treasures, left after the Revolutionary War, disappeared for a while. Only a few Masons knew where they were hidden and what became of them after the nation's capital was designed and built. The secret was described in coded symbols, an esoteric road map if you will."

"What does that mean?" Green asked.

"It means that the map was intended for or likely to be understood by only a small number of people with specialized knowledge. They were the higher-ups in the Mason order, the Master Masons. I'll come back to the coded map in a few minutes," Bautista said.

"Many people do not know this simple fact. Freemasons invented these United States. Many principles that appear in our Constitution came right out of the Freemason's Constitution like:

free speech, freedom of religion, right to assembly, balance of power, and more.

Washington, D.C. was built by Freemasons for Freemasons. There are Masonic codes all over the city and they all have specific meanings. The obvious symbols are the Mason's stone working tools: a stone cutter, square, compass, hammer, and a trowel. These are symbols of the origin story.

There was an architectural revolution in the 12th century in Europe. Masons built structures of magnificent proportions that are still standing this very day and will probably be standing many centuries from now. They used their secret and sacred geometry knowledge to build these structures. The knowledge came from the Master Masons. They were the Freemasons, free to move from area to area, from job to job.

That knowledge was used to build all the great structures in Washington, D.C.: the White House, the Washington Monument, and the Capitol Building. Ah yes, the Capitol Building, a temple in and of itself. I'll explain in just a moment."

"You mention treasures, Senor Bautista. Are the treasures in the Capitol Building?" Pecos asked.

"You're a wise man, Pecos," Bautista said.

Pecos smiled and said "gratias" as his puffed up chest almost popped the buttons off his shirt.

"That's what most people would think. And that would make sense. Let me regress for a few minutes. Some say that the streets of Washington, D.C. are a secret grid, a treasure map if you will.

Washington, D.C. was designed on what was known as the Pythagorean right triangle which is 'a' squared plus 'b' squared equals 'c' squared. This right triangle is the foundation of all masonry and it symbolizes their power. In D.C. it symbolizes a map.

George Washington and a few others used this triangle to lay out the Capitol Building, the Washington Monument and the White House with each structure being at a point on that triangle. The cornerstone for the Capitol Building was in the middle of the diamond shape boundary of Washington, D.C., which is a 100 square mile area. The point where the Washington Monument was supposed to be built was too marshy so the actual location was moved apiece – on a knoll nearby. Incidentally, what eventually became the Washington Monument, an obelisk, was originally going to be a statue of George Washington on a horse."

Bautista then picked up a pencil and started drawing.

"The Masons loved to use geometry. It was what they knew. For example, take the square and draw a circle in it like this. Now draw four lines outside the circle from the sides but stay inside the square. That will form four small triangles. Now from left to right, draw parallel lines going diagonally across the circle connecting the points of the inner bases of the triangles to form something similar to railroad tracks. Do the same from right to left. Now you have what appears to be crisscrossing railroad tracks. There gentlemen, that is a treasure grid. Every place where two lines meet or intersect, those are possible places where the treasure would be hidden. There are 16 possible Masonic hiding places in this particular treasure grid. This grid laid inside the diamond shape boundaries of Washington, D.C."

"But were they actually hidden there, the treasures I mean?" Short asked.

"You bet they were, on two of those intersections, plus under the Capitol Building. Two years after the original foundation stone for the city was laid, that was the first corner of the 10 mile square I talked about, George Washington led a Masonic ceremony setting down the cornerstone for the Capitol Building. The location for the Capitol Building was then known as Jenkins' Hill; now it's called Capitol Hill."

"The building looks like a temple," Burns said.

"You are very perceptive sir," Bautista replied. "Actually it was indeed meant to look like a temple. In fact, it was first known as the 'Temple of Liberty'. But let me go one step further. It wasn't just a symbol of a temple. No sir, it was a literal temple, a temple of Freemasons.

When you analyze the structure, you find that it has architectural features, and other characteristics that basically give it a direct link with Biblical temples."

"Like what?" Dakota asked.

"Things like: it's a stone structure, it has underground entrances, secret chambers, it's designed using Freemason sacred geometry, and there are even 40 pillars on the floor beneath the main floor just like the Dome of the Rock in Jerusalem. Yes, gentlemen, the Capitol Building is more than just a Masonic

Temple. It is a recreation of Solomon's Temple. And there lies the mystery of the remaining treasures. Some of the original Solomon treasures, which became the Templars' treasures, combined with other Freemasons' treasures, were hidden in the secret chambers of the new Solomon Temple, the Capitol Building."

"Are you telling us that we are going to raid Washington, D.C.?" Burns asked.

"Not at all sir, the treasures are no longer there."

"Then where are they?" Short asked.

"That I will not tell you yet. But I will, sooner than later," Bautista said. "We now have old Knights Templar treasures and Freemason treasures which combine to form a cache worth multimillions. But it doesn't stop there gentlemen. There's more.

I connected the Templars to the Freemasons. Now I will show a relationship between some Freemasons of the South who were Southern sympathizers and another secret society, one that was the most powerful and subversive that ever existed in the United States.

It was during the Civil War when the intersection of these Southern Freemasons and this other secret society occurred. This other secret society was known as the Knights of the Golden Circle or the KGC. They believed in the Southern cause. They were indeed, Southern sympathizers. They had plans to take over the world markets in cotton, rice, sugar cane, tobacco, and other crops grown in the South using slave labor. They wanted to expand beyond the South by means of war to Mexico, Cuba, and the Bahamas. The Civil War halted their expansion and set back their plans, permanently. Most of the KGC members joined up with the Confederates.

Once there were about 100,000 members, maybe more. Lincoln's assassin, John Wilkes Booth, was a KGC member as was that infamous outlaw from Missouri, Jesse James. But there was a more notorious rebel than the two I mentioned. He was the Confederate General named Albert Pike: a slave owner, and was thought to be a war criminal. They say his soldiers scalped and tortured captured Union soldiers.

Besides being a Confederate General, he is the Grand Commander of the Scottish Rite Freemasons, a branch of Freemasonry. He is extremely powerful in the Masons and most influential. He is recognized as a genius. He is a lawyer, poet, author and playwright, and speaks seven languages."

"How does he play into all of this?" Burns asked.

"It was eventually thought that the Knights of the Golden Circle organization was in fact a Scottish Rite Masonic organization," Bautista replied.

"Was that just speculation or was there proof of this?" Burns asked.

"Good question, some say there was proof," Bautista said. "Union troops raided a Confederate headquarters in the South. What they supposedly found was telling and shocking. They found a KGC codebook, identical to the ciphers of the Scottish Rite Freemasons – right down to every single cipher, according to the historians of my secret society."

"Now you're talking over my head," Dakota said. "What do you mean by cipher?"

Bautista looked at Dakota and said,

"A cipher is a secret or coded way of writing a word or message. For example, a letter that looks like an upside down 'f' might represent a 'g'; an upside down 'a' might represent a 'u'; and an inverted capital 'B' might represent an 'n'. Therefore the three coded letters put together might spell 'gun'. That's what I mean by a cipher.

Here is what is important. When the Civil War ended in April of 1865, most of the Confederate's gold disappeared. The gold was actually hidden by the Knights of the Golden Circle. Leading the burial of the Rebel treasures was none other than Albert Pike. It took his genius to layout a treasure grid using esoteric geometric formulas."

"So what happened to the gold?" Burns asked.

"Ah, that is the next question which I will clear up," Bautista remarked. "When the War ended, that Rebel gold was lost forever – I mean, that's what was thought. But in reality, it wasn't lost. Instead, years later, it was secretly taken to another location where it was combined with treasures from many secret societies. It was placed with the original Templar treasures and Freemason treasures and others. The combination of all of these treasures is now worth more than one hundred million dollars."

Burns looked at Short, and Short back at Burns. It was now obvious to them, that the treasure Bautista had said was beyond their wildest dreams, really did exist. But there were still a couple more questions which needed to be answered.

"Why were the treasures combined and where are they hidden? Do you really know the answers to those questions?" Burns asked.

"Of course I do!" Bautista snapped back. "I wouldn't be telling you all of this if I didn't."

"Well then, continue with the rest of the story," Burns said in an anxious manner.

"I intend to do just that. There is a motto of the Scottish Rite Masons that we used in our secret society. However, we had a hidden meaning. The motto is 'From chaos to order'.

But listen my friends, this is probably a good time to break for dinner. We can finish up this discussion tomorrow because it gets a bit complicated from here on out."

"Nonsense," Burns replied, "keep going."

Bautista paused and looked at the others. They all appeared to demonstrate the same enthusiasm as Burns, so Bautista continued,

"All right then, the motto, 'From chaos to order' brings me to the last secret society – the most dangerous the world – yes, the entire world – has ever known. It's the secret society known as the Illuminati. Have any of you heard of the Illuminati?" Bautista asked.

He wasn't surprised that no one had, so he continued,

"The origin of the Illuminati goes all the way back to 1776. It was founded on May 1st of that year by a man named Adam Weishaupt. He was a professor of Canon Law and practical philosophy at the University of Ingolstadt in Bavaria, in the Federal Republic of Germany. He copied many of the Freemason's laws and rituals. He joined the Freemasons to learn those things and then used some for his secret society.

An owl became the Illuminati's symbol. Keep that in mind because I will come back to that later. The owl represents wisdom and knowledge. The word Illuminati itself means 'enlightened'.

The Illuminati have a history of conspiring to control world affairs. I believe they were responsible for the French Revolution and some say they might have even financed the later years of the American Revolution. They act from the shadows to control world affairs and mastermind events, like the two Revolutions I mentioned, by planting agents in governments and businesses in order to gain political power, and to influence and establish what some call a New World Order."

"What does that mean?" Burns asked.

"Do you mean the term, New World Order?"

"Yes."

"Having been a member of this secret society, I can tell you exactly what it means. It refers to secret power elites, men of stature, puppet masters if you will, who have a globalist agenda to eventually rule the world through an authoritarian world government. This New World Government will replace sovereign nations as we know them today. Yes, gentlemen, this secret society is dedicated to the annihilation of all national sovereignties."

"That sounds ridiculous," Green said.

"Really? It's happening, my friend – it's happening right now! You can see it all over our nation's capital. If you look around Washington, you will find the Illuminati symbol, the owl, everywhere in the capital city. Even the great seal of the United States, which is a pyramid with an eye on top of it, has a secret Illuminati meaning. The pyramid symbolizes strength and duration, and the eye symbolizes that the Illuminati is watching over our nation and controlling its activities. It's the all-seeing eye.

Lastly, to prove that this New World Order theory is real, on the back of the Great Seal of the United States, it reads, 'Novus ordo seclorum' which is Latin for 'new order of the ages'. Meaning, the New World Order is here and it is working. This slogan came out of three congressional committees.

Gentlemen, what does that tell you?

However, I want you to think about this very important point; this secret society can rule the world because they have the wealth to do so. What I am telling you is this, whoever has control of that one hundred million dollars will have the power to rule the world. That could be us gentlemen – I'm telling you – that could be us.

And now my anxious friends, I will tell you the name of the amalgamation of secret societies I belonged to, the guardians of the largest treasure trove in the world. Its meaning is 'the gathering of the enlightened', the gathering or collection of all the secret societies I mentioned – an amalgamation of all of their treasures and wealth - all with the same goal. They are known as the, 'Illuminati Congrego'."

CHAPTER SIX:

Judgment Day in Abilene

"Be courteous to all, but intimate with few, and let those few be well tried before you give them your confidence," Bautista said.

"Gentlemen, that quote was from the most famous Freemason of the Founding Fathers, George Washington. I have always believed this quote had merit, especially in my position, and it has specific relevance in our relationship.

For us to work together on this project, we must have trust in each other. You can demonstrate trust in me by accepting this job and raiding the secret society I belonged to for their treasures. However, it is difficult for me to determine what I need from you that will convince me that I can trust you."

Bautista paused and then turned around and walked over to the fireplace to stoke the logs. Burns and the others looked on wondering what Bautista was going to ask of them. It was true that the mysterious man had shared a goodly amount of information with them, known only to a few. What possibly could Bautista ask in return, Burns and the others wondered?

Bautista walked back over to the group. The look on his face had changed. The enthusiasm he showed, while explaining the secret societies and their wealth, had vanished. Instead, the group was now looking at a man capable of killing and torturing you without hesitation. It was his eyes – you could see it in his eyes. The evil in his eyes gave away his malicious soul. Even Burns, as malevolent as he was, was taken aback.

Then Bautista spoke as the others looked on in a state of anxiety.

"Gentlemen, I will not ask you to give up something valuable in return for trust. Instead, I want you to know this. If I am betrayed in any way, my assassins will hunt each and every one of you to the ends of the earth if necessary. You won't know when the final and lethal blow will occur. It could be in the light of day or the dark of night. It may not be soon, it may be later. They will stalk you - play with your emotions - until that final day when you feel that knife slicing across your throat or that bullet penetrating your skull that sends you to your eternal resting place, in the belly of a coyote. I hope I make myself perfectly clear, my friends."

"You do," Burns said. Burns wanted to verbally fire back at this psychopath but he knew better and understood Bautista's position – it was the incredible amount of money involved.

Then Bautista's demeanor changed.

"Now gentlemen, tell me about the numbers you have to raid the location of the treasures," Bautista requested. "I am referring to the number of men you have in your gang."

Burns thought about it for a while and then said, "There are fourteen."

"That should be sufficient. Are they at your immediate service?"

"They will be when the time comes," Burns said.

Burns included the three who were once part of his brother's gang: Johnny Dane, the explosives expert; Kenny Burkley, the sniper; and Doctor Eddie Hawkens, train robber and family doctor. All three were in the middle of their trial. Burns knew that he had very little time left to bust them out of jail before they were convicted of their heinous crimes, fitted with new neckties with 13 coils, and had their necks stretched beyond repair on the gallows in Abilene.

"They will be when the time comes? What does that mean?" Bautista asked.

"Well I guess I can tell you. There are three men with special expertise who are not readily available to us at this moment. They are incarcerated. Mr. Brinkman has plans to break them out of jail. When he does, his gang will be at full force and ready to go."

It was a long day for everyone. The meeting went way beyond dinner time. They finally sat down for a nice meal at 7:30. After dinner, the men went out on the porch and sat around sipping on Tennessee mash and smoking cigars Bautista ordered from Cuba.

"You know my friends, Cuban cigars are known to be the best cigars in the world. They produce a lot of cigars down there in that Caribbean island. I heard that in 1859, there were 10,000 tobacco plantations and 1,300 cigar factories in Havana. I get as much pleasure smoking a Cuban cigar as I do watching a pretty Spanish senorita in a full colorful skirt and black boots dancing to an old Spanish folk song."

As the sun was sinking into the Pacific, a servant walked around lighting oil lamps on the porch and in various locations in the courtyard. After a while Burns conjured up enough courage to ask a question. It wasn't fear that made him think first, it was probably how to ask the question to get an affirmative answer. The reason it took him a while was because he figured the question or more accurately, the demand, might demonstrate a lack of trust. He did not want to go backwards on the trust issue as it might jeopardize everything.

"Mr. Bautista, please don't take this wrong, but you know there is a lot at stake here for both of us. I'm sure Mr. Brinkman would like to send about three men to the location of the treasure, check it out, observe the lay of the land, and make plans before we raid the place. So you will have to trust me and disclose the location of the treasure before we leave here."

"That is a reasonable request. Tomorrow I will reveal the location of the treasure and the people guarding it," Bautista said.

It was a long night for the guests because the next day's meeting promised to be both interesting and important.

After breakfast the next morning, they all once again met in the study. Burns and the group were more than ready to find out where this huge stash of treasure was located. The servant Jose brought in a fresh pot of coffee, Arbuckle's brand, and placed it on the marble top stand with the cups. Bautista asked everyone to help themselves to a cup of coffee before they started.

While they were doing that, Bautista rolled up the two maps on the table and put them aside. Then he rolled open another map and put weights on the corners so it laid flat.

When everyone had their cups filled, they walked over to Bautista. Pecos looked at the map, smiled, and said, "I know that place you have circled, Senor."

"Well, that's good but let me do the talking," Bautista said.

"Si Senor, I'll be as quiet as an owl swooping down on a field mouse," Pecos said as he gave Bautista one of his infamous arrogant grins. Ole Pecos did not like being told what he could and could not do – he never did – tolerance was never his strong point. Dakota looked at Pecos and worried that he was becoming a loose wagon wheel. It didn't just start now; it had been going on for months. Something was different about Pecos. Something that was hard to explain. Dakota saw it. It was worrisome to him. He felt that Pecos was becoming unpredictable – even dangerous - he might even jeopardize this project.

"Gentlemen, this morning I will reveal to you the whereabouts of the Illuminati Congrego's treasures. The treasures are moved every two years. They are currently in Mexico. I told you that this secret society has a master plan and they finance wars to upset the status quo so that they create chaos in an attempt to set the stage for their New World Order.

They financed the Mexican Wars against Spain and even Santa Anna's War against the Republic of Texas. But they are a patient lot who have been working in the shadows for over a hundred years."

"If they have been financing wars, how do they replenish their wealth?" Green asked.

"Excellent question. They participated in gold and silver rushes – staked out claims – and had their ore melted down and turned into gold and silver coins. They were there for just about every gold rush in the United States and around the world. For example: the Georgia Gold Rush in 1828, the California Gold Rush of 1848, British Columbia in 1850, Pike's Peak in 1859, New Zealand in 1861, Montana in 1862, Vancouver Islands in 1864, Australia in 1872, the Black Hills of Dakota in 1871, and many more. They have a network of thinkers, soldiers, assassins, and workers. I was an assassin and a thinker, the gold diggers are the workers.

Now it's time to talk about the location. Let's look at this map of North America which includes Mexico. Gentlemen, the multimillion dollars, which I spoke about, are located across the Rio Grande, straight south of El Paso, Texas. Originally, the amalgamation of treasures happened right here near the Gulf of Mexico in Veracruz. But it could not remain in that area because of the Spanish-Mexican Wars; so it was moved northward toward the Rio Grande and closer to the United States.

You might recall that I said that the Pythagorean Theorem or triangle is the foundation of all Masonry. Some say it symbolizes the Mason's power. Well the Illuminati Congrego uses that theorem as well to create a treasure grid. In fact gentlemen, that was my responsibility along with two other brothers of the Illuminati."

"I'm probably getting ahead here but since you defected, would they not come up with another hiding place for the treasures?" Burns asked.

Everyone looked at Bautista wondering if he had an answer for that very pertinent question.

"You are very perceptive, Mr. Burns. I will be giving you the alternate hiding place – the place where the treasure is now. What I didn't tell you is that I have an insider who is also interested in the treasure. When we confiscate the gold, he will be defecting as well and we will be giving him a share of the prize. I know the current location of the treasures on the grid. It all has been planned out in advance," Bautista said.

Burns began to realize that this Bautista person seemed to be every bit the genius Albert Pike was. The more Bautista talked, the more Burns salivated. He had to be careful not to give himself away by exposing the avarice pouring out of his very soul - his greed was his spiritual uplifting and his eyes were the windows to his soul. Everyone knew that the Brinkmans lived to indulge themselves in excessive wealth and power. It was a sickness with them – a sickness that Cole Brinkman hoped would be cured with the Illuminati Congrego's treasures.

"Please get to the point, Mr. Bautista. Where are the Illuminati's treasures now?" Burns asked.

"I will tell you after we come to an agreement on the distribution of this great wealth. Whatever we come away with, it will be a 50/50 distribution – 50% for me and my men, and 50% for you and your men. Are we in agreement?"

"We are, but there is one thing bothering me. Why is it that you and your men don't raid and steal the treasures without our help? Why do you need us?" Burns asked.

"Because my men are assassins, not thieves. I am very familiar with the success your brother had robbing the Carson City Mint. Oh I know eventually it caused their demise because of the workings of a traitor. But the fact is plain and simple - they got away with the gold. It was a magnificent feat. I figure Jerod Brinkman's brother Cole, your boss, will be just as clever and figure out how to take out the Illuminati guards and successfully make a clean getaway with the treasures. That's why I came to your gang," Bautista said.

"Well, I can assure you, you came to the right people. I have another question. Why did you defect and why are you interested in fifty million dollars?"

"I have my reasons. That's all you need to know."

Burns figured Bautista had no intention of sharing any more personal information, so he asked,

"Now, where do we go to find the treasure?"

"It's being guarded in an evacuated Franciscan monastery across the Rio Grande in Juarez, Mexico. This area was well traveled in the mid and late 1600's. The location was known as Paso del Norte meaning 'the North Passage'. It was a route to the north and the southern Rocky Mountains. The mission, Mision de Nuestra Senora de Guadalupe became the first Spanish expansion and development in the area. Eventually commerce, between Santa Fe and Chihuahua, passed through Juarez. El Paso and Juarez were pretty much connected in everything until the 1848 Treaty of Guadalupe Hidalgo established the Rio Grande as the border between the United States and Mexico.

The old adobe monastery is abandoned now; that is, by bona fide Franciscans. However, gentlemen, the Illuminati Congrego are hiding their treasures in that monastery. They will be there for the next six months. Then the treasures will be moved again to a location deeper into Mexico.

The time and location is perfect right now for the heist. There's no time to waste. If we intend to do this thing, it must happen soon, before the treasure is moved again. Time is of the essence, gentlemen. If the treasures are moved again, prospects of a successful attempt to confiscate it will diminish greatly."

"Like I said, Brinkman will want to send about three men to check the place out. What do we look for there? I mean, how many guards will be posted?" Burns asked.

"First let me say that sending only two of your men is sufficient. I'll explain in a minute. As far as the Illuminati are concerned, they try to keep a low profile. You will see what appear to be Franciscan Friars working in the gardens outside. That's a ruse. They are not friars at all. They are guards and are heavily armed underneath their robes.

The Knights Templar I told you about wore special garments to identify themselves. They wore white surcoats with one red cross, and white mantles also with a red cross. The red cross was a symbol of martyrdom; to die in battle was considered a great honor, and they believed it would assure them a place in heaven.

Well, these guards are wearing the symbol of the Illuminati. Look for an owl on the front of their Franciscan garments. The owl symbolizes wisdom and all-knowing. The Illuminati believe they are the elite who are the only ones with the knowledge of how to rule the world and conduct world business. I will remind you again, this is a very dangerous organization. However, they are not invincible."

"We will take your suggestion and send only two men," Burns said. "I'll make the decision for Mr. Brinkman right now. We'll send Short and Green."

Short looked at Green and said, "I'm game, how about you Green?"

"I'm good with that also," Green replied.

"Good," Burns said, "Dakota and Pecos, since you have experience breaking criminals out of prisons, I'm sending you two to Abilene to bust Dane, Burkley, and Hawkens out of jail."

"How do you know about our prison breaks, Senor Burns?" Pecos asked.

"Your boss and my boss were brothers, remember? They talked all the time. They were in the same criminal network. I know everything because I'm Cole Brinkman's attorney. That's all you need to know," Burns said in an arrogant fashion.

Pecos looked right back at Burns and squinched up his eyes in such a way as to say, "I didn't like the way you came back at me with that attitude".

Burns paused and then said to Bautista,

"Let's make our plans right now. Give Short and Green directions on how to get to the Illuminati's hideout."

Bautista agreed and he spent the next ten minutes pointing at the map and giving specific instructions on how to get to Juarez and from which direction to approach the monastery. He suggested that they stay at least 300 yards away so as not to be seen – they would need to pack binoculars.

Then Bautista asked,

"What are your plans now Burns - I mean, as far as you are concerned?"

"Are we free to go at our choosing?" Burns asked.

"Yes you are."

"Well then, we'll do our jobs and keep you posted."

Then Bautista added,

"There are just two more things I didn't tell you yet. Since I will not be going with you when you raid the Illuminati hideout, you will be taking my surrogate, Harrington. In fact, he will be with Short and Green to do a reconnaissance of the hideout. He is very handy with a six-shooter like your men. His instructions are to keep me informed every step of the way. He knows how to reach me.

The second thing is this. I know we agreed to trust each other, but I'm no fool. There will be three of my men in the shadows who will know your location at all times. These three men were assassins for the Illuminati who defected with me. They will be dogging you every step of the way – you won't see them – but they'll be there all right – day and night – all day, every day. They will watch your men from the shadows. Any wrong moves or double crosses will be dealt with immediately and without mercy.

Now my friends, when do you plan to leave here?" Bautista asked.

"If you are finished with all of your threats, I'll tell you," Burns replied.

Bautista didn't respond - didn't smile - just nodded.

"If we leave within the hour, we can be back in San Francisco before nightfall," Burns said.

"Good, Harrington, you get your gear ready and leave with these gentlemen," Bautista said.

"Yes sir," Harrington responded.

The six men (Burns, Short, Green, Pecos, Dakota, and Harrington) left for San Francisco as planned and headed back to Diamond Lil's place before heading over to the hotel. When they arrived at the Palace, Diamond Lil was nowhere to be found. They saw Bret Stone over by the stage. So Dakota walked over to Bret and said,

"Tell Lil that we're here to see her. We just got in from out of town."

"That will be hard to do," Stone said.

"Why's that?" Dakota asked.

"She's not here. She packed up and left with two gentlemen. She told me to run things while she's gone. She didn't even introduce me to the two men."

"Well how long did she say she'd be gone?"

"She said it could be a few weeks. She didn't really know."

"Who do you think those men were?" Dakota asked.

"I have no idea. I told you that she didn't tell me who they were and I didn't meet them either. Now if you don't mind, Dakota, I have a business to run."

Dakota walked back to the group with a perplexed look on his face. He told the group what he just learned. Everyone was confused when they heard this surprising revelation. It just didn't make sense. Burns was especially worried since he exposed many of his gang members to a person who now had disappeared with a couple of strange men.

"It's late," Burns said. "Let's go over to the hotel. After you take your luggage to your rooms, come on over to my room and we'll have a short meeting and make some plans."

It took about thirty minutes but they finally arrived at Burns's room. Burns wanted to speak freely but with Harrington in the room, he couldn't. Burns did not trust Bautista at all. He felt that Bautista could pull a double cross on him, kill them all, and make off with all the loot. But Burns (a.k.a. Cole Brinkman) was planning a fancy Brinkman double cross himself. However, his double cross would have to come quicker than Bautista's.

Of course there was the matter of those assassins who were supposedly tailing them – they would have to be dealt with – somehow, and at some time. Burns would worry about that later, when the time was right. For now, he told the group to move on as planned: Dakota and Pecos would head to Abilene; Green, Short, and Harrington, would check out the Illuminati Congrego's hideout, and Burns would head back to Pueblo, Colorado. Burns told Short to meet him in Pueblo at his office when they got back from Mexico. He gave Short a direct order to take no one to the hideout outside of Pueblo until he gave the word.

FINDING THE ILLUMINATI CONGREGO HIDEOUT

Short, Green, and Harrington planned to take the Southern Pacific Railroad first thing the next morning, after breakfast. They purchased their tickets at the San Francisco Depot at about 9:00 a.m. and caught the 10:15. Green loaded his horse in a freight car but Harrington and Short would have to buy their horses at a livery stable in El Paso.

The route took them from San Francisco to Los Angeles, through Yuma, Arizona Territory, onward to Tucson and finally to El Paso, Texas. Green and Short sat together while Harrington sat by himself the whole trip. It was risky for Short and Green to ride a train because they knew that Judge Isaac Parker probably had a marshal and a posse out looking for them. Plus their pictures were most likely hanging in every post office and marshal's office north, south, east and west of the Indian Territory. That's why they kept their pistols fully loaded and were ready for action at all times.

They arrived at their destination two days after they boarded their train in the Bay City. Short took charge of everything. There was no problem with the others in that regard. Short was the closest to Burns. Plus he was also the closest to Brinkman, the others accurately conjectured. Short was also a strong leader, wiser than most outlaws, and slicker than grease on a wagon wheel axle. He could con a con man into thinking the con man's mother was Short's own lost mother. Short proved his mettle over and over again in Brinkman's eyes.

The first order of business in El Paso was to sign into a hotel, incognito of course, and then purchase horses and tack for Short and Harrington. Short thought it was best for him and Green to stay in their rooms and let Harrington make the purchases. Short was a thinker. He told Harrington to procure a pack mule too since they did not know how long they'd be out on the trail.

After Harrington made the purchases, he walked over to the telegraph office to send a wire to Bautista to let him know that the three arrived in El Paso as planned and without incident. Then he went back to Short's room where Short and Green were hanging out.

"Any problems buying the horses, mule and tack?" Short asked.

"Not at all, now what do we do?"

"Let's figure out what we need to take along with us to Juarez. We probably need to figure we'll be in Mexico for about three days – that's probably the max."

The three agreed on the food, supplies, and a good pair of binoculars. Short pulled out a wad and handed Harrington a hundred dollars in greenbacks and told him to go across the street to the general store and make the purchases and then take everything back to his own room. Their plan was to leave at first light the next morning before the townsfolk began stirring.

The three ate their dinner in Short's room that evening. Harrington bought their food. Short sat by his window, constantly looking out onto the street. He was a confident gunfighter, but he knew that Judge Parker would probably have his best men searching for them with warrants for their arrest. He knew that they would be willing to take them back alive – that was Judge Parker's preference. In that way Parker could hang them after their "fair trial" and they were found guilty of anything that would require a capital punishment. Nobody was going to make a fool out of Judge Parker and live to tell about it.

At about 8:15, right at dusk, two men rode to the front of the hotel.

"Green, come on over here and look at this."

"What is it?"

"Two men just rode up in front here. They both have badges. Do they look familiar to you?" Short asked.

Harrington just looked on while Short and Green stared out of the second story window.

"They sure do. Those two guys work for Judge Parker. They were in the room with us when Parker was handing out warrants. They offered to go after a bank robber headed to Kansas," Green said. "Do you think they're looking for us?"

"Of course they are."

"They could be after someone else," Harrington offered.

"Could be, most likely not – best stay in our own rooms until just before first light tomorrow morning," Short said.

"I don't think so. Let's not take a chance. Let's leave later tonight when the streets clear out. We're gonna need time to saddle up and pack down the mule. We can find a place on the other side of the Rio Grande to catch some shut–eye," Green said.

"Green's right," Harrington remarked, "I think we need to leave tonight."

"All right, let's plan to leave just after 1:00 a.m. if the town is shut down by then," Short said.

Harrington and Green went back to their rooms. At 2:00 a.m., the three had their horses saddled, mule packed, and saddlebags full, and then they quietly trotted out of town toward the river. They crossed the Rio Grande using the wooden bridge that linked Texas to Mexico.

Bautista's directions had specified that the Illuminati Congrego's hideout, the old Spanish mission, was about eight miles south of the border. But before they got anywhere close to that snake pit, they wanted to rest among some large boulders for a few hours since they had very little sleep. They were lucky that there was a rustler's moon on this night because it gave them enough light to navigate in an unfamiliar territory.

At sunup, Green built a fire and he cooked up some bacon and beans and boiled a pot of coffee. Short saddled up the horses hitched to the picket line in case they had to make a fast getaway due to stray Apache off the reservation or Mexican bandits working the area. They had no idea who or what they would encounter down here south of the Rio Grande. Harrington rolled up the bedrolls and tied them behind the saddles using the leather saddle strings.

When their bellies were full, Green kicked dirt on the fire and the three packed up the rest of their gear and continued on their journey southward, staying off the main road – if one could call it such down here in the poor country.

After riding for a while, they weren't sure how close they were to the mission so they asked an old Mexican man with a weather-beaten face, sitting outside of his small wooden shack, directions and how far the mission was from their present location. In broken English he said, "Half mile, just o'er hill, in part box canyon. Mission been empty many years."

Short flipped a one dollar coin to the old man and thanked him. Then they moved on. Now their hearts were beating a little faster as they were coming ever so close to the Illuminati's clandestine location and their treasure trove.

As they approached a hill, Short said,

"Let's dismount here. I bet the mission is a few hundred yards on the other side of this hill – that's what I gathered from that old Mexican fella. Let's tie our horses to these mesquite trees and walk to the top. I'll bring the binoculars."

About ten feet before they reached the peak, they bent over and walked in a stooped position. Then they crawled on their hands and knees the last three feet. When they looked over the hill, now lying on their bellies, Harrington said in a volume just above a whisper,

"There it is."

"That's it for sure, the old mission," Short said.

Short began looking through his binoculars.

"What do you see?" Green asked.

"I see exactly what Bautista said we would see. There are a few monks out in front…I see one, two, three, four. There are four…wait, here come four more through the wood gate. It looks like they're relieving the four on the outside because the first four are now going inside."

"I wonder how many more there are around this compound," Green remarked.

"Yeah, I wonder," Short replied. "We know there are at least eight here – probably more though."

"I don't think Bautista ever gave us a real number about how many are actually guarding this treasure. It would also be helpful to know what's beyond those gates and that adobe wall surrounding those buildings," Green replied.

"Look over there, on the other side of the mission - there's a taller hill. From that vantage point we can probably look down into the courtyard. That's where we need to go," Harrington said.

"Yeah, I agree, let's go get the horses and ride over there," Short replied.

They scooted backwards until they could stand up without being spotted. Then they quickly walked back to their horses. While they were untying their horses Green asked Short,

"Could you see the owl emblem on their cloaks with your binoculars?"

"I saw it – it wasn't big – but it was there all right - right on their chest – plain as day – just like Bautista said."

"I didn't see any firearms," Harrington remarked.

"Of course you didn't. They had them hidden underneath their robes," Short replied.

The three saddled up and rode around the back side of the ridge to the taller hill on the other side of the old mission. It took about ten minutes to get there and then another twenty to climb up the rocky hillside to the peak. When they reached the peak, once again lying on their bellies, Short began looking over the place with his binoculars.

"Dang."

"What is it?" Green asked.

"There's a Gatling gun in the middle of the courtyard facing the gate. There's one person sitting behind it. You don't need binoculars to see it."

"I also see a chapel and a couple other buildings - wonder which building the treasures are in?" Harrington questioned.

"I don't know. But this sure is a great vantage point to position a sniper. Those Illuminati fellas will be easy pickings from up here," Short said. "All and all, I only counted nine men so far. Let's hang here for another hour or so and see if any more men show their faces. Man, my hands are getting itchy to run my fingers through all of that gold, silver and jewels," Short remarked. Then he looked at the other two and said, "I think this is going to be easier than what we thought."

DAKOTA AND PECOS TRAVEL TO ABILENE

All six men had left San Francisco on the same day. While Short, Green, and Harrington took the southern route to their destination, Burns, Dakota, and Pecos took the First Transcontinental route to theirs. Burns exited the train in southeast Wyoming and then caught a train south through Denver and onward to Pueblo, Colorado. Dakota and Pecos continued on to Abilene, Kansas. Their previous gang's hideout was just outside of Abilene, so they knew the area well.

The trial for Johnny Dane, Kenny Burkley, and Doctor Eddie Hawkens was in full swing. The three decided to be co-defendants and tried together. They had nothing to lose doing it this way – that's what they figured – they knew they would be found guilty and hung either way.

Dakota and Pecos arrived in town on the third day of the trial. The prosecution had just finished calling their witnesses and now it was the defense's turn to call theirs to the stand. That part of the procedure would begin the next day.

Before Dakota and Pecos had arrived in Abilene, they agreed that it would be wise not to be seen together, so they split up when they exited the train. They both unloaded their horses and headed to the hotel to sign in with their aliases. Dakota signed in first, Pecos about 10 minutes later. After each signed in, they walked their horses over to the livery stable to board them.

When they belonged to Jerod Brinkman's gang, they spent most of their time at the hideout outside of Abilene. So they were not overly concerned that they would be recognized. However, it was still wise to be cautious. If anyone did recognize them, it would most likely be the barkeep, or a soiled dove working one of the saloons – that's all.

Dakota and Pecos were smart enough to lay low until nightfall when they could sneak behind the jailhouse and talk to their old buddies through the back barred windows. The hotel they were staying in was located in both a precarious and opportune location; precarious because it was right across the street from the sheriff's office, opportune because, from Dakota's second story street-view window, the two outlaws could keep an eye on the sheriff and deputies coming to and going from the jailhouse. That's what they did the rest of the day and evening.

At 11:00 that night, the two walked out of the hotel and onto the boarded walk. The street was pretty much vacant. Albeit there were quite a few horses hitched in front of the few saloons down the street. However, all the other establishments were closed.

Dakota figured the sheriff had gone home – they saw him ride off earlier – a few hours ago. They also surmised that one deputy was guarding the prisoners, because they saw the other deputy walk into a saloon. They accurately deduced he was now off duty as well. The sheriff and two deputies seemed to be the only law in town. That's one more deputy than what Abilene had when their last gang hung around this railhead town.

After looking to their right and then to their left, the two desperados cautiously walked across the street and entered the alley adjacent to the jailhouse. Then they went around the back. The window was at the height of Dakota's face so he didn't have to stand on anything to look in. Pecos could not see in though. If he wanted to, he had to jump up and down because there wasn't anything around to stand on. So Pecos stood guard while Dakota got the attention of the gang members.

Dakota looked through the window and saw the three stretched out on their cots. Dane and Burkley were in one cell and Hawkens was in the other. They were all sawing wood.

Dakota looked around on the ground for a rock. He picked up one about the size of a one dollar gold piece and tossed it through the bars at Dane and hit him smack on the nose. Dane grabbed his nose and yelled "ouch" and cursed, waking up Burkley. Luckily the deputy was sawing wood as well while slumped in a chair behind the sheriff's desk and didn't hear Dane yell. When Dakota stopped laughing, he made sure the deputy was still snoring; then he called out in a whisper,

"Psssst, Dane, up here."

Dane glanced up and saw Dakota, and then looked over to make sure the deputy was still sleeping. He was, so Dane stood up and walked over to the window. Burkley got up as well and Dane motioned to Burkley to keep an eye on the deputy.

"You are a welcome sight Dakota. Looks like you need to bust us out again," Dane whispered.

"Yeah, this is getting old and dangerous. I have half a mind to let you guys rot in jail this time."

"Rot? There won't be any time for that. The trial is almost over and they are gonna hang us as sure as I'm lookin' at ya."

"We'll bust you out tomorrow night."

"Who's we?" Dane asked.

"Pecos is here with me. We'll pass a pistol to you before we come through the front door tomorrow."

"The deputy keeps the door locked and he won't open it for anybody, except…"

"Except who?" Dakota asked.

"Except his girlfriend, Lola. She's a song and dance whore who works at the Watering Hole down the street. She comes by sometimes after work – but not always."

"Which watering hole?" Dakota asked. "There's about ten on this street."

"No, that's the name of the place, the Watering Hole. It's under new management. The deputy told me that."

"What does this gal look like?"

"She's short, real short – probably the shortest girl there. Her hair is as red as fire and she seems to always wear green."

"We'll grab her after work tomorrow night and bring her over. Here, you best take this gun now but keep it hidden until tomorrow night."

"It sure is good to see you again Dakota. You came at the right time. Looks like there ain't gonna be no amnesty."

"I reckon not," Dakota said as he smirked.

Just then the deputy changed his position in his chair, the chair squeaked, and Dane hurried and got back into his cot as did Burkley. Dakota ducked, waited a few seconds and then stood up and looked in again, making sure the deputy didn't wake up and hear them. He didn't.

Pecos and Dakota went back to their room and caught some shut-eye.

The trial continued early the next morning in the Abilene Courthouse – right at 8:30. The defense had only one witness and he turned out to be a hostile witness at that, doing the defense no good but helping the prosecution. The judge decided that it was time for the closing arguments. The prosecution gave about thirty minutes of arguments and an appointed defense lawyer gave about ten minutes. A fair trial was nowhere to be found in this town – at least for these three criminals. The prosecution passed on their second closing arguments, so the judge gave the case to the jury. The jury deliberated for only one hour and came back with their verdict.

After the trial and sentencing, the sheriff walked over to the telegraph office and sent a wire to Allan Pinkerton in Chicago. It read,

Burkley, Dane, and Hawkens found guilty as charged. Will be hung in three days in the town square on Saturday at 9:00 a.m. Will send you another wire after the hanging. Dane laughed out loud when the judge handed down the sentence. I think he's gone crazy.

Dakota and Pecos laid low that day. Dakota snuck out once to get food for two meals to eat in, but that's the only time he left the room. Pecos stayed in Dakota's room and kept an eye on the jailhouse. At about 3:00 that afternoon, Pecos saw a man wearing a long black coat and sporting a top hat enter the jailhouse. It was the hangman getting a good look at the convicted criminals.

Two carpenters were already pounding their hammers, nailing together wood, building the gallows. By the end of the day, they had the three trapdoors in full operation. This was the gallows they had used in the past. After a hanging they would disassemble it and store the wood away in an old shed behind the courthouse until the next hanging. It was not a good idea to leave gallows up in the middle of the street – could chase off some newcomers looking to settle down in Abilene. Settlers were always moving in from the East or passing through, searching for land with good fertile topsoil for raising crops. Cattlemen referred to them as sodbusters. They meant it as a pejorative term.

While the two desperados were keeping an eye on the front of the jailhouse from Dakota's room, Pecos asked,

"Hey Dakota, are we sitting five on two horses when we break the three out of jail?"

"What do you mean?"

"We need three more horses. Where are we gettin' three more horses from?"

"From the livery stable. You'll steal them later tonight before I grab that Lola girl."

"When were you gonna tell me this?"

"Relax Pecos, I've got it all figured out. Here's what we're gonna do. That saloon will probably close about midnight. The livery stable will be shut down for the night. You go over there at 11:30. The doors to the stable will be closed but not locked. They generally aren't."

"What if they are?"

"Then break them down. Once you're in there, saddle up three horses and take them to the back of the jailhouse and wait there for me. We'll keep our two saddled up in front of the hotel. I'll wait across the street from the Watering Hole Saloon."

"How do you know which watering hole?" Pecos asked. "There's several on this street, ain't there?"

"Trust me on this one Pecos, I know. Like I said, I'll wait across the street from the Watering Hole and watch to see where that Lola girl goes. If she heads to the jailhouse, I'll just follow her there. If she goes another direction, I'll nab her and take her to the jailhouse. You just have those three horses ready to go."

"Do I get to kill the deputy and that girl Lola, or kill the deputy and take Lola with us?"

"Neither! What the hell has come over you Pecos? Why do you want to kill everyone? No you aren't gonna be able to kill 'em. We'll gag and hog-tie 'em and lock 'em in a cell. We'll have about a seven hour head start on the posse if everything goes according to plan."

At 11:15 p.m. they put their plan into motion. Pecos walked over to the back side of the livery stable while Dakota meandered over to the Watering Hole Saloon. When he arrived there, he looked over the double swinging doors to see if he could spot Lola. He saw three floozies table hopping. One was Lola for sure. She was easily identifiable and fit Dane's description perfectly.

The saloon wasn't crowded at all. It was a weekday night. Most of the action happened on Friday nights and the weekends.

There may have been about fifteen in the saloon, some playing cards, others just drinking. About half were out-of-towners passing through - saddle bums and drifters one would surmise.

After Dakota spotted Lola, he waited across the street and sat on a bench with his hat pulled down so no one would recognize him. After all, he did spend a little time in a saloon down the street when his old gang had their hideout just outside of Abilene, the hideout that Pinkerton had raided and took out Jerod Brinkman and his gang. If someone recognized him or Pecos, that could blow everything.

While Dakota sat there waiting for the saloon to close, Pecos was able to open the back door to the livery stable. He drew his pistol just in case one of the stable keepers was somewhere in the stable sleeping on a bed of hay. Some did that – mostly the poor old fellas who made an honest but meek living just to have a place to stay and enough money to fill their bellies with whiskey and grub. But this stable had no such person. Horses and a few mules were the only creatures consuming oxygen in this equine establishment.

Pecos saw a small kerosene lantern by the door so he lit it and kept the flame low – he made just enough light to see. There were plenty of horses to choose from all right. He held up the lantern and looked around for the tack. He searched for a few minutes and finally found a small room that contained saddles and bridles. He then went to work saddling three horses.

Pecos knew it would be difficult walking out with all three at one time. So when he finished saddling them, he took one horse out the back door, walked it over to the back of the jailhouse, and tied it up. Then he went back for the other two and turned off the lantern when he left. He found a small crate in the alleyway and used it to stand on to look inside the back jail window to make sure the deputy was alone. He was. He was up this time sitting at his desk, reading a newspaper.

Pecos noticed that Dane and his other two pals were lying on their cots with their eyes wide open. They knew it was getting close to breakout time.

Dakota sat calmly and patiently across the street waiting for the saloon to empty out and close its doors. A few were walking out now. The girls were always the last ones to leave – that's how it always was. They were paid to stay until the last patron left.

Pecos wasn't so calm though. He was becoming impatient and rubbing his magic potion pouch for luck. He was ready to get this thing over with. His trigger finger was getting itchy too.

As the last customer left the saloon, the girls began walking out. The barkeep had walked them to the door and saw them off. He spotted Dakota sitting on the bench across the street but paid little attention and just went back inside, closed the doors and began sweeping the floors. Two of the girls turned to the left and Lola turned to the right. It appeared Dakota was in luck. Lola seemed to be walking over to the jailhouse to visit with her boyfriend.

Dakota stood up and started walking in the same direction. Then he looked back at the other two girls before he made the decision to cross the street. They were talking to each other and carrying on as they walked, so he quietly snuck across the street and behind Lola.

He cocked the hammer on his single action revolver, stuck the gun in her back, and at the same time put his left hand over her mouth and pulled her backwards into the alley adjacent to the jailhouse as she kicked and tried to scream. However, the little filly was easy to manhandle because of her petite size. She struggled some until Dakota said,

"Calm down and don't say a word Lola, or I'll blast you right here where you stand. If you do what I say, you and your deputy boyfriend won't get hurt. Do you understand?"

She shook her head yes. Dakota still had his hand over her mouth and the barrel of his gun pressed into her back. Then he said,

"Here's what I want you to do. I want you to calmly knock on the jailhouse door like you always do. When he opens the door, just walk in like normal. Any questions?"

She shook her head no.

"OK then, I'm going to remove my hand. If you scream, I will first carve up your pretty little face and then put a bullet through it. Do you understand?"

Lola shook her head yes. Dakota slowly removed his hand from her mouth. She said nothing. Her hands were shaking and her knees were knocking. She was scared out of her wits.

"Start walking toward the door now and knock like you normally do."

She walked up to the door still feeling that hard cold steel from the end of the barrel of Dakota's six-shooter jammed into her back. She knocked on the door four times and waited.

"Is that you Lola?"

"Yes."

The deputy slid the bolt and opened the door. Dakota pushed her in and to the floor and told the deputy to put his hands up. The deputy had a startled look on his face. While Dakota held the gun on the deputy, he ordered Lola to get up and close the door and bolt it. The three incarcerated gang members stood up and walked over to their cell doors. Dane pulled out his hidden pistol and pointed it at the deputy.

"Now deputy, there's two guns on you, mine and Dane's," Dakota said.

The deputy looked over at the cell and was shocked to see that Dane had a pistol pointing at him as well.

"Here's what I want you to do. Grab those keys off the wall and open up those two cell doors. Then you walk into one cell and Lola, you go into the other one; then I want both of you to lay face down on the floor. Dane, when he lets you out, run across the street and get two ropes off our horses. Make sure no one sees you."

The deputy unlocked both cells and he and Lola did as Dakota ordered. Dane ran across the vacant street, collected the ropes, and brought them back. Then Dakota told Dane, Burkley and Doc to gag and hog-tie the two. When that was accomplished, Dakota locked the two cell doors and tossed the keys in the corner.

"Let's go. Your horses are out back. We're headed east to Missouri," Dakota said.

They ran out of the jailhouse, closed the door and rode out of town as fast as lightning.

"Why are we goin' to Missouri?" Dane yelled to Dakota as they were riding.

"We're not. We're doubling back and heading west to Colorado. I said that to throw off the posse."

Before they turned around to the west, they stopped to cut the telegraph wires on the east side of town. Then they rode on the outskirts of town to the west and did the same to those wires as well. Now all the wires were down leading in and out of Abilene and it would take the townsfolk hours the next morning to hook them up again.

The five sat on leather, riding most of the night, and then camped in a secluded wooded area. They and their horses needed the rest. They were all plum tuckered out.

After some shut-eye, they woke up about an hour past sunup. Pecos had a slab of salted sowbelly, pinto beans, cornbread, and coffee stashed in his saddlebags; Dakota carried a coffee pot and skillet in his. Doc and Burkley collected wood for a fire while Dane stood guard in case of the unlikely possibility that a posse somehow picked up their trail.

When the Abilene sheriff went to the jailhouse at seven the next morning, he was shocked to find the criminals gone and Lola and the deputy hog-tied in the cells. The sheriff was livid.

Being a gentleman, he opened Lola's cell first and untied her, then he did the same with the deputy. The deputy couldn't apologize enough.

"Save your apologies, what the hell happened here?"

The deputy explained and said that the outlaws were headed toward Missouri.

"How do you know that?"

"I heard one of the jailbreakers say so. He said so - plain as day."

"Lola, you have no business over here at night especially when we have people locked up. You could get yourself killed. Go home now. Go ahead, get out of here," the sheriff said. He was riled at her, but tried not to let his anger show; although he wasn't too successful in that endeavor.

Lola didn't say a word. She glanced over at the deputy and then walked out and went home.

The sheriff told the deputy to start rounding up a posse. Then he said,

"I'll wake up the telegraph operator and tell him to send off some wires about the jailbreak. We'll see if we can't get help rounding up those outlaws."

That idea went nowhere, because they eventually discovered that all the wires were down. A posse was formed in about two hours and they rode hard to the east trying to pick up a trail that did not exist.

Meanwhile, the five criminals were eating breakfast. Dane and the other two had a lot of questions. While they were chowing down, Doc asked,

"From where I sit, it seems to me that you two must have had a good reason to bust us out of jail. Believe me, we're grateful. You saved our necks. But what's up with you risking yours, Dakota?"

"Well I don't want to get mixed up in all the details but we broke you out because we're joining up with another gang and we need your help for a heist. Our old boss Jerod Brinkman has a brother. His name is Cole. Jerod was in cahoots with his brother. They had some sort of network – a criminal network. We didn't know it but we were part of the network when we worked for Jerod Brinkman."

"The sheriff told us something about that. He read us an article in a newspaper and questioned us about the network. In fact he said he had a hankering to beat the information out of us in back of the jailhouse – he never did – but he sure acted like he was gonna," Burkley said.

"What's this Cole guy like, Dakota?" Dane asked.

"Don't rightly know. He keeps his identity a secret. He's not like our old boss. As far as I know, there are only two people who know his true identity, his lawyer named Burns and his ramrod named Short. We met both out in California."

"California, what were you doing in California?" Doc asked.

"We were visiting Dakota's old flame, a gal named Diamond Lil. She's as pretty as a young red roan filly I had back in Mexico," Pecos said.

"Look, let me get to the point," Dakota said. "We're joining up with this new gang. They found us in El Paso before we traveled to California. My friend Lil put us on this guy who belonged to a secret society – he claims he was an assassin for them and some type of thinker or administrator. He said a bunch of secret societies got together and pooled their money."

"Yeah, he called it an immigration, migration, infestation, or something like that," Pecos said.

"No he didn't," Dakota said. "He called it an amalgamation."

"An amalgamation of what?" Doc asked.

"I'm gettin' to that. He called it an amalgamation of secret societies and their treasures for the purpose of a New World Order."

"Sounds like a bunch of hogwash to me," Burkley said.

"Me too at first," Dakota replied. "But this guy, who lives in a mansion in California mind you, is for real. He knows everything about their history, how much gold they have, who's guarding it, and where it's located. Like I said, he knows everything about it. Not only that. I told you he was an assassin for the group. This guy is dangerous. If you say you're in with him, and he gives you the scoop, you don't want to crawfish. He'll hunt you down and torture you before he cuts you up and feeds your innards to the coyotes."

"You're bogged down in the mud man, get to the point," Dane said.

"We're joining up with Cole Brinkman's gang to steal one hundred million dollars in treasures from this secret society. The gold, silver and such are across the Rio Grande in a Mexican town south of El Paso. It's hidden in an old abandoned adobe Spanish mission. Part of the gang is checking on the place right now. We are headed to Pueblo, Colorado where the gang has its hideout."

"How many are in this gang we're joining up with?" Dane asked.

"I don't know exactly, twelve or fifteen all totaled I guess – don't rightly know for sure," Dakota said. Then he stood up, poured the remaining coffee on the fire, kicked some dirt on it and said,

"We do well now to finish our grub and get back in the saddles before the posse picks up our trail."

Dakota walked over to his saddlebags and removed two loaded six-shooters and three boxes of ammunition. He passed the pistols to Doc and Burkley and gave all three a box of ammunition.

"We'll get holsters in some town along the way and get you some different clothes to wear too. You guys smell worse than polecats," Dakota said. "By the way, after we steal the treasures, we have unfinished business in Hays City."

"What's in Hays City?" Dane asked.

"It's not what, it's who. Our friend Rusty Blake, remember him – the traitor – the Pinkerton agent? His real name is Barnes. He's a preacher now. We're gonna ride to Hays City and kill him and his new wife, Kathleen, Brinkman's adopted daughter."

"They got married, eh?" Doc asked.

"Si amigo they got hitched, and we're aiming to put them in their eternal ditch," Pecos said as he laughed out loud at his own joke.

It was a long journey to Pueblo; about 270 miles – give or take 30 or 50 – mostly give.

SHORT, GREEN, AND HARRINGTON RIDE BACK TO PUEBLO

"We've seen enough here," Short said. "Let's ride back to El Paso. When we get there, I'll send a wire to Burns and tell him that we're on our way back."

After they crossed the Rio Grande and arrived in El Paso, the three had plans to sign into a hotel. It was about 3:30 in the afternoon and they felt it best to lay over in El Paso for the night and head north at sunup after breakfast. They also thought it wise to catch a train the next day instead of sitting in the saddle for 500 plus miles for days on end.

They rode over to the telegraph office first thing. Green and Harrington sat on their horses while Short went in and sent a wire to Burns that read,

Attorney Burns
Pueblo, Colorado

Found mission. In El Paso for the night. Headed back tomorrow. Will take a train. See you in a couple of days.

Short

When Short came out, he stood there and looked to his right and then to his left and then said,

"Let's sign into the hotel down the street now and come back and get us a square over there at Emily Kay's Steakhouse - sounds pretty inviting. I could use a thick steak, how about you guys?"

"We're with ya," Green said.

The three rode down the street to the Railroad Stop Hotel. When they were situated in their rooms and such, they rode up the street to the restaurant. They picked a table for four near the kitchen. Short sat with his back to the wall – a wise idea since he made more enemies than friends over the years. He knew how Hickok met his demise up in Deadwood – he wasn't going to make the same mistake.

After they ordered their steaks, potatoes, and beers, Short began quizzing Harrington which didn't sit real well with him.

"Tell me Harrington, how long have you known Bautista?" Short asked.

"Long enough to know that he says what he means and means what he says."

"Yeah, well how long is that?" Short pressed on.

"Look, I don't know why that's important. I've known him for years. I grew up in Half Moon Bay and my family and his family were very close and neighbors for years. The hacienda he lives in now belonged to his mother and father who were immigrants from Portugal. The Bautista you know grew up to be every bit as mean and should I say as lethal as his father, and then some. Not many people knew he went away to join up with that secret society, but I did. He and I have been best friends for years. He used to tell me secrets that could get him and I both killed. Make no mistake about it. Bautista has no conscience. He believes in no God. He will do what is necessary to take what he wants."

Just then the waitress brought over their beers. Green held up his in a toast. The others followed.

"Here's to becoming filthy rich," Green said. The others held up their glasses as well and then they all took a few sips of the warm home brew ale which was more appropriate for fence runners in the Bad Lands up north than for the three who considered themselves to be future heirs to a secret society's copious amount of treasures.

After dinner they rode down the street to the Buckhorn Saloon for a few drinks. The place was filled with saddle tramps, Mexicans, a few half-breeds, drifters, and cowboys of all sorts. It was loud and noisy. The men tried to talk over the piano player and the two singing dance hall girls who were fishing for the right pitch while hitting a bucket load of sour notes.

This place was no Diamond Lil's. However, it did serve up some pretty fine corn squeezin' from Tennessee albeit one needed to dig pretty deep in his pockets for that fancy sour mash. Now if you were short of cash, it did offer up some freshly made backroom rotgut, which burnt all the way down and out. Oh, it was no match for a tenderfoot from the East all right - that was for sure – but it was affordable at five cents a shot. The three outlaws hung around for a few drinks. They were greeted by a few table hopping ill reputes, but those $10 an hour floozies were sent on their way to find another table to do their audacious beseeching.

Afterwards the three companions rode their horses over to the train depot to purchase train tickets for the ride back to Pueblo the next day. Short had the telegraph operator at the station send Burns a telegram to alert him that they would now be arriving late tomorrow night, around 10:30 or so.

Once their tickets were bought, they saddled up again and rode over to the livery stable where they bedded down their horses for the night, giving them a handful of grain, along with hay, and water. Then they headed for the hotel and called it a day, except for one. Harrington snuck out of the hotel and down to the train station to send a telegram out west to Half Moon Bay. He then went back to his room, undetected by the other two.

On the next morning Short, Green, and Harrington loaded up their horses on a freight car and caught the 7:05 to Pueblo. When they reached their destination later that night, Burns met them at the station and had rooms reserved for them at the Golden Nugget Hotel, named for the Colorado Gold Rush of 1859.

Burns told them to get a good night's rest and meet him for breakfast in the hotel's restaurant at 7:30. He said that breakfast was on him.

"Will Cole Brinkman be joining us in the morning?" Harrington asked. "I'm anxious to meet him."

"I am too," Green said.

"We'll see, but I rather doubt it, but we'll see," Burns said.

The next morning when all three walked down to the restaurant, they found Burns already sitting at a table. He was there enjoying a cup of coffee with another person. Harrington and Green assumed it was Cole Brinkman.

The man seemed tall, built like a boxer, tough looking almost like a mountain man and sported a full face beard and a mustache. He looked like the type of person who could run a criminal organization and not take anything from anyone. In other words, he looked as though he could handle himself in any type of situation which presented itself. He even wore a fancy nickel-plated six-shooter at his side.

When the three walked up to the table, Harrington extended his hand to the gentleman and said,

"Mr. Brinkman, I presume."

The gentleman stood up, smiled, and said,

"No sir, I'm Charles Goodnight. I just came down from my room. Mr. Burns here saw and recognized me and asked if he could buy me a cup of coffee. I just finished it and I was getting ready to leave."

Green and Short also introduced themselves to Mr. Goodnight before he left. He was in town to wrap up a cattle deal with a local rancher.

When the three sat down with Burns, he went on to explain what he knew about Goodnight, who was well known in this part of Colorado because he founded the Rock Canyon Ranch in 1869, eight years after the Colorado Territory was established and the original seventeen counties of the new territory were founded of which Pueblo was one.

Goodnight lived in Pueblo for about seven years and then moved to the Texas Panhandle where he helped establish the JA Ranch. JA stood for John Adair who was an Irish businessman. Adair had the money and Goodnight had the knowledge.

The land was perfect for ranching and raising cattle; there was plenty of grass and water.

Goodnight was famous for a lot of things; one being the fact that he created the first chuck wagon for cattle drives to the railheads up north. He also herded feral longhorns and drove them up what would became known as the Goodnight-Loving Trail. The trail originally stretched from Young County, Texas to Fort Sumner in the New Mexico Territory, north to Colorado, through Pueblo and to Denver.

The Comanche Indians were always a threat to other Indian tribes and European settlers. They were the dominant tribe who inhabited the Southern Plains. They were known for capturing women and children of weaker tribes, and settlers, and selling them as slaves to the Spanish and later Mexican settlers. Many times they would keep young captive white women and assimilate them into their tribes where they would eventually become brides of Comanche warriors.

One such captive was Cynthia Ann Parker, an American of European descent. She was captured in 1836 somewhere between the ages of eight and eleven. Her Comanche name was pronounced in English as Nadua meaning "someone found". She lived with the Comanche for twenty years, and completely disremembered her white European ways.

She married a Comanche chieftain named Peta Nocona and bore him three children. One became the famous and last free Comanche chief, Quanah Parker.

In 1857 Charles Goodnight became a Texas Ranger. In 1860 Goodnight was known for leading a posse against a Comanche camp where Cynthia Ann Parker was living with Peta Nocona. They recaptured Cynthia Ann at the age of thirty-four. However, she spent the rest of her ten years on this earth refusing to adjust to life in the white society.

Goodnight's cattle drive partner Oliver Loving died on September 12, 1867 at age 57. It was in the spring of 1867 when Goodnight and Loving made ready for their third cattle drive. Comanche bands were still creating havoc on the Southern Plains. Loving went ahead with a scout named Bill Wilson for contract bidding. It was recommended that they should travel at night because of the threat of Indian attacks, but they did not. Instead, they traveled during the day.

Loving was seriously wounded in an Indian skirmish at Loving Bend on the Pecos River. He sent Wilson back to the herd for help. In the meantime some Mexican traders found Loving and transported him to Fort Sumner where he died of gangrene. Before he died, he asked Goodnight to carry his body back to Texas after he died, and bury him in Weatherford, Texas. He was buried in the Greenwood Cemetery on March 4, 1868.

Burns knew most of this story and conveyed what he knew about Charles Goodnight to the men over flapjacks, skillet fried sowbelly, biscuits and gravy, and eggs over easy.

CHAPTER SEVEN:

The Raid

"I'm headed over to my office," Attorney Burns said. "Have another cup of coffee and then come over for a meeting. Short will show you the way. Come through the back door though and we'll meet in my back room. I'll take the information about what you learned across the Rio Grande and I'll get it to Brinkman right away."

Burns picked up the tab for the entire breakfast and then strolled over to his office. He entered his office through the front door but kept the shade pulled down and the "Closed" sign in place. He did not want to be disturbed while he met with the gang.

Fifteen minutes later there was a knock at the back door. It was Short, Harrington and Green. Burns opened the door and said,

"Come on, hurry up, and get in here."

When the three entered, Burns stepped out, looked to the left and then to the right to see if anyone saw the three enter. There was no one around so he quickly closed the door and locked it.

"Help yourselves to a cup of coffee, men. There's a fresh pot on the stove. You'll find the cups on a shelf right above it."

The three did and then they sat down at a round table that seated four. Burns had a large map on the table. It showed all of Texas and Mexico. He started the conversation.

"I want you three to tell me everything about how to get to the location of the mission and what you saw there. I'll take your information and give it to Brinkman. He'll draw up a plan and we'll go from there."

"I'm surprised Mr. Brinkman doesn't want to hear this firsthand," Green said.

"By now you know what his policy is," Burns snapped back. "He will always remain incognito. That's why he continues to be able to do his business outside of a jail cell instead of from the inside. That's the last time I'm talking about that. Now listen up, when we're done here, you three will head out to the hideout and stay there until Brinkman orders you otherwise. Nothing will happen until we hear from Dakota and Pecos about the jailbreak. Now let's hear what you have."

Short was the one who took charge of giving Burns most of the information. He stood up, grabbed one of the pencils on the table, and drew a circle around the location of the mission. He then described what they were up against when it was time to raid the place and take custody of the treasures.

"Sir, the location of the secret society's hideout is exactly where Bautista said it would be, across the Rio Grande right here in Juarez, Mexico," Short said as he pointed to the map.

"Tell me something about the terrain around the mission."

"Yes sir, there are a couple of ways in and out of the place by horseback but really only one good road for wagons. That's probably the way they took the treasures in and that's the way we'll take the treasures out."

"Quick question, how deep is the Rio Grande where we'll be crossing. I mean can we drive wagons through it?" Burns asked.

"Sir, you won't have to worry about that. There is a sturdy bridge which crosses the river from El Paso into Mexico."

"Good, now tell me what you saw at the mission: how many guards, what type of ordnance, and things like that."

"We did not see many guards. All told we counted nine. But obviously, there had to be more inside the buildings."

"What buildings? Tell me something about the buildings."

"This place is like a fort. There is an adobe wall surrounding three buildings. One is the mission church with a bell tower."

"Could you see any guards in the tower?"

"No, but there had to be somebody there. It would only make sense," Short said. "There are two other buildings, one on each side of the church. They are probably some type of sleeping quarters. It's anybody's guess which building the treasures are in. Also, there is a slight problem."

"What's that?" Burns asked.

"There is a Gatling gun in the middle of the courtyard facing the front gate."

"How is that a 'slight' problem? It sounds like it could be a 'big' problem."

"It's a slight problem; the person sitting behind the Gatling gun can be picked off from a hilltop. I didn't tell you yet but we have a terrific vantage point. There is a mountain or it's more of a tall rocky hill on the south side of the mission. Actually, there are several hills around the mission, but this one is the tallest – the one on the south side. We can position a sniper on that hill to take out the guy behind the Gatling gun."

"That's good, we have just the man for that job," Burns said. "Tell me what else you saw there."

"Like I said, the place doesn't seem to be heavily guarded. We saw four on the outside and then four men coming out to relieve them. I have no idea how many more men are in those three buildings, but we should assume that there are a lot more. It only makes sense, if we're talking about one hundred million dollars."

"What type of pistols or rifles were they toting?" Burns asked.

"We didn't see any."

"What? You mean they weren't carrying any weapons?"

"I didn't say that. I said, we didn't see any weapons. They were probably hidden underneath their robes. They were wearing monks' garments and had the owl insignia on their robes signifying they were Illuminati, just like Bautista said."

"A couple more questions. How far across the Rio Grande is this mission?"

"I would estimate about seven miles, wouldn't you say that guys?" Short asked.

"I would say so," Green said.

"At least that," Harrington confirmed, "maybe eight to nine miles."

"OK then, now one last thing. Show me on the map the route we will take after we cross the bridge into Mexico."

Short outlined his thoughts on that subject as he pointed to the map on the table. When Burns thought he had enough information, he told Short to hold up on taking them to the hideout – he told everyone to stay at the hotel instead. He also mentioned that there would be a group meeting after Dakota and Pecos came back from Abilene with the other three new gang members. That's when they would all travel to the hideout - in two groups.

Short told Harrington and Green to go get on their horses. He said he needed to talk to Burns in private and would be out in a few minutes. After Green closed the door, Burns asked,

"What do you want to see me about?"

"It's about Green. I know he's been with us a few months now, but I don't trust him."

"What do you mean you don't trust him!" Burns yelled back. "You're the one who recommended we let him join up with our gang. Why are you questioning his loyalty now?"

"Because a few times he dropped out of our sight. One time in El Paso, I asked him where he had been. He knew I saw him go into the telegraph office. He told me he sent a wire to his mother in Missouri to wish her a happy birthday."

"Why would you question that?"

"Because when he first joined up with us, and after a few drinks, he told me his family lived in Iowa. He was pretty juiced at the time though. I don't know if he was sober enough to know what he was talking about or not."

"Let's be realistic here. When was the last time you had one too many and didn't know what state you were from? That sounds troubling to me. I don't like it. Keep an eye on him. Have Jerry at the telegraph office tell us if Green tries to send a wire from there. Tell him not to send it until we can read it."

"Will do," Short said.

PECOS, DAKOTA, AND THE THREE DESPERADOS HEAD WEST TO PUEBLO

After the five ate breakfast, they saddled up and headed due west, staying off the main trails and skirting Kansas cow towns. Hays City was on the way. Dakota was tempted to stop and kill the traitor Barnes himself but he thought it would be wise to let it be for now. He overheard Burns say that Cole Brinkman wanted to perform the deed himself since it was his brother who Kathleen killed.

At nightfall on the second day, they snuck into the town of Ellsworth, which once was known as the wickedest cow town in Kansas. Ellsworth was a booming cow town back in the early 1870's. It has been said, "Abilene was the first cow town in Kansas, Dodge City was the last, but Ellsworth was the wickedest". Hays City had not been far behind Ellsworth in that regard. However, those days were history now. There was no longer the smell of Texas longhorns, the constant bellowing of cattle, loud shrieking train whistles blasting away several times a day, or rowdy Texas cowboys shooting up the town. Peaceful and tranquil would now describe this once unruly cow town. That's why it was a great place to break into the general store near midnight – the streets were vacant and the townsfolk were snuggled up in their warm beds.

The five broke into the back of the general store and stole clothes for Dane, Burkley, and Doc. They also lifted saddlebags and filled them with jerky, ammunition, canned beans, and other cold food rations. They easily pilfered their way throughout the shop until the owner who had his residence upstairs heard the noise and came down with a lantern and a shotgun.

Pecos saw the light from the lantern shining down the stairwell and alerted the others who then hid in various places in the store. Pecos waited at the bottom of the steps and when he had a chance, he stuck his foot out and tripped the owner. The store owner fell flat on his face and dropped both the lantern and his shotgun. Pecos pounced on him like a bobcat on a jackrabbit, rolled him over, and pummeled him with his fists before he knifed him in the gut, just after Dakota yelled,

"No!"

Dakota's plea to not kill the man fell on deaf ears. Meanwhile, the lantern had shattered and sent a trail of oil followed by reddish-orange tongues of fire which raced along the wooden floor.

"Let's get out of here before the town wakes up!" Dakota frantically shouted.

They ran out the back door, the three threw their stolen saddlebags over the withers of their horses and then they all jumped on their mounts and rode hard and fast before the entire building went up in flames. The fire eventually took out a whole block of businesses. The store owner's body was so charred that it was impossible to determine how he died. Nobody suspected foul play.

When the five stopped several miles west of Ellsworth, Dakota laid into Pecos for killing the store owner. Once again, Pecos demonstrated that killing was becoming easier for him with each life he took. Dakota was becoming bothered about this – killing was not Dakota's way of solving a problem.

The group now rode southwest to Garden City, Kansas, a newly formed town northwest of Dodge City, where they stole more supplies. This time they got away without an incident. Their journey then took them on to what would soon become known as Cheyenne Wells, Colorado, straight west to Colorado Springs, and finally due south to Pueblo.

When they reached Pueblo, they signed into two different hotels, at different times, using aliases. Everyone stayed in their rooms except for Dakota. He went over to Burns's office and informed him that all five had made it safely back from Abilene.

"Do you think you were followed by a posse?" Burns asked.

"No we weren't. We got a clean getaway," Dakota said.

"That's good, real good. I'll tell Brinkman that you men are back and see what he wants to do now."

"Will we be meeting Mr. Brinkman soon?" Dakota asked.

"Not likely," Burns said. "Stay out of sight for now. Short will tell you our next move."

Dakota told Burns where they were staying and then went back to his room. Burns met with Short that afternoon and told him to set up a meeting with everyone at the hideout outside of Pueblo in two days. Green and Harrington were also staying in a hotel in town waiting for word from Short on what would happen next. Burns remembered that Bautista said that they needed to act fast because the Illuminati Congrego did not like to keep their treasures in one place too long.

On the next day Short got word to everyone that they were having a meeting at the hideout outside of town. He gave directions to Dakota for his group. Short would personally lead Green and Harrington to the hideout. The meeting was set up to start at 11:00 tomorrow morning. The gang was supposed to be at the hideout at least one hour before the meeting.

In the meantime, about 4:30 in the afternoon, Green walked over to the telegraph office, wrote out a message and asked the operator to send it immediately. The operator began to tap out the message while Green was standing directly in front of him. When he finished, the operator said,

"That will be four bits."

Green took a couple of coins out of his pocket, dropped them on the counter, and then walked out of the building, quickly returning to his hotel room. The telegraph operator, who was being paid by Burns, closed his front door, pulled down the shade and went out the back door down the alleyway to Burns's office. He knocked on the door. Burns opened it and told him to come in. The operator passed the wire to him. Burns read the telegram and then asked,

"Did you send this?"

"No sir, I pretended I did, but I didn't. Green thinks I did."

"Good man, go find Short. I believe he's eating an early supper over at Cora's Café. Hurry now."

"Yes sir."

The telegraph operator wasted no time and ran over to the café. Short was just finishing dinner when the operator walked into the café and gave him the message to head over to Burns's office as soon as he could. He whispered to Short that Green tried to send a telegram and that Burns was holding it.

Short called the waitress over and asked for his bill. She wrote it out and he paid the cashier on the way out. Burns already had the closed sign up on the front door of his office so Short went around back. He didn't knock – he just walked in – he knew Burns was expecting him. He closed the door behind him.

Short asked, "Did you want to see me?"

"You bet I do. Here read this. Green was sending it to Chicago. Go ahead, read it out loud so it sinks in."

Short looked at it and even before he began, he knew there was trouble, serious trouble.

It read:

Allan Pinkerton
Chicago, Illinois

Brinkman's hideout is just west of the town of Pueblo, Colorado. Have not met Brinkman yet nor have I been to the hideout. Will get back to you later.

Green

"I had a suspicion that he was up to something, but didn't know what."

"Now you know," Burns said.

"Jerry didn't send the message, did he?"

"No he did not, but Green thinks he did."

"At least he doesn't know you're Brinkman."

"That's not the point. The point is, now we have to dispose of him. I'll let you do that since you're the one who brought him into our gang. You, Harrington, and Green ride out to the hideout together early tomorrow morning. About halfway there, let him have it in the back. After you kill him, tell Harrington why you had to do it, and then you two bury the body. Do you have any questions?"

"No sir."

"Good, then I'll see you and Harrington at the hideout tomorrow morning. That's right, I'm going there for this one occasion, but as my alias," Burns said.

Short passed the note back to him. Burns tore it up, and tossed it into the waste can as Short was walking out the door. Burns then slammed the door in anger.

The next morning, Dakota, Pecos, Dane, Burkley and Doc got an early start and headed out to the hideout a couple of hours before the meeting was set to begin. Burns was already there waiting to talk to Short about the plans regarding the heist in Mexico. Tom O'Hara was staying at the hideout and he introduced himself to Dakota and the other four and showed them to their sleeping quarters. Burns stayed in an office going over his plan of attack on the mission based on the information he received from Short, Harrington and Green. He was not going to be the one to convey the plans to the group, Short was. Brinkman would continue to be Attorney Burns.

Cole's hideout was different than his brother's. Jerod's hideaway had been a lodge – a fancy one at that. Cole was not like his brother. He was more pragmatic with his money – more thrifty – didn't like to flaunt his wealth. Cole's place was a ranch in a secluded area with a small house where the meetings were held, and a bunkhouse where gang members slept.

He had about a hundred head of cattle on the place out in the pasture, but that was just for show. Most of the cows were too old to breed and the two bulls were far beyond their prime. Cole wasn't really interested in having his men tied up managing a passel of cattle – no sir – this was not one of those so-called "working ranches".

O'Hara was in charge of pretending to be the owner of the ranch, and getting rid of any strangers who happened to stumble onto the place by accident. It was his option on the method he used to "get rid of strangers". But it was also his responsibility to cover up any unfortunate residual remains from unforeseeable but planned "accidents" in the pastures.

To pretend like everything was normal, Short met Green and Harrington at the hotel and suggested they go to breakfast at Cora's Café. Green was in a jovial mood because he thought his message to Pinkerton had been safely delivered. In fact, he felt a sense of relief, more so than he'd been feeling for a few weeks.

Neither Green nor Harrington had exact directions to the hideout – Short was going to show them the way. So Short gave them a bum steer and led them south of the hideout into a barren area on an old narrow dirt road. Short was leading the way, Harrington followed, then Green. Short stopped about three miles outside of Pueblo in what appeared to be a desolate area, got off his horse and said,

"Keep following this path; it will lead you to the hideout. I'll catch up with you in a few minutes, my horse picked up a pebble."

He pretended to remove a stone from the horse's left front shoe, and then climbed back on his sorrel and trotted toward the two. Then Short pulled out his six-shooter and yelled out,

"Hey, Pinkerton man!"

No one turned around but Short shot Green twice in the back anyway. Green fell off his horse. Harrington turned around just in time to see Green slump, then fall to the ground.

"What did you do that for?" Harrington yelled.

"Because we've got a fox in the henhouse, or we did. That guy there is a Pinkerton man."

"A Pinkerton man, Green is a Pinkerton man? How did you know that?"

"He tried to send a telegram to Allan Pinkerton late yesterday afternoon. The telegraph operator works for us and he gave Burns the wire. That's how."

"What do we do now? Are we gonna bury him?"

"Nah, leave him for the cougars, coyotes, and buzzards. That's the proper burial for a Pinkerton man. Jump off your horse and remove his holster and pistol."

Harrington did and then he mounted up again and asked,

"Now what?"

"Follow me, the hideout is not that way, it's this way," Short said as he turned his horse around. They traveled to the east about a half a mile then they headed north another two miles to the hideout. Short ponied Green's horse. They didn't say a word all the way back. Harrington was still in shock that Green was a plant working for Allan Pinkerton.

When they arrived at the ranch, O'Hara asked where his buddy Green was.

"Your buddy Green is filling the bellies of a flock of buzzards," Short said.

"What's that supposed to mean?" O'Hara asked.

"Our buddy Green was a dang lowlife mangy dog Pinkerton man. He almost gave away our hideout to Allan Pinkerton. Jerry didn't send the wire but gave it to Burns. Burns gave it to Brinkman, and I followed his orders. Now he's buzzard bait. Like I said, he's filling the bellies of a bunch of buzzards right now as we speak. I hope his Pinkerton guts don't make those buzzards puke. Is Burns here?"

"Yes, he's in the office. Are we going to meet Brinkman today?"

"Not likely," Short said.

"Why are you and Burns the only ones who are privileged to know who Brinkman is?" O'Hara asked.

"Because Cole Brinkman does not want to be shot in the back by a gang member he thought he could trust. Plus, he has no intention of rotting in jail the rest of his life. Burns and I met with him last night. We covered the plans to take out the mission south of the border. I'm meeting with Burns one more time now to make sure I have all the details to cover them with you guys. Hang out with the new guys for a while. I'll be with Burns for an hour or two."

Short went in and met with Burns for at least two hours going over every little detail including the responsibility of every gang member. They reviewed drawings, maps, responsibilities, ordnance needed, horses, wagons, crates and such. Burns thought of everything.

He was like that, the quintessential planner of heists. In the past year, his gang members successfully robbed banks in Denver, Colorado Springs, the Boulder area, and Cheyenne, Wyoming just to name a few. They also held up stagecoaches in Kansas, Nebraska and Wyoming stealing gold shipments and payroll runs.

They never lost a man. Cole's men were excellent marksmen, and skilled at what they did. They planned thoroughly, hit hard and fast, killed if they had to, and always left a cold trail. They were the best of the best in their field of criminality. And they all had a voracious desire for wealth.

Cole Brinkman, like his brother Jerod, was never content with his fortune; he never satisfied his appetite for wealth; he always hungered for more. He was able to keep loyal gang members because they shared in the booty and had a safe haven to call home.

Short called O'Hara into the office and told him to have the gang assemble in the parlor in fifteen minutes. He said he was ready to go over the heist with them. The gang was anxious as well to get moving with the project. Only a couple of the men really knew the full magnitude of the venture but they were spreading the word to the other gang members that this heist was different – it could be a rewarding adventure or a really dangerous undertaking.

Now the gang was assembled. They were all waiting in anticipation – waiting to hear the plan. Short walked into the room with Burns. He had a drawing in one hand and a map of Texas and Mexico in the other. In the room, besides he and Burns were twelve other men.

Short started the meeting.

"Men we have a job to do. It's an unbelievable opportunity. The rewards will set all of us up for the rest of our lives. When it's all over, you can go straight, leave the country if you wish and start a new life. My point is that you'll have enough money to do whatever you want.

As you all know by now, we have brought several members of Jerod Brinkman's gang into our gang. We did that for a reason. We need their expertise in their given fields to pull off this heist. Plus they were loyal members.

In case some of you didn't know this, our boss Cole Brinkman worked with his brother Jerod planning robberies around the Midwest. None of us really knew they were working together. That came to light after Jerod was killed by his own adopted daughter in a raid by the Pinkertons on Jerod's hideout.

Our gang like Jerod's gang has a code. If there is a traitor in our midst, we will hunt him down to the ends of the earth and kill him or her. Jerod had a traitor in his gang – a Pinkerton plant. He was their safecracker and an undercover Pinkerton man. He went undetected. He's the one who alerted Pinkerton to Jerod Brinkman's hideout and got half the gang arrested and the others killed including Jerod Brinkman.

Cole Brinkman has sworn vengeance upon Rusty Blake and his wife, Kathleen. Rusty Blake is his alias. His real name is Barnes, Reverend Barnes. He's a preacher in Hays City, Kansas. After this heist, our boss and whoever else he chooses will be making a trip to Hays City to punish the preacher and his wife Kathleen. It was Kathleen who pulled the trigger to kill Jerod Brinkman.

With that, let me introduce everyone in this room starting with the new members of our gang who came from Jerod Brinkman's gang. By the way, they were known as the 'Professionals' because of their unmatched skills. The Mexican wearing that oversized sombrero and that 12 inch wicked looking blade on his belt is Pecos. Don't let his height fool you. He's deadly with that blade and known as one of the fastest gun hands south of the Red River, right Pecos?"

"Si Senor."

"Standing next to Pecos is Dakota Wilson. Dakota is well known for being one of the fastest guns north of the Red River. Pecos and Dakota are not only known for being quick on the draw but if any of you get caught by the law, these two know how to break you out of jail. That's another one of their expertises. Also, just so you know, I would not test the speed of their gun hands – many have – no one has lived to tell about it.

The next reprobate I want to introduce to you is Johnny Dane. Johnny likes to blow things up, right Johnny?"

"You bet I do."

"Dane is our explosives expert. Whether it's dynamite or nitro, it doesn't matter. As long as it blows things up, it makes Dane happy."

Dane nodded in the affirmative and grinned from ear to ear. He was happy to be out of jail and to be able to blow things up again.

"The man standing next to Dane is Kenny Burkley."

Burkley raised his hand at the group and nodded in a shy fashion.

"Burkley is a marksman with a rifle. He and his brother Bobby were snipers in the War Between the States. Both he and his brother were in Jerod's gang. His brother was killed in the Pinkerton raid at Jerod Brinkman's hideout.

Kenny and his brother took out the guards at over 200 yards at night when Jerod Brinkman's gang robbed the Carson City Mint in Nevada. Kenny is a deadly shot. We have a specific plan for him. Is your aim still good Kenny?"

"Yes sir, but I don't have a rifle and scope any longer."

"Not to worry Kenny, we took care of that for you."

"Standing next to Kenny Burkley is Doctor Eddie Hawkens. He's known as Doc. He was in prison for robbing a train and was broken out by a few of our new members here. Doc is handy to have around in case any of you get shot in the line of duty. Welcome aboard Doc."

"Thank you, good to be here. But's it's going to be tough to patch up wounds when I no longer have medical instruments and bandages."

"Don't worry Doc – we have you covered.

Those are the five men who came to us from Jerod Brinkman's gang. Now, for the sake of these five new members, I will introduce the members of Cole Brinkman's gang.

The person you all met who looks like your typical cowboy from Texas and who operates this ranch is Tom O'Hara. Tom is also fast with a gun, actually does have ranching experience and can rope and ride with some of the best vaqueros out of Mexico, California, and Texas. He's also educated but don't hold that against him. Tom comes from a long line of rustlers. His father was a rustler, his father's brothers were rustlers, and Tom's brothers were rustlers. Tom did his share of rustling too but he was the only O'Hara who was never caught and hung. He knows how to skirt the rope."

O'Hara laughed and said, "That's right. I have evaded a stretched neck since I was ten."

"Now, Tom has five ranch hands working for him here at the hideout. However, each one of them has participated in all of our heists. They're loyal and good with a gun. They are Slim, Jimmy, Colorado, Brisco, and Matt."

They all raised their hands when their names were called out.

"You all know who I am; for the sake of our new gang members, I'm John Short. I'm the go-between you and our boss Cole Brinkman. This other gentleman is Attorney Burns. You can just call him Burns. He and I are the only ones in this gang who will ever know Cole Brinkman's true identity. He's Brinkman's lawyer.

The last person I want to introduce to you is Ben Harrington."

Harrington nodded to the group.

"Harrington was our contact with a gentleman by the name of Carlos Bautista who has hired us to do a job. We will be splitting the loot with him. Dakota, Pecos, Burns, the now dead Pinkerton agent Green, and I met with Bautista. He has a ranchero in Half Moon Bay, California. He's of Portuguese descent and looks to be as mean as a south Texas badger. But I'll let Harrington tell you more about Bautista and the organization he belonged to. Go ahead Harrington, make your case."

"All right, first let me say that after meeting all of you and hearing about your expertise, I believe Mr. Bautista has selected the right men for the job. This will be a great undertaking. The prize, if we are successful, is beyond your wildest imagination. Mr. Bautista is a defector of a secret society known as the Illuminati Congrego. The name means a congregation of the enlightened.

This secret society is an amalgamation, a merger if you would, of many secret societies, some of whom you may have heard of – the Freemasons, the Knights of the Golden Circle, the Illuminati group, and others of lesser known names. They have also pooled their wealth and treasures, treasures that go all the way back to the secret Christian society known as the Knights Templar.

They have combined their wealth for one main reason, to rule and direct world affairs. You see with the money they have, they can virtually rule the world."

"How much money are we talking about?" O'Hara asked.

"You better be sitting down when I tell you this. I'm talking about one hundred million dollars."

"Did you say one hundred million dollars?" one of the ranch hands asked.

"That's exactly what I said. Whoever has that kind of money has great power."

"How do you know all of this stuff if it's a secret society that has this money?" O'Hara asked.

"My boss, Mr. Bautista, whom I have known for many years, was a member of this secret society. He was an assassin for them and then an administrator. He is hiding out in California. He also has an inside man working for him who will remain anonymous. I'm not supposed to tell you this but I will; Bautista is not his real name. If the secret society knew where he was, he'd be dead by now along with me and a few others who work for him. So it should be obvious to you that once you are verbally exposed to this information, your lives could be in danger as well."

Everyone appeared very sober at this point. But it wasn't like they hadn't put their lives on the line before. Each and every one was a notorious outlaw who would be sentenced to hang by any judge, in any county, because of their past evil deeds. They were all murderous felons.

THE PLAN

After Harrington spoke, Short took over again.

"Like Harrington said, the loot we are going after is one hundred million dollars. When we get it back to this location safely, that's when we will split it up. Our gang's share is actually fifty million dollars. The other fifty million bucks belong to Bautista and his group.

I am not going to sugarcoat this for you. This is going to be a dangerous mission. Some of you may not make it back alive. We'll be up against some really ruthless and trained assassins who are guarding the treasures. If there is any one of you who feels he does not want to be part of this venture, then speak up now."

Both Short and Burns looked into the eyes of each man, one at a time. It was obvious – no one wanted to back out of this proposition. The rewards were too great.

"I'll take a 'no response' as an answer to tell me you are all in. So, let's get into the plan and what everyone's responsibilities will be. Gather around this table and I'll show you on this map where we are headed."

Everyone moved in close. Short unrolled the map of Texas and Mexico and placed candleholders on all four corners to hold it in place. Then he rolled out a drawing of the mission and the surrounding hills. He held it in place with a pistol on one side and a heavy hunting knife on the other. He pointed to the areas on the map and the drawing as he talked.

"Our target area is across the Rio Grande in Juarez, Mexico - right here. It's about eight miles south of El Paso, Texas. There's an old Spanish mission there which is fortified by an adobe perimeter wall. It encloses the entire mission. There are three buildings behind the walls. One is a chapel. There is a substantially large building on each side of the chapel. They are probably sleeping quarters or storage buildings of some kind. We don't really know.

What we do know is the loot is in one or all of those buildings."

"How are we gonna get into the compound?" O'Hara asked.

"I'll get to that in a minute," Short responded.

"What about the guards? The place has to be crawling with men," Dakota remarked.

"We really don't know how many men there are behind the walls. There were nine visible to us when we were scouting the place out. Four were outside and one inside. The one inside was sitting behind a Gatling gun, in the middle of the courtyard, which was aimed right at the front gate."

"Ay, chihuahua! Who's the first one going through the front gate?" Pecos asked.

"You are, Pecos," Short said.

Pecos put his hand in his pocket and began rubbing his magic potion pouch.

Harrington began laughing because he knew what the real plan was.

"Don't worry Pecos, we have a plan for that Gatling gun," Short said as he smiled.

"You said you counted nine men, where were the others stationed?" Dakota asked.

"The four who were guarding the outside were relieved by four more men while we were there. The four who were replaced then went through the gate and closed and barred the gate shut. They then went into the building on the south side of the chapel. It appears the gate is always closed and barred except when the guards switch out. By the way, all of those men were wearing Christian monk robes. It's their disguise."

"How do we know they are not monks? I don't want to go to hell because I killed a bunch of priests," O'Hara said. "It's a bad thing to kill priests."

"You don't have to worry about going to hell for killing priests. You'll probably go to hell for a lot of other reasons," Short said.

Then he continued,

"Those men are not real monks. All of them had an insignia on the front of their garments. It was an insignia of an owl. That's the symbol of the secret society known as the Illuminati. The owl stands for wisdom, the enlightened, all of that nonsense. But make no mistake about it; these guys who are dressed as monks are trained killers. We figure they all have sidearms hidden under their robes.

Now, let's go back to the beginning. We are leaving for El Paso by train the day after tomorrow. We'll be taking our horses with us. There are two trains that head south each day; the 8:15 in the morning and the 2:10 in the afternoon. Half of us will be on the 8:15 and the other half will be on the 2:10. I already have our tickets. Here's the list of who will be on the 8:15. I'll call you out in pairs. That's how you will sit on the train:

Slim and Jimmy; Harrington and Doc; Pecos and Burns; and I will be sitting by myself. Here are your tickets."

Short passed out the tickets to the first group.

"Now, here are the arrangements for the 2:10:

Dakota and Colorado; Brisco and Matt; O'Hara and Dane; and Burkley, you'll be sitting by yourself. Here are your tickets."

Short then passed the tickets out to that group. Then he continued,

"Now, when we get to El Paso, we'll sign into the same hotel. We'll stay one night in El Paso. Sign in using an alias. Take your horses to the livery stable when you arrive in town. Stay in your hotel rooms except when you go out for meals; and don't bunch up in the restaurants.

We are going to need five wagons. They'll be waiting for us at the livery stable. I already placed an order for them. Slim, Jimmy, Colorado, Brisco, and Matt, each of you will be driving a wagon. We'll buy the wagons when we arrive in town. There will be a canvas in each wagon along with crates. We'll cover the treasures after we pack them. By the way, you'll be hitching your horses to the back of your wagons.

Now, we are not taking a train back to Pueblo. We'll all be escorting the wagons back to our hideout. We'll load up on food when we cross back into El Paso, then we'll immediately head north. Are there any questions at this point before I go on?"

No one spoke up.

"OK then, here's the plan once we get to the mission. Let's look at this drawing of the compound. I told you that there is a Gatling gun in the center of the courtyard. That's why we broke you out of jail, Burkley. You will be traveling around the back side with O'Hara and climb to the top of this hill right here, south of the mission. From that view, you can look right into the open courtyard. I want you to take out that person behind the Gatling gun. Stay in that location and take out everybody you can as they come running out of the buildings. Chances are they'll head for the Gatling gun too.

That's why, O'Hara, I want you to aim at the gun itself, and put it out of commission. Burns, bring their rifles over here."

Burns walked over to the corner and picked up two new Winchester repeaters with scopes and passed them to O'Hara and Burkley. Oh they were beauties all right - never been fired. Burns also gave them two boxes of ammunition each and a special scabbard to attach to their saddles to hold the rifles with scopes.

"Do you two have any questions?" Short asked.

"Yes, do we get to keep these rifles when it's all over?" Burkley asked.

"If you want to, they're yours."

Burkley rubbed his hands up and down the stock and said, "Oh I want to. That's for sure."

"All right then, let's continue. The ones who are driving the wagons will stay back until Dakota, Burns, Pecos, Doc and myself take out the four guards on the outside. Our sign to move in will be when we hear Burkley's and O'Hara's gun shots. We'll all charge from different directions with our guns blazing, and knock them out hard and fast. They won't know what hit 'em.

Dane, you then go for the large wooden double gate and blast it wide open. We have a bag of dynamite over in the corner for you with matches and cigars in case that's your means of lighting the fuses. I probably don't have to tell you this but if it's a windy day, cigars work pretty well."

"Thanks for the information but I can assure you that I am not a novice at this," Dane said in a sarcastic manner.

"No you're not. That's why we busted you out of jail my friend," Short said.

"Once the gate is open we'll all ride in, even the wagons at this point. If we have to, we'll use the wagons for cover. Again, Burkley and O'Hara we are depending on you to take out as many guards and men as possible. We aren't taking any prisoners.

Now, once we take control of the place, we'll all pitch in and load up the wagons with the loot, cover everything with the canvases, and immediately head back to El Paso where we'll pick up some grub and then ride on to Pueblo.

That's the plan. Are there any more questions?" Short asked.

"Yeah, what happens after we split up the loot?" Dane asked.

"When you get your share, you're free to go. If there really is one hundred million dollars behind those walls, we can all retire from this business and go straight. You may need a manual on how to do that," Short said as he laughed and added,

"That's all I have. Now, there's whiskey, brandy, and glasses over there on the table by the window. Help yourself. Some of the ranch hands will be cooking up some beef steaks for us this afternoon. They'll be ready in a couple of hours. There are also a few decks of cards over there and a box of cigars. Help yourselves to anything you find.

We'll all be staying here on the ranch until we catch the train to El Paso. Let me make myself clear on that; I don't want anyone leaving this ranch until we catch the train to El Paso. O'Hara and Burkley, I suggest you try out your new rifles and get used to them. The rest of you get better acquainted. Your lives will depend on each other when we get south of the border."

That was the end of the meeting. It was now a waiting game. Everyone was feeling relaxed and loose now but that would soon change when they boarded their trains to an unfamiliar destination and an unknown future.

O'Hara and Burkley immediately gathered up a few cans from the trash and took them out to the pasture to shoot their new rifles and sight in their scopes. They spent over two hours sharpening their shooting skills at 100 yards, then 200 yards and finally 300 yards. O'Hara was not surprised at Burkley's marksmanship skills. After all, he had been a sniper in the Civil War. However, O'Hara was no neophyte either. He had been a buffalo hunter in the Northern Plains when the government's plan was to wipe out the great herds to get rogue Sioux to come back onto the reservation. Wiping out the buffalo herds meant eliminating the Sioux's food and clothing source.

The ranch hands cooked the steaks and pinto beans and baked corn bread in Dutch ovens out on the campfires. The whiskey was flowing freely, and there were a few card games being played.

As usual Pecos was drinking too much and got into a brief fracas outside with a ranch hand. Pecos accused Slim of being a no good yellow-belly gringo because ole Slim made fun of the huge sombrero Pecos was wearing after he jokingly greeted Pecos with a Mexican slur. Dakota was outside with Pecos at the time and told him to ignore it because the guy was just having a little fun. Pecos was having none of it though so he punched Slim in the gut and then hauled off and decked him with a hard right wallop to the chin. Dakota walked away in disgust. He had enough of Pecos.

Burns was outside at the time and broke up the fight and helped Slim up. He told Pecos to cool off and go back inside. Pecos told Burns to mind his own business. Needless to say, that did not sit well with Burns; but he backed off because he did not want to give away his identity by showing his authoritative side.

After the meal, Burns rode back to town. He had a small house at the end of Main Street. Burns wasn't married now, but he was at one time. His wife died a few years back from consumption. It always worried him that he may have picked up the disease from her and it would eventually rear its ugly head, but he never showed signs of having it, at least not yet.

Cole Brinkman knew that Pinkerton had a desire to catch up with him and end his criminal career like he did with his brother Jerod. Cole also figured that Pinkerton was also after his other brother but Cole hadn't heard from him in about four years. He had no idea if he was dead or alive.

When Cole arrived in town, he took great pleasure in sending an anonymous wire to Allan Pinkerton in Chicago. It read:

Allan Pinkerton
Chicago, Illinois

This is to inform you about one of your agents named Bobby Green. After his flesh and innards fill the bellies of the buzzards, his bones will be scattered around the West by wild curs and coyotes. Thought you needed to be made aware of this to inform his next of kin.

A friend of Cole Brinkman

It gave Cole Brinkman satisfaction to send this morbid wire to Pinkerton. When Allan received the telegram, he was visibly upset and madder than a cornered rattler. He tore it up and threw it in the waste can. Now he had to meet with the wife of another agent and inform her that her husband had died honorably in the line of duty. He would have to tell her a lie that her husband's body was buried in an unmarked grave out west somewhere in the Arizona Territory. He really had no idea where Green was slain.

When everything settled down at the ranch, and most of the gang was sauced from drinking all day and sleeping in their bunks for the night, Pecos sat up on the side of his bed and began putting on his boots. He never did take his clothes off because he had something else in mind. He figured he could get away with sneaking out because Short stayed in the ranch house and not the bunkhouse with the rest of the men.

Dakota did not drink as heavily as the other cowboys and gang members so he was not knocked out like the rest. The ranchers always kept a lantern burning with a low wick so if they had to get up during the night to go to the privy, they wouldn't trip over someone's saddle, boots, or a misplaced chair.

Dakota heard someone moving around and opened his eyes to see who it was – he was a light sleeper. He caught a glimpse of Pecos leaving with his sombrero on. It was a sure thing Pecos wasn't making a trip to the outhouse wearing his hat. So Dakota hurriedly put on his pants, a shirt, and boots and slowly meandered between the bunks to the door. Then he opened the door, walked out, and quietly closed the door behind him. He stopped and looked around. There was a Comanche moon this night – a full moon – so it was easy to see across the pastures.

However, Dakota did not have to look very far. He only had to look toward the corral. There was Pecos saddling up his horse. Dakota walked over to Pecos and grabbed Pecos's arm and pulled him down just as he began to climb into his saddle.

"Where do you think you're going, Pecos?"

"I'm goin' to town. There's a little senorita waiting for me there."

"We were all told to stay here at the ranch, you heard Short; everyone is supposed to stay right here until we head to town to board the train."

"Don't worry amigo, I'll be back before sunup. Nobody will ever know I left."

"If you leave now Pecos, I'm through sticking up for you."

"Bueno, I have no problem with that."

Pecos laughed, put his left foot into his stirrup, grabbed a handful of mane, and pulled himself into the saddle. Then he turned his horse into Dakota, knocking him back some, and rode off into the night. That was the last straw as far as Dakota was concerned. Dakota went back into the bunkhouse. It took him about thirty minutes before he dozed off and began sawing wood like the rest. It sounded like a lumber mill in that bunkhouse – it always got that way after a long day of drinking.

Pecos didn't ride back to the ranch until the next morning at around 8:00 while everyone was eating breakfast. Short chastised Pecos for leaving during the night. However, what was even worse, Burns was eating breakfast at the café in town and saw Pecos come out of the saloon that had an all-night brothel upstairs. That was also the last straw for Burns. Now he had to do something about Pecos – but what – and when?

It was now the day before the gang would catch their trains to El Paso. After breakfast in the bunkhouse, Short told everyone to strap on their holsters and meet him in front of the ranch house. He asked O'Hara to help him with a couple of boxes. While the gang was waiting, Short and O'Hara walked out of the house carrying two heavy boxes. They were loaded with ammunition. Short told the guys to gather around. Then he and O'Hara reached into the two large boxes and handed out small boxes of cartridges to the gang.

"I want all of you to spend the morning doing some target shooting. Take turns; I don't want you fellas to accidently shoot each other with all the bullets flying around. When you go through your box, clean your pistols and hang out the rest of the day. You can play cards, work around the ranch or just sleep all day. I don't really care. But what you can't do today is drink. Those are direct orders from Brinkman himself."

"Are we ever going to meet this Brinkman?" Pecos asked.

"No you're not," Short said.

"No problem, I know who he is anyway," Pecos whispered out loud as he turned and walked away.

Short walked behind Pecos, grabbed Pecos's left shoulder with his right hand, forcibly turned him around, and asked,

"What did I hear you say, Pecos?"

"Say? I say nothing, amigo," Pecos remarked as he smirked and walked away.

After target practice, the rest of the day was uneventful for everyone. Many of the gang members sat around by themselves, cleaning their pistols and rifles and just contemplating about the next few days ahead. Several cornered Harrington throughout the day and asked questions about his boss Bautista, the secret society, and their treasures. Harrington was more than happy to talk to them and answer their questions.

A few played some friendly poker and other card games just using chips - no money was exchanged. That was another one of Short's orders. Sometimes big money losers can become a wee bit aggravated and lose their tempers subsequently causing eruptions into verbal and physical disputes. Short didn't want any of that this late in the game.

Burns rode out to the ranch house in the afternoon to check on things and to meet with Short. He just wanted to be sure everyone understood the plans and they were all set to go. They had a brief discussion about Pecos's attitude. They both had Pecos pegged – he was a loose cannon and had the ability to jeopardize the operation. Burns told Short that he would handle the situation – not to worry.

On the next morning, a couple of the ranch hands got up at 3:30 and began making breakfast for everyone: Biscuits and gravy, bacon, eggs, and coffee. The food was cooked on the wood burning stove in the bunkhouse. The clattering of the iron skillets, the coffee boiling and the aroma of the bacon frying woke everyone up early. The gang members were quiet during breakfast

– there wasn't much talking going on – just a lot of thinking, and a lot of wondering.

After breakfast, the ones with the 8:15 a.m. train tickets started to put their gear together and filled up their saddlebags with just the essentials – ammunition and a few extra clothes. The 8:15 a.m. group – Slim, Jimmy, Harrington, Doc, Pecos, and Short rode out at 7:00 toward Pueblo. The latter group watched them ride off. Burns was already at the depot when the first group arrived. They all greeted Burns but didn't have much to say to each other as they sat in the depot waiting for the morning train to arrive.

Burns walked over to the depot master and asked if the train was on time. The telegraph operator heard the question and answered,

"I received a wire about ten minutes ago saying it was. It's coming from Cheyenne, making a quick stop in Denver, and then coming directly to Pueblo. It should be here right at eight bells."

At 7:55, the train whistle began blowing. You could hear the shriek a mile down the tracks. Everyone stood up and walked out on the platform to watch the train roll in. The gang members then gathered their horses which were hitched up behind the depot and walked them up the side ramp to the platform getting them ready to load onto the freight car.

All of the trains out west had two to three freight cars for boarding horses – it was just a normal thing around those parts. On the floor there was always hay for eating on top of straw for bedding. The trouble was that reeking manure and foul smelling urine were mixed in and the cars weren't cleaned out for a few days or sometimes a week. They were virtual rolling barnyards.

On occasion, freshly used cattle cars were employed to haul horses. That made some of your high society-type westerners uneasy loading their horses in mushy rank cow manure laden railcars, especially if they wore their Sunday go-to-meeting boots for business meetings.

After the horses were loaded, the depot manager moved the loading ramps away from the freight cars and the gang members found their seats. There were two passenger cars. The men split up in different cars but stayed with their seat assignments. Slim and Jimmy, and Harrington and Doc sat in the front passenger car. Pecos and Burns sat in the last row in the second passenger car which was next to the freight car. Short sat in front of those two.

The train pulled away from the depot right on time at 8:15. After a few hours into the trip, the train began to travel through a desolate area. The terrain was rocky and filled with nothing but sagebrush and mesquite. There wasn't much else to see out the window.

Burns began striking up a conversation with Pecos. Short was sitting directly in front of them and listening. There was no one in the seats directly across the aisle from them. Most of the passengers shied away from the cattle or equine freight cars for obvious reasons.

"You know Pecos, you seem like a very smart man."

Pecos looked at Burns and said,

"You think so, Senor?"

"Yes I do. I bet you really know who I am don't you?"

"Si Senor, I can see it in your eyes. I can see it by the way you talk, and now by the way you move."

"Who do you think I really am, Pecos?"

"You are Jerod Brinkman's brother. You are Cole Brinkman, I think. I'm pretty sure of this. Si, I know for sure, you are Cole Brinkman."

"Wow, you have me all figured out don't you, Pecos?"

"Si, Senor Brinkman."

"Do you like cigars, Pecos?"

"Si."

"I have a couple of Cuban cigars here in my pocket. They are the best. Let's go out back on the gangway connection and have a smoke. I want to tell you something else about me that most people don't know. I don't want anyone to hear it, especially Short."

They both walked out on the noisy back platform of their passenger car. Burns pulled out one cigar from his coat pocket and gave it to Pecos. He then pulled out a match, lit Pecos's cigar and then said,

"Your friend Dakota told me you carry a lucky potion pouch in your pocket. Can I see it?"

"Sure."

Pecos put his left hand into his pocket. When he did, Burns quickly put his left hand around Pecos's neck at the Adam's apple. Pecos's eyes bulged out as Burns squeezed tightly. Pecos reached up with his right hand and grabbed Burns's left wrist. But in a split second, Burns pulled out his pistol, stuck the barrel in the Mexican's gut just below the sternum, pointed it upwards, put two quick .45 slugs into Pecos's heart, and pushed him backwards off the train. Pecos was dead when his body slammed against the ground and rolled down a steep embankment.

Burns calmly put two cartridges into the empty chambers. Then he holstered his six-shooter, straightened out his suit coat, walked back into the passenger car, and sat down with Short. They quietly looked at each other. Burns nodded his head once. Short knew what that meant. Short smiled, looked out the window, and said nothing.

Burns put his head back, pulled his hat down, and dozed off.

When the first train was approaching El Paso, Texas, the second train had just rolled up to the station in Pueblo at 2:00 p.m. - Dakota, Colorado, Brisco, Matt, O'Hara, Dane, and Burkley were boarding that train.

The first order of business for the group which arrived in El Paso was to walk their horses over to the livery stable and then sign into the hotel using false names. Short told everyone to stay in their own rooms until dinner time. Then to eat their dinners in the hotel's restaurant sitting only two at a table if possible. After dinner they were to go back to their rooms until they heard from Short again. Short and Burns were planning to hold one last meeting when the second group arrived very late that night.

After Short paid the stable manager for boarding his horse for one night, he took care of procuring the five wagons, four long ears, and six horses to pull the wagons. He preferred to use all mules for hauling back the treasures, but the stable only had four available.

When the first group was at the livery stable arranging to have their horses boarded, it was Doc who looked around and noticed Pecos wasn't with the group, yet Short had his horse and was trading it for a stockier steed to pull a wagon.

Doc walked over to Short and asked,

"What happened to Pecos? His horse is here, but I don't see Pecos anywhere."

"He got off at the last stop."

"Why didn't he take his horse?"

"He was in a hurry."

Being an educated man, Doc did not have to ask twice. He knew that Pecos had a propensity to act unpredictably and could jeopardize this very important mission. He surmised that Pecos got off involuntarily between stops while the train was barreling down the tracks; his conjecture was precise.

The men waited in their rooms as ordered until dinner. After dinner, they went right back to their rooms and waited again.

The second train arrived later that night. They too walked their horses over to the livery stable. The stable attendant was not around, so they found empty stalls to use, removed their saddles, and gave their horses enough hay and water to last the night.

Then they all walked over to the hotel together. There wasn't a clerk on duty at the time. He had retired to his room two hours earlier. Short though was waiting in the lobby for the men and met them when they walked through the door.

"I see everyone made it," Short said as he greeted them. "Sign in; the book is on the counter. I already paid for your rooms. After you sign in, I'll give you your keys and room numbers."

They all walked over to the counter and took their turns signing the hotel book with phony names – they had to - some of their pictures and names were on wanted posters hanging over at the post office.

"Take your gear up to your rooms and meet me in my room in fifteen minutes. I'm in room 201. Here are your keys and room numbers: Colorado, room 211; Dakota, room 212; Brisco, room 214; Matt, 215; O'Hara, 216, Dane, room 217; and Burkley, room 218. See you all in fifteen minutes."

Short then went up to Doc's room and told Doc to inform the earlier group to meet in Short's room in fifteen minutes. Doc got a glimpse of Dakota walking into his room, room 212. He waited until the halls were cleared and then quickly walked over to 212 and knocked on the door. Dakota cracked his door to see who it was, then opened it and let Doc in.

"Hey Doc, glad to see ya made it OK. Do you know what room Pecos is in?"

Doc put a somber look on his face. Dakota knew something was wrong.

"What's the problem, Doc?"

"Pecos didn't arrive here with everyone else."

"What do you mean? Wasn't he on the train with you guys?"

"Yeah, but when we arrived, he was gone. I believe either Short or Burns threw him off the train somewhere in New Mexico just before we reached El Paso."

"You mean they killed him?"

"I'm sure of it. I knew you and he were close. I just thought you ought to know ahead of the meeting. He was in bad standings with Short and Burns and probably Brinkman. It's best if you leave it alone."

"I will; thanks for the information."

Dakota felt bad about the news but in a way, he wasn't surprised. No sir, Pecos was becoming reviled by many of the gang members. He began acting foolishly and irresponsibly and Dakota actually thought that it was just a matter of time before the line would be drawn. It just happened sooner than Dakota expected. But he thought Doc's advice was prudent, so he just let it be.

Everyone arrived at Short's room on time. Some sat on the few chairs in the room, some sat on the bed, and the rest stood up. Short and Burns stood. Then Short spoke,

"We are leaving El Paso to cross the Rio Grande at 7:30 tomorrow morning. If you want breakfast before we ride out, I suggest you get an early start. I won't tolerate anyone being late. I want the 8:15 group to eat at the café directly across the street. The 2:10 group should eat here at the hotel's restaurant. Drop your room keys at the desk before you eat and have your gear with you. If you get any questions from anyone, you're here on business. That's all you have to say.

Let's go over our plans one last time. We all need to ride out of town together. There's a main road leading out of El Paso to the Rio Grande. I'll lead the way. We'll be crossing over a bridge into Mexico. Once we get into Mexico, we have about a seven to eight mile trek. We'll stop about three hundred yards out from the mission and wait for Burkley and O'Hara to get into position on the south hilltop. Our signal will be when we hear Burkley and O'Hara begin their volley toward the Gatling gun and anyone else they see in the courtyard.

What happens when we hear the gunshots, Dakota?"

Dakota stood there and thought about it for a few seconds and then said,

"I believe you, Doc, Burns, and I will charge in and kill the Illuminati guards on the outside of the compound, right?"

"That's right," Short said. "What happens next?"

No one answered. Then Short looked at Dane. Dane stared back at Short for a few moments and said,

"I guess I'm up now. After you take out the guards, which I assume will be pretty dang quick, I'll come riding in and blow the gate wide open. I'll know how many sticks to use once I see the size of the gate."

"That's right Dane, but only give us two minutes to get our job done. That should be all the time we need to take out the guards.

Slim, what happens after the gate is blown wide open?"

"I gather you guys will ride in first with your guns blazing and then the wagons will follow."

"Good, but I want the wagons to move toward the entrance immediately after the explosion. Don't stop for anything. Ride right into the courtyard. Got that?"

"Yes sir."

"We'll use the wagons for cover if we have to. However, by now we should have taken out any and all resistance. If not, all of us will battle until we do.

Are there any questions?"

Short looked around the room. There were no questions so Short continued,

"Burkley and O'Hara, stay in position until you see us ride through the front gate, and the opposition is put down. Then ride over to the compound.

Once the opposition is neutralized, we'll find the gold and treasures and load up all we can into the five wagons and our saddlebags. We may not be able to take all of the one hundred million dollars, but we're gonna sure try. When we get loaded we'll throw the canvases over our cargo and head back north to the border. We'll all ride back to Pueblo together and split up the loot there. Harrington, you'll need to contact Bautista and see how he wants to collect his share."

"What about food? We can't eat gold on the way back," O'Hara said.

"Not to worry. One of the wagons has water and rations in it. I thought it best that we take care of it now rather than afterwards," Short said. "Are there any other questions?"

"I have one. Who's hitching up the horses and mules to the wagons?" Slim asked.

"Good question, the livery stable owner will be doing that for us. All you need to do is to make sure you guys driving the wagons tie your horses to the back of them," Short said. "Are there any more questions?"

There weren't, so Short told them to go straight back to their rooms, get a good night's sleep, and make sure their guns were fully loaded in the morning. Short went over to Burns's room to discuss a few last minute details. They talked about Harrington and Bautista and the possibility of pulling a swindle on the two.

"I would like to think we could get away with a double cross, but I'm not sure we can," Burns said. "That Bautista fella said he would have assassins watching every move we make."

"Do you believe him?" Short asked.

"I don't know if I do, or if I don't; but I do know one thing, I don't think I want to find out. There is something mighty evil about that man. I think that if we crawfished on the deal, we might find ourselves in the same bellies of the buzzards that munched on Green. Anyway, it sounds like there's more money in that mission than anyone of us can spend in three lifetimes.

After this is all over, I'm taking Dakota with me to Hays City so he can point out that little weasel, Rusty Blake for me, or whatever his name is. I'm planning on putting a well-placed slug in his and his wife's head for killing my brother Jerod. Then I'm eventually moving on to Canada and that's the last I'll be heard of. I intend to find me a woman up there and settle down. What are you going to do Short? How are you going to spend your money?"

"The War was tough on my family down in Mississippi. We had a plantation in a small town just east of Vicksburg. The land is still in my parents' name. I'm aiming to go back there and start up a ranch and hire some cowhands to run it. I'm gonna build me a big ole two story plantation house like I grew up in, before those dang Yankee blue bellies burnt it to the ground. I'm not one of those guys who think the South will rise again. I'm not even one of those guys who hold a grudge against the northerners. I figure it wouldn't do any good. I just want to start a new life, and be able to afford to get out of this business of getting shot at."

"Well, after this one last job, we'll all be able to do that," Burns said. "You better go back to your room now. We both need to get a good night's sleep. We need to have our senses and wits about us tomorrow."

Many of the gang members laid in their beds with their eyes wide open staring at the ceiling for hours wondering what the morning would bring - others were able to doze straight off - stress causes different reactions in different people.

Short was one of the last ones to unwind and saw wood that night, but he was one of the first ones up. So he went from room to room knocking on doors to make sure everyone would be getting up and going on time.

The men packed up their gear and went to their respective restaurants for coffee and breakfast. No one skipped their first and only real square for the day. After breakfast they meandered over to the livery stable one by one and made ready for their journey. There wasn't much talking – just a lot of quiet thinking.

It wasn't long before they were ready to cross the Rio Grande into Mexico. Slim, Jimmy, Colorado, Brisco, and Matt climbed into their buckboards after they tethered their saddled horses to the back of their wagons. The others mounted up on their steeds. Burns, Short and Harrington led the way, followed by the five wagons and then the rest of the men.

It was early yet and there weren't many people stirring around town. A few who were roaming the streets saw the group riding out, but thought nothing of it. The thinking was that they were heading across the border for several loads of freight.

On the way to the mission, the outlaws passed many small farms and cattle ranches. They had many look-seers but no one asked them any questions. They were all armed to the hilt and they were gringos who looked like you should pay them no mind – for your own good.

Even though the distance was just a few miles to their destination, it seemed like hours because the anticipation was building as the time passed.

Short backed his horse up some and began telling the men to check their weapons one last time. "Don't leave a chamber empty."

Their nerves were on edge now. Reality began sinking in as they approached their last holding point before their charge.

"About one half mile to go men, pass it on!" Short shouted back.

"One half mile to go!"

"One half mile to go!"

Dakota riding the drag, raised up his hand to let the point men know that he got the message. Short waved back.

Short slowed the movement so the wagon wheels wouldn't make too much noise as they approached the mission. The wheels were freshly greased so the noise was at a minimum – but even with that, five wagons with squeaking boards could be heard a pretty good distance as they traveled over a slightly rocky and bumpy terrain.

When they reached their destination, about three hundred yards from the mission, Short held up his hand for everyone to stop. They couldn't see the mission from there but Short knew it was right around the bend. Then he waved Burkley and O'Hara to come forward. They quickly trotted up to Short.

"Burkley and O'Hara, this is our stopping point. Your location is that tallest hill over there. That's south of the mission. Position yourself by those three large pine trees up there. You'll be able to see down into the courtyard from there. As soon as you see your targets, start blasting away. That will be our signal to move in. Ride around this hill. It will eventually get you over to the south hill. Now ride hard, get in place, and let 'em have it," Short said.

"You got it," Burkley replied.

Burkley and O'Hara spurred their horses hard and galloped fast into the wind riding this side of the small north hill, then behind the west hill and over to the taller south hill. There was an opening between the west and south hills – a passageway of sorts. They could see the back part of the adobe wall surrounding the mission as they rode across that passage and onward to the tall southern hill.

When they reached the base of the hill, they hopped off their horses, tied their reins to some tree branches, pulled their rifles from their scabbards, and began climbing. It was a fairly steep climb. But that wasn't the only problem. There was a lot of loose rock - it was easy to lose your footing. What also added to the difficulty of the climb was the fact that they were both carrying a rifle with a scope in one hand, while using their free hand to help them move safely up the hill. It was important to keep their rifles from banging against the rocks so their scopes would not be knocked out of alignment.

It took longer to reach the top than they anticipated. About four feet from the peak Burkley whispered to O'Hara,

"Wait, let's crawl from here so we're not spotted. We'll lay down by those pine trees. We're supposed to be able to see everything from there."

They got down on their knees and crawled up to the peak the best they could, maneuvering with one hand to the ground and the other hand holding their weapons in the air at shoulder height. When they reached the top, they positioned themselves between two of the pine trees, and laid flat on the ground. Then they both put their rifles to their shoulders in a firing position and looked through their scopes.

"Where's the Gatling gun that's supposed to be in the middle of the courtyard?" O' Hara asked.

"I don't know; I don't see it. In fact, I don't see anyone or anything in the courtyard. Something's wrong," Burkley said. "Let's get back to the horses."

Just then a voice behind a boulder yelled out,

"Drop your weapons!"

The two were startled when they heard the demand. They saw two men in black hats and black dusters holding six-shooters walk out from behind a large boulder. They were about thirty feet away. Burkley whispered to O'Hara, as the men approached,

"I don't know who these guys are, but I'm not gonna die here in Mexico."

Burkley quickly raised his rifle and shot at the two men. O'Hara did the same. They shot them dead on the spot.

"Who the hell are these guys?" O'Hara asked.

"I don't know. I guess they're members of the secret society," Burkley said. "Let's go check them out."

O'Hara and Burkley walked over to the dead bodies that were stretched out flat on their bellies. O'Hara stood there with his rifle pointing at the slain men, just in case they were still alive. Burkley laid his rifle down, got down on one knee, and turned one of the bodies over. Then he moved the black duster aside so he could look for some type of identification. He patted around the chest and found a wallet.

He opened it and looked inside. He was shocked at what he found. He pulled what looked to be a membership card out of the wallet and said,

"Dagnabbit, look at this. These sneaky ambushers are the scum of the earth – low-life snakes. They're dang Pinkerton men."

"What? Pinkerton men?"

"That's what I said, Pinkerton men. We've been tricked."

"Say, isn't…?"

"Yes, he's wearing the exact same color hat and coat…I'll kill that weasel when I see him," Burkley said.

In the meantime, the rest of the gang heard shots coming from the top of the south hill and assumed Burkley and O'Hara had taken out the Gatling gun and the man behind it.

"That's the cue men, let's ride!" Short shouted.

Short, Harrington, Doc, Burns, and Dakota rode hard and fast down the path. Dane followed fifty feet behind them carrying a saddlebag full of dynamite. They spurred their horses as they charged around the bend in the road. All five had their six-shooters drawn and ready to unload at the sight of the Illuminati guards.

But when they approached the adobe walls, there was no one out front. Dane rode in behind them and put the dynamite in place by the large wooden gate and lit the fuses.

O'Hara and Burkley ran back to the top of the hill and began waving their rifles in the air to warn the group. The horsemen didn't see them because they were focused on the dynamite that was about to blow.

O'Hara and Burkley kept trying to get the attention of the gang to no avail. But just when the dynamite blew, O'Hara fell backwards to the ground.

Burkley looked down at him and saw a bullet hole in his forehead. A sniper picked him off. Burkley began running frantically down the hill, slipping and sliding on the loose rocks. He lost control of his descent and dropped his rifle but did not take the time to pick it up. Instead, he kept traveling down the hillside – he was in a heap of hurry to get back to his horse and warn the others. To make things worse, he had no idea where that sniper was positioned.

When the five men driving the wagons heard the explosion of the dynamite, they whipped their mules and horses and rushed toward the compound. With the gate wide open, Short, Dane, Doc and Harrington rode in. Burns told Dakota to wait outside the compound with him until there was an all-clear sign. Burns thought there was something strange going on since there was no one around the outside like they anticipated and no resistance when his gang entered the courtyard.

The wagons came rolling up and went straight through the entrance and inside the courtyard. Short and the others did not see the Gatling gun or any Illuminati around. He thought they either came too late and the treasures were moved, or they had been hoodwinked. Nevertheless, he was going to check out the three buildings. He ordered Slim, Colorado, and Jimmy to jump off their wagons and each check a building for the treasures.

The instant they jumped to the ground, shutters on the buildings flew wide open, rifle barrels appeared in the windows, and lead began flying, whistling all around them.

"It's a trap!" Short yelled out as his horse spooked from the gunshots and reared up. Seconds later Short took a bullet to the chest and fell off his horse. He was dead when his body slammed against the ground. Then Harrington fell to the ground - he hit it hard.

The teamsters ran behind their wagons for cover and commenced firing. The fusillade of bullets rang out sounding like a war zone. They then began untying their horses from the back of their wagons with one hand while continuing to fire toward the open windows with the other, but they were shooting wildly and missing their marks because they were trying to control their horses which were spooking and rearing from the barrage of gunfire.

Dane and Doc rode their horses out of the compound and met up with Dakota and Burns. All four began riding hard back toward the border. Burkley met them at the first stop area. They momentarily halted and Burkley frantically yelled,

"What about the others?"

They looked back and saw Jimmy, Colorado, and Slim riding fast toward them – their horses were galloping at top speed. Matt and Brisco were killed in the courtyard. Then a shot rang out and Jimmy fell backwards to the ground while his horse kept running toward the outlaws. He was hit by a Pinkerton sniper's bullet.

"Let's get the hell out of here before we all get killed!" Dakota yelled.

They kicked the sides of their horses, leaned forward in their saddles, and rode straight for the border. There was no stopping now. At this point only two of them knew who ambushed them: Burkley and the Pinkerton agent who infiltrated the gang.

CHAPTER EIGHT:

A Whiskey Indiscretion

The gang of thirteen had now dwindled down to seven. As they rode toward the border, there were an unknown number of Pinkerton agents dogging their trail. The detectives were dead set on capturing or killing everyone in Brinkman's gang - they mostly had killing on their mind - too many jailbreaks – the Pinkerton men intended to put an end to that now.

Colorado took charge of the group and told everyone to follow him.

Colorado was part of another gang before he joined up with the Brinkman gang. He worked cattle for John Tunstall in the New Mexico Territory. Tunstall was a rancher and merchant in Lincoln County. He was the first man killed in what eventually became known as the Lincoln County War. On February 18, 1878, Tunstall, was shot and killed by a crooked deputy. Colorado, Billy the Kid and others were working cattle when they heard the gunshots. They rode toward the sounds and found their boss shot in the chest. He was already dead.

Colorado rode with Billy for a while, killing the ones involved. Colorado turned into a cold-blooded killer just like Billy. On December 23, 1880, Pat Garrett and his posse captured Billy the Kid and three of his gang members at their hideout in a small shack. One gang member was killed, Charlie Bowdre. He took the first bullet on the way to the outhouse.

Colorado was out gathering wood at the time behind the shack and heard the gunfire and hid behind some brush and watched as the Kid and his gang members surrendered. He hung around the area for a while, hiding in the shadows to see what would become of Billy.

Billy the Kid went on trial in April, 1881 in Mesilla, New Mexico Territory. After two days of testimony, Billy was found guilty for the murder of Sheriff Brady. On April 13th, he was sentenced by the judge to hang on May 13, 1881. The legend goes that when the judge said,

"Billy Bonney, you are sentenced to hang until you are dead, dead, dead."

Billy the Kid responded,

"You can go to hell, hell, hell."

Well, Billy the Kid never did hang for his crime. He escaped from the Lincoln County Jail on April 28, 1881, killing two more lawmen, Deputy Bob Olinger and Deputy James Bell.

It was after the sentencing in Mesilla that Colorado headed north to Pueblo and joined up with the Brinkman gang.

Colorado knew the area well so he figured that he and the Brinkman gang could ride to the outskirts of Mesilla, or La Mesilla as it was sometimes called, which was about forty-nine miles from El Paso. It was a long ride but they had no choice – they had to ride as far as they could to keep a safe distance from the Pinkertons. Colorado figured they could camp out there, pick up some grub, and maybe rob the small bank to get some cash.

The seven desperados rode hard for about twenty five miles, changing from gallops to fast trots, and then back to gallops. Colorado suggested that they hug the Rio Grande all the way back. It would be their North Star and a way to get drinking water for their steeds.

The outlaws' horses were all lathered up from the ride. It was time to give them a rest. When they stopped to water their horses about halfway to Mesilla, Burkley got a bit rowdy. He knew better than anyone what happened back in Juarez. He shot and killed two Pinkerton men and watched O'Hara take a bullet to the head from a sniper. He was furious - the whole plan fell apart and he was almost captured and killed. It reminded him of when he belonged to the other Brinkman gang, the "Professionals".

"What the hell happened back there? Does anyone have a clue? I'm taking over this gang now before anyone else gets killed. We are heading back to Pueblo and regrouping," Burkley said.

"Who says you're in charge?" Colorado asked.

"I did, that's who."

Burkley stood up and undid the leather which was holding the hammer of his pistol in place, and challenged Colorado to get up and draw. Dakota stepped in and said,

"Wait a minute. We don't need to lose any more men."

"Back off Dakota, if you know what's good for you," Burkley said.

Now everyone gathered around as it looked as though there was going to be a gunfight between Burkley and Colorado.

"Hold up now," Burns said. "There's not going to be any gunplay among my gang members - at least not today."

"Your gang members!" Burkley yelled. "Who the hell made you boss?"

"I did. I'm Cole Brinkman. Now back off."

Everyone stood there in disbelief and looked at Brinkman for a few seconds. Then Brinkman said,

"That's right. I'm Cole Brinkman. And now that my cover has been blown because of your stupidity, I'll gun down anyone who doesn't listen to my orders. If you don't think I can outdraw you, try me – try me now – come on – get on with it!"

Burkley hooked the leather back on his hammer and backed off.

"Now, who can shed some light on what the hell happened back there?" Brinkman asked.

"I can," Burkley said.

"Well go ahead then," Brinkman demanded.

"When O'Hara and I reached the top of the hill, we could see that there was not a Gatling gun in the courtyard, neither were there any men. Two men came out from behind a boulder and ambushed us. I got the bead on them and killed them both. I checked them out and they were Pinkerton men."

"Pinkerton men?"

"That's right. We tried to warn you but you guys never saw us. When we were standing on top of the hill trying to get your attention, a sniper shot O'Hara right between the eyes. He never knew what hit him. He fell dead on the spot. That's when I ran down the hill to join up with you."

"Well then, either the Illuminati moved the treasures out before we arrived and the Pinkertons moved in or…"

"Or what?" Dakota asked

"Never mind, what else do you know, Burkley?" Brinkman asked.

"The two Pinkerton men I killed up on that hill were dressed in black coats and black hats. That's what they wore when they attacked your brother's gang at our hideout outside of Abilene. Now it's obvious that we have another Pinkerton man in this gang besides Green. There's only one man wearing all black. That was probably to keep from being shot."

Burkley then looked at Slim.

Slim backed up and said,

"You're crazy, I always wear black. I'm not a Pinkerton agent."

Slim could see the fire in everyone's eyes – it was no use – these outlaws were now convinced that Slim was the traitor. As he was backing up, he put his hand by his six-shooter. When he made that gesture, Burkley and Brinkman drew and drilled Slim full of holes.

"Throw that scumbag's body into the river," Brinkman said.

Dane grabbed his hands, Colorado grabbed onto his feet, and they flung Slim's body into the Rio Grande. The gang was now down to six.

"What do we do now?" Dakota asked Brinkman.

"It will take a while but we'll rebuild our gang. Then we'll revisit with Bautista and ask him where the Illuminati's treasures have been moved to. Now that we got the last Pinkerton off our backs, we have a future, a future full of treasures. We won't give up until it's ours; I don't care if we have to go deeper into Mexico to get it."

"Sir, that's great but don't you think we better get back on our horses and head north? If those were Pinkerton agents back there in the mission, they're probably trailing us," Doc said.

"Yeah, let's saddle up. Colorado, show us the way," Brinkman ordered.

"You got it! We're about twenty-five miles outside of Mesilla."

The outlaws continued to ride leather following the river to Mesilla not really knowing if the Pinkerton agents were hot on their trail. Mesilla was a small community adjacent to the southwest corner of Las Cruces in the Dona Ana County. It was an established colony by 1850. But it was under a constant threat of attack by Apache warriors. Because of this, Fort Fillmore was built by the United States Cavalry to protect the settlers.

During the first two years of the Civil War, 1861 – 1862, Mesilla served as the capital of the Confederate Territory of Arizona. It was known as the hub of the entire region. Mesilla was eventually recaptured by a group of volunteer California Union soldiers and became their headquarters in Arizona until 1864.

In the 1870's and early 1880's, Mesilla was well known around the territory for its cantinas and festivals. Billy the Kid and his group along with other notables of the time were attracted to the area. Two major stagecoach lines, the Santa Fe Trail and the Butterfield Stagecoach, passed through Mesilla on their travels to the east and west.

Mesilla ceased to become the focal point in the region around 1881. The Atchison, Topeka, and Santa Fe Railroad naturally chose Mesilla as the town to lay tracks and build a railroad stop with a depot and spur. But the town asked for too much money for the land rights. Subsequently, Las Cruces stepped in and offered the railroad free land. That changed everything in the region. Las Cruces would now become the place that expanded in population and commerce.

Colorado kept tabs of these events. That's why he directed the gang to head to Mesilla and steered them away from Las Cruces. It would be easier knocking off a bank in Mesilla and making a clean getaway.

It was nightfall when they approached the town. The gang didn't have any grub to eat so they had made plans to buy some rations to stuff in their saddlebags, chow down at a cantina, and then knock over the local bank before sunup after they grabbed some sleep on the outskirts of town.

Just as Colorado predicted, the town was dead – not much stirring. Brinkman thought it was wise to head to the general store first before it closed. The storekeeper had just walked out of his store and locked the front door when Brinkman walked up to him and said,

"I'll give you an extra fifty dollars if you open up again and let us buy some provisions. We're traveling to Texas tonight to round up another herd of cattle to drive north."

The storekeeper stuck the key back into the keyhole and opened up his store to the outlaws. The others were sitting on their horses in front of the store when Brinkman waved them in and told them to bring in their saddlebags. They all did except for Dane. His saddlebags were loaded with dynamite left over from south of the border.

While the men were walking in, the store owner lit three kerosene lanterns so everyone could see the contents in the store. They collected their goods, paid the store owner, and Brinkman politely thanked and handed him the $50 that he promised.

The men walked back outside and slung their saddlebags behind their saddles and tied them with their leather saddle strings. Then Brinkman said,

"Let's all eat at that cantina across the street. We're probably safer if we all stay together."

So that's what they did. Every time someone walked through the door, they all looked up and reached toward their guns. They were jumpier then frog legs frying in a cast iron skillet.

When they finished their meals, they checked out the bank – both the front and the back. Then they rode just outside of town into a wooded area and found what they considered a safe place to bed down for a few hours. The men took turns standing guard to watch for Pinkerton agents who might ride up on them. Although they would not easily be detected – the area was surrounded by a lot of trees and brush. There was no moon on this night either.

Brinkman woke up at about 4:00 in the morning and then proceeded to wake everyone else up.

"Come on boys get up, we have a bank to rob. Saddle up and load your guns. We'll eat breakfast north of town after we rob the bank."

The crew was moving mighty slow. The stress from the day before had them worn down. Stress tends to do that to a fella. But Brinkman was determined to get a cracking so he hurried them up. After they saddled their horses, he gathered everyone together and gave them the plan.

"We'll break in through the back door. Dane, you blow the safe. Take a look at the size of it and determine how many sticks you need just to blow off the door. I don't want to blow up the whole building. Not that I care about the building. It's just that it would be hard to collect our money that way.

When you have that figured out, go ahead and light the fuses. We'll all wait out back. When it blows, Dane, you, Doc and Burkley run in and empty the safe. Gather what you can. Dakota, Colorado, and I will wait outside and stand guard. Once we have the loot, we'll continue our ride north along the Rio Grande.

There's one last thing, when we ride out of town, I don't want anyone firing their pistols into the air like the James-Younger Gang did after they robbed banks. We aren't the James-Younger Gang. Those novices got themselves caught up in Northfield. We'll ride out fast and make as little noise as possible. Maybe no one will spot us heading north. Are there any questions?"

No one had a question so they spun their cylinders one last time to ensure every chamber had a cartridge in it. Then they saddled up and rode into town. The streets were dark in those wee hours of the morning. There were only two street lights lit, one at each end of Main street. They were fairly dim at that, beings they had short wicks. This was perfect for a bank robbery. They rode down Main Street at a walk so the sound of pounding hooves would not call attention to them.

When they approached the bank, they quietly rode around to the back. Burkley, Doc, and Dane got off their horses and handed their reins to Colorado. Colorado knew that the explosion would most likely spook the horses so he dismounted in order that he could better control the horses after the blast. He then realized that four rearing horses would be too hard for one man to handle so he passed off one set of reins to Dakota.

Burkley was a professional lock picker. He had the door open in seconds. He smiled at Dane and Doc because this bank was easier to get into than most. Burkley came with a lot of bank robbing experience from up northern Missouri way. If anyone knew how to break into a bank, it was ole Kenny Burkley.

Doc found a kerosene lantern and lit it so Dane could see the size of the safe and determine how much dynamite to use. It wasn't a large safe, about 6 feet tall and 5 feet wide. Just about what he figured for this small town. Dane concluded 2 sticks of dynamite would be sufficient. So he told the others to leave the building.

He positioned the sticks by the bottom door hinge, lit the fuses, and ran outside. He used short wicks so the dynamite blew the moment he stepped out of the bank building. After the blast, the three ran back into the bank to get the loot. The safe's door was still attached and hanging from the top hinge. Burkley held it aside with one hand while Dane grabbed sacks of money from the inside and passed them to Doc and Burkley. When their arms were full, they ran outside, stuffed their saddlebags, grabbed their horses, mounted, and rode out to Main Street and north of town.

The deafening sound of the explosion woke up the townsfolk. Lights from kerosene lanterns began to appear one by one in second story windows up and down Main Street. Many local merchants lived above their businesses. Almost every room lit up in the hotel on the south side of the street as well.

Tom Kiefer, owner of the General Store across the street from the bank, opened up his second story window and shouted to the left and then to the right.

"The bank's been robbed! The bank's been robbed!"

By the time the town's marshal figured out what had happened, Brinkman's gang was long gone. Tom Kiefer told the marshal that there were several strangers, Texas cowboys, in his store the night before and they told him they were riding to Texas to gather another herd of steer to drive north.

It took the marshal about two hours to form a posse. When he did, they all headed south, while the bank robbers headed north.

Brinkman and his gang rode about 25 miles before they stopped and camped again. They accurately figured they got a clean getaway. There were also no signs of Pinkerton agents on their tail. When they counted up the money, they had about $21,000 in cash - a nice haul for a bank heist - unless of course you were Cole Brinkman. No amount of cash was ever enough for him - especially after missing out on the big haul south of the border. So the next heist was an easy decision.

About 35 miles south of Albuquerque, they came up on a Santa Fe Stagecoach. It was known to carry passengers and railroad payroll to the south. Colorado gave that important piece of information to Brinkman. It was the strongbox they were after.

The gang was riding to the north when they saw the stagecoach at a distance headed their way. Brinkman told all of them to pull up their bandannas over their faces, and unholster their pistols.

As the stagecoach approached the group, the outlaws shot their guns into the air to slow up the stage. The teamster pulled back on the reins to get the horses to slow up and then put his boot on the brake handle and pushed it forward. When the stagecoach came to a complete stop, Brinkman told the man riding shotgun to throw his weapon to the ground. The man held his double barrel 10-gauge shot gun in the air and was getting ready to toss it when Burkley shot the man.

"You didn't have to do that!" Dakota yelled.

The man riding shotgun was hit in the shoulder – it wasn't a fatal wound.

Colorado jumped off his horse and opened the stagecoach door and told the passengers to get out as he held his gun on them. There were only three passengers on board, a railroad executive and a lady with her 9 year old son.

In the meantime Brinkman told the teamster to throw down the strongbox. It wasn't easy to lift – it was full of gold pieces. But he found the strength because his adrenaline was running high. Multiple six-shooters pointing at your head will do that to a person. This was the first time this young teamster had ever been held up.

Burkley jumped off his horse and shot open the heavy duty padlock. They hit the jackpot! There was about $40,000 cash in the box in sacks of $20 gold pieces and large denomination bills. They didn't know the exact amount at the time, but there was a lot there.

While Burkley was removing the cash from the strongbox, Doc climbed up on the stagecoach and looked at the wound of the man riding shotgun. He was an older fella, in his 60's. He had no business riding shotgun at his age. Doc told the man to see a doctor as soon as they arrived in the next town. The bullet went straight through him. Doc assured the man that he would survive the wound. The old man appreciated Doc's concern.

Colorado frisked the railroad executive and found a huge wad on him. He then thanked the man after he lifted the man's gold pocket watch as well.

Brinkman then ordered the passengers to get inside the coach and he told the teamster to move on out. The driver whipped the reins, and off they went. The stage was originally headed for Las Cruces but with a wounded man aboard, they had no alternative but to stop in Socorro first, about 40 miles down the road, straight south.

The outlaws did not want to ride into Albuquerque, it was just too risky. So they headed northeast to Las Vegas, New Mexico Territory. Colorado new this place well. It was a stopping off place on the Santa Fe Trail and a hot spot for drinking, gambling, and women. It also had a reputation for being as lawless as El Paso.

The railroad arrived in Las Vegas in July of 1879. Gambling houses and brothels brought in the likes of thieves, robbers, murderers, and gunmen. Billy the Kid hung out there for a while with Colorado. Even Jesse James was said to have visited the town. For ole Jesse, it was a place to hide out between train robberies.

In 1879, Wyatt Earp was a deputy marshal in Dodge City with his brother James. Wyatt received a letter from his brother Virgil, who was in Prescott, Arizona Territory at the time, telling him about the opportunities in a new silver mining boomtown named Tombstone. Wyatt thought the prospects were good, and with Dodge City calming down and becoming civilized, he decided to head southwest. He, his common-law wife Mattie Blaylock, his brother James, and his wife Bessie headed southwest. They stopped in Las Vegas, New Mexico Territory first to do some gambling. That's where Wyatt met up with his friend Doc Holliday and Doc's companion, Big Nose Kate. Wyatt, Virgil, James, Doc, and their common-law wives arrived in Tombstone in December of 1879.

A few years had passed since the Earps and Doc Holliday gambled in Las Vegas, New Mexico Territory but it was still a town that was wide open and a safe place for outlaws, for all practical purposes, to get a drink in a saloon and rob another bank, at least in Brinkman's mind.

However, reality was, with the population growing now due to the coming of the railroad, it just might be a little too risky to rob a bank in Las Vegas. Dakota talked Brinkman out of it. Brinkman reluctantly accepted the suggestion, but didn't agree with it. Dakota was worried that Brinkman's greed was getting the best of him, and his desire for excessive wealth could eventually take the whole gang down. Dakota noticed changes in Brinkman - there were signs - it was the way he talked – the things he said – the way he acted - that had Dakota concerned. That missed opportunity in Juarez messed with Brinkman's mind.

Between the lost opportunity in Juarez and his brother Jerod's death, Brinkman had a strong desire now to kill anyone who was associated with Pinkerton. It was in the saloon in Las Vegas after several drinks that Brinkman decided to split the gang up, for the time being. All six of them were sitting at one table. They were all drinking, some more than most. Brinkman was in the group of "some more than most".

The saloon was smoky, it was late at night. The only ones left drinking in the saloon were a few gamblers, some vagrants, saddle bums, and several young drovers on their way back to Texas. There were a couple of table hopping soiled doves making the rounds for upstairs' business, but Brinkman told them to stay clear of his table.

Brinkman took a swig of whiskey and then said,

"Men, this is where we split up. Dakota and I are going to travel to Hays City and kill Rusty Blake. I think they call him Preacher Barnes now. He was the lowlife yellow belly Pinkerton agent who got my brother killed. Then we're going to kill his wife Kathleen. She's the one who pulled the trigger and shot my brother in the back in coldblood.

I want the rest of you men to go back to the hideout in Pueblo and wait for our return. When Dakota and I come back from Hays City, we'll work on rebuilding our gang and then a few of us will travel out to California, meet with Bautista again and find out where the Illuminati Congrego moved their treasures. I guarantee you, we will be getting our share of that one hundred million dollars – that's for sure."

"Boss, is it safe to go back to Pueblo?" Colorado asked. "The Pinkertons may be waiting for us there."

"Nonsense," Brinkman said. "Short killed Green before he ever knew where the hideout was."

"What about Slim, could he have sent a wire to Allan Pinkerton without us knowing about it?" Burkley asked.

"Not likely, you guys don't know this but the telegraph operator in Pueblo works for me. If anyone tried to send a wire out of Pueblo to Pinkerton, I would know about it. That's how I discovered Green was a Pinkerton agent."

"Could Slim have sent a wire from El Paso before we headed to Juarez?" Doc asked.

"No, nobody went close to the telegraph office after we arrived in town. I kept tabs on that myself. I had my ways. Trust me; no one sent a telegram to Pinkerton," Brinkman said.

CHAPTER NINE:

The Gang Splits Up

"Well then let's toast to safe travels, good health, and our future wealth," Brinkman said as he held up his glass of whiskey.

They all held up their glasses and downed the backroom made rotgut and the dregs in their glasses. This late at night and after several drinks, the barkeep began slipping the inebriated outlaw gang his less than prime New Mexico homemade corn mash. It was an old outlaw town trick used in these parts of the new frontier.

"Colorado, do you know the way back to the hideout from here?" Brinkman asked.

"Yes sir, we'll head north to Cimarron, New Mexico Territory and on to Raton Pass. That's a mountain pass on the Santa Fe Trail along the Colorado-New Mexico border. I know that path well. During the Civil War it was the most used route into New Mexico by the Yankees.

Once we ride through the pass, it's a straight shot north to Pueblo. I'm thinking it's about a two hundred fifteen mile journey. So it will take us a good eight to ten days to get there."

"How do you know so much about this area?" Dakota asked.

"They don't call me Colorado for nothing. I grew up in Colorado Springs and then worked in the coal industry in Trinidad, Colorado. That was backbreaking work. I hated it. I really wanted to work in the cattle industry so I moved south to Lincoln, New Mexico Territory. That's where I hooked up with the Kid – you know – Billy Bonney."

"What about you boss, which way are you headed?" Colorado asked.

"I'm going onto Kansas. I'm letting Dakota lead the way. He's been up in that territory before. What about it, Dakota?" Brinkman asked. "Which way are we headed?"

Dakota thought about it for a minute, and then said,

"It doesn't make sense to ride on horseback all the way to Hays City. It's too far – probably about four hundred fifty miles – maybe further than that. It would take us too long to get there - too many hours and days in the saddle. My back isn't fit for riding on hard leather that long, and I'm sure that's the same way with you, Mr. Brinkman.

The best idea would be to ride on horseback to Amarillo, Texas. We could probably make it there in six days. Then we can catch a train in Amarillo to Dodge City."

"Why Dodge City? Why not Hays City?" Brinkman asked.

"Because I could be identified by Luke Barnes or Kathleen if they're near the depot. That would put an end to everything. I think it's best to get off the train in Dodge City and then ride on horseback to Hays City. We should be able to make that ride in three to four days. In that way we could ride into town when we saw fit."

"Then that's what we will do," Brinkman said. "Now let's call it a night. It's too late to hit the trail. I don't think we have to worry about a posse. Let's sleep here at the hotel tonight, eat breakfast together in the morning, and then go our separate ways."

"One last question before I forget. How are we going to stay in touch?" Colorado asked.

"We can't and we won't until Dakota and I leave Hays City after we take care of Barnes and his wife. Then we'll send you a telegram that we're on our way back. The telegraph operator, Jerry, will get it to you.

Let's walk our horses over to the livery stable now and then sign into the hotel."

They all staggered over to the livery stable pulling their horses behind them. The stable was locked up - the stable manager already went home. Not many businesses stayed open after sundown except for the saloon, the brothel, the hotel, and the small sheriff's office.

There was a corral outside for latecomers after closing. Many drifters left their saddles, saddle blankets, and headsets draped over the top rails. However, if you were one of the unlucky ones, you could be shopping for new tack in the boot and leather shop in this rowdy town.

The six men put their horses into the corral, removed their tack and carried all of it over to the Rio Pecos Hotel which was named after the Pecos River that flowed just east of town. As usual, they signed in using fictitious names. The hotel had an attached restaurant named Ma's Tater House; that's where they agreed to meet for breakfast at about seven o'clock. It was ironic that four of the six men left standing in Cole Brinkman's gang were survivors from Jerod Brinkman's gang.

It wasn't long before they were sleeping and snoring away. However, it seemed such a short time before the sun on the eastern horizon shown through their windows and lit up their rooms the next morning – morning comes fast when you're all tuckered out from stress on the mind and whiskey in the gut.

They all meandered down to the restaurant, each toting their saddle over their shoulder with one hand, and the rest of their gear in their other hand. Their heavy saddlebags full of loot were draped over their other shoulder. They had more leather surrounding them than a plump longhorn steer on a lush prairie.

Black coffees were the priority, and then came the biscuits and sawmill gravy with country ham, eggs sunny side up, and two flapjacks on the side. In this establishment Ma herself took the order. And to make things simple, you just ordered one coffee and one breakfast. Ma would determine each day what that breakfast would be – that's just how it was in Ma's Tater House.

"Does everyone remember the plans we put together last night?" Brinkman asked. "I know we were all hitting the bottle pretty hard."

"I'm good with ours," Colorado said.

"I'm good with mine too," Dakota added.

The six desperados ate quickly and paid their bills. On their way out, they passed the sheriff and his deputy walking in. They all looked at each other, slightly nodded, and went on their ways. When they walked onto the street, Brinkman said,

"Let's get the hell out of this town while we still can."

"Do you want to knock over the bank here first before we leave?" Dane asked.

Brinkman merely looked at Dane like he was a crazy man. Dane accurately interpreted the look and kept his trap shut the rest of the way to the corral.

Within 10 minutes they were saddled up and on their separate ways: Brinkman and Dakota heading east to Amarillo; Colorado, Burkley, Doc and Dane, riding north to the Raton Pass.

Brinkman had given most of the stolen loot to Colorado to put in the hideout's safe. He also gave him the combination to the safe's lock. Previously to now, only Brinkman and Short knew the combination. Colorado was becoming the new ramrod, taking Short's old position. Brinkman would rather put his trust in one of his original gang members than one of his brother's. That's just how it was.

Colorado and his group were making good time. During the second night out on the trail, they camped near Springer, New

Mexico Territory near the Cimarron Cutoff of the Santa Fe Trail. There wasn't much activity anymore along the Santa Fe. No sir, the railroad was replacing the need for the famous old route.

They stopped in Springer first to buy some rations, and then they rode a couple of miles northeast to set up camp along the Canadian River. That was a good place to water their mounts. There was also a nice meadow there for the horses to feed. They didn't stay in Springer overnight because the town marshal and his two deputies were roaming the streets and making their presence well known. It didn't appear to be a safe place for outlaws to hang a hat for a night – too risky.

However, they did take a few minutes to quench their thirst at the Cimarron Pass Saloon. It was Dane's idea. Dane was one to take more chances than the rest. He had proven that all the way back to when he unholstered his .45 and blasted his double-dealing partner point blank in the back of the head a few years ago in a cantina in Santa Fe, New Mexico Territory. He did that evil deed with the sheriff of the county eating lunch at the next table over. It was bad judgment on his part. But that's how it was with Johnny Dane. His good judgment brain cells went missing in action when he turned 17 and ran away from a good home.

While the four were sitting around the campfire on the bank of the Canadian River chowing down on beef steaks they picked up in Springer, Dane came up with an idea that didn't sit well with Colorado or the other two.

"Why do we have to go back to the hideout in Pueblo? Let's face it, it's gonna take a long time before we can rebuild our gang and go after those treasures again. I say we split the money we have in our saddlebags right now and go our own separate ways."

"I say if I see your hands in those saddlebags, you'll have a well-placed bullet in your back," Colorado said.

Burkley and Doc looked at Colorado and then back at Dane. They were ready for Dane to pull on Colorado but Dane knew better. Colorado was a quick-draw, faster than anyone sitting around that fire.

"It was just a thought. I was just joshing anyway," Dane said as he knew he better just back off and leave it alone if he intended to ride another day. He knew of Colorado's reputation with his gun hand. Dane was reckless, but he still possessed a few rational brain cells in that hard cranium of his.

Colorado suggested that they take turns guarding their camp. There were still drifters along the Santa Fe Trail – some were outlaws just like themselves. Most of the time, outlaws distrusted other outlaws on the trail, and for good reasons. Colorado took the first shift, then Burkley, and then Doc. At this point none of the three trusted Dane to take a shift. They left him sleep. That became the plan for the rest of their journey.

Brinkman and Dakota had a little rougher go than the other four. There wasn't much civilization until they reached their destination. They traveled a little further north so they had plenty of water for themselves and their horses. A straight eastern path to Amarillo was not practical – it was dry desolate land. They took the path along the Canadian River which flowed southeast. They were able to pick up grub at a few small towns along the way. However, they had to sleep under the stars for many nights which was not too pleasing to Brinkman. He was more of a city type dweller than a frontiersman.

When the two rode up to the location where the Rita Blanca River and the Punta de Aqua River converged with the Canadian River, they came across a large trading post that had a small cafe, and a bar made out of three old wine barrels and four sawmill scrap pieces of wood left over from a shed that was built out back. It wasn't a fancy bar, but it did the job.

The log building had been standing for years. It was musty smelling from the dampness and as dark as a cave from the lack of sunlight. The structure was originally built with a few windows, but they were knocked out several times by raiding Comanche a while back. The owner got tired of replacing the glass in the windows, so he boarded them up.

Dakota and Brinkman were happy to get a good square at this rustic Texas Panhandle establishment. When they finished eating their meal, they bellied up to the bar and downed a couple mugs of warm beer. While talking to the owner, an unshaven man in his early 70's, they found out that there was a small boarding house about sixteen miles due south where they could get another good meal, sleep inside, and even get a shave and a bath. The town was known as Vega and homesteaders were starting to settle into that area.

"Perfect!" Brinkman said, "Perfect!"

"Are you cattlemen?" The owner asked.

"No, why do you ask?" Brinkman questioned.

"Have you ever heard of a man named Charles Goodnight?"

"I have. Met him once too up in Pueblo."

"Well he's lookin' to hire a few good men to cowboy on his JA Ranch in the Palo Duro Canyon southeast of Amarillo. He was just in here about two weeks ago – passing through. He said to put out the word that he's hiring. I told him I would. He's a well-known man in these parts you know. Why he and his partner have about one hundred thousand head of cattle grazing on a million acres or more of grassland."

"Wow, that's a lot of land and a lot of cattle," Dakota said.

"Sure is, the JA Ranch spreads out over six counties. You know, I think that's too much land for just a couple of men. What do you think?"

"I think he's a lucky man with all of that wealth and power. Yes sir, he's a lucky man," Brinkman said.

The two raised their mugs to the old timer, guzzled down their room temperature brew, and off they went to find a shave and a haircut, a bath, and a good night's sleep under a roof in a new settlement named Vega.

In the meantime, the other four gang members had just arrived in Walsenburg, Colorado. There was a boarding house there where they could stay the night and pick up a meal. The night was uneventful. They went over to the small saloon after dinner for a few drinks and then headed back to their rooms. They were all anxious to sleep on a feather bed instead of on a bed of dirt and pebbles.

They ate a good hot breakfast for a change and then they saddled up and rode 35 miles to the St. Charles River, which was now only about 15 miles outside of Pueblo. That's where they made camp for one more night. Colorado cooked up some beans and bacon for supper. It was the last time they would have to eat a saddle bum's meal. There was real food waiting for them at the hideout.

After they ate, they just sat around the campfire and chatted for a while. Ole Doc wasn't in a talkative mood. Instead of joining in on the conversations, he laid out his bedroll, put both hands behind his head and just stared at the stars, and listened to the coyotes sing their song in the moonlit shadows of the ponderosa pines. It was a beautiful night, no clouds in sight; every star was sparkling in the sky like the heavens winking from up above. A quarter moon produced just enough light to be able to witness a predator horned owl quietly swoop down from a perch on a pine tree branch to pounce on an unsuspecting field mouse. Doc was oblivious to the talk around the campfire.

"What's the plan when we ride into Pueblo?" Burkley asked.

"Well, I'll tell you what I think we ought to do," Colorado replied. "I think we should all get a shave, a haircut, and a bath. You guys are all gettin' pretty dang putrid smelling. I don't want to spend the next four weeks with you in the bunkhouse in your present state. If you guys don't use some soap tomorrow, you're sleeping in the barn."

"You don't smell like no sweet petunia yourself, buster," Dane retorted.

They all laughed and then Burkley asked, "Do you think it's OK if we use some of our loot to buy some new clothes tomorrow at the Mercantile?"

"Brinkman would have it no other way. We'll do it and burn these clothes in the fire pit when we get to the ranch. There's no help for them anymore," Colorado said.

Dane had a bottle of whiskey he stashed into one of his saddlebags. He walked over to get it, sat back down on a log near the fire, popped the cork, and took a big ole swig. Then he passed it to Colorado – he did the same – and then passed it to Burkley who took two swigs and finished the bottle. He then passed it back to Dane. Dane held it up to the light to see and jokingly said,

"That last swig was supposed to be mine. I was hornswoggled by a sniper."

They once again laughed and then the laughter turned to silence as they all stared into the campfire for several minutes as if the bright orange and yellow flames hypnotized the hardened criminals – a bright warm campfire on a dark cool night will have that kind of an effect on a fella, especially if worry consumes his every thought.

"Well boys, it's time to get some sleep. I want to get an early start tomorrow so we can arrive in Pueblo at a decent time, get all cleaned up, buy some new clothes, and get back to the hideout where we know we'll be safe. I don't think any lawmen are dogging our trail, but we can't be one hundred percent certain of that. I'll take the first shift," Colorado said.

"Burkley, you take the second, and Doc, you take the third."

"Still don't trust me, eh?" Dane asked.

"Sure I do, Dane. You just look like you need more sleep than the rest of us," Colorado replied.

"Well that there may be a true statement since I'm the oldest," Dane said.

The four woke up right at first light, ate some jerky, saddled up, and rode on to Pueblo. They didn't even take time to stoke the fire and boil some coffee. They all agreed to hit the trail and get a cup of that good Arbuckle's at the café in Pueblo. The lady that owned and operated the café was from Louisiana – sort of a Cajun queen – at least that's how she described herself. Most wranglers had other names which might suit her better.

Anyway, in her establishment, you could order either Arbuckle's coffee which was preferred by most, or that Louisiana chicory which was sometimes as thick as mud and as black as bituminous coal.

Beings they were only 15 miles out from Pueblo, the journey was relatively short, timewise. It only took a few hours to arrive in town. The first order of business was to visit the "Cajun queen's" café and get a cup of Arbuckle's and a piece of her homemade apple pie.

When they walked into the cafe all dirty, dusty, and smelling like polecats, heads were turned – first their way – then the other way. The patrons were happy and thankful that those saddle tramps ate and drank fast and left the establishment quickly.

After they left the café, Burkley and Dane headed for the barber, and Doc and Colorado went shopping for clothes and some canned goods in the Mercantile General Store. The barber had two bathtubs in the back room. Two Chinese girls would fill the tubs with hot water. They would also help scrub your backs and wash your hair if you paid them enough. The two men thought the service was worth the money – back rubbing and hair washing was all the Asian girls were allowed to do though. For all practical purposes, this was a respectable barber shop and bathhouse. The local ladies' society insisted on it.

When the two were done bathing, and they smelled like roses due to the imported French soap they used, they each got their shave and haircut.

Doc and Colorado then walked into the barber shop and took their baths, in clean water of course. Burkley and Dane went over to the general store and bought their new clothes. Within an hour and a half, the four men, looking as clean and groomed as Easterners, left for their hideout.

When they arrived thirty minutes later, they were laughing and carrying on. They had made it safe and sound. They rode up to the ranch house, dismounted, and clove hitched their reins to the rail. Then Colorado said,

"Men, the first order of business is to take these saddlebags inside and put all the money into the safe. Then we'll put our horses into the corral, and rest for the next several days. How does that sound to you saddle tramps?"

"Sounds good to me," Burkley said.

They all untied their saddlebags and slung them over their shoulders. Colorado walked to the door and unlocked it. They all walked into the kitchen. But when they went into the parlor,

shots rang out, and then
more shots rang out, and then yet
more rang out; and then…
there was dead silence.

In just 25 seconds, 48 shots were fired, and the four ruthless outlaws were drilled with lead, riddled with holes, and lying in their own pools of blood. It was a morbid sight in that gunsmoke filled room. Most folks would not be able to handle the scene.

The fusillade from the firearms could be heard in the east, all the way to Pueblo, because of the winds blowing strongly out of the west. Only a few knew what just took place – the how - the why. Most townsfolk had no clue.

CHAPTER TEN:

Showdown in Hays City

"How soon do you think we'll be in Dodge City?" Brinkman asked.

"I think we'll probably be on this train for another four hours. That's my guess," Dakota replied.

The two outlaws had boarded the train in Amarillo early in the morning after they walked their horses up the ramp into the freight car. The train left the station for Dodge City, Kansas at 7:10 a.m., right on time. There were two passenger cars hitched up, but only enough people on board to fill one.

The two men had cleaned up at a boarding house in Vega before they reached Amarillo, but they were able to freshen up again in Amarillo, as well, the night before they boarded the train. They also bought some clean clothes from the general store – it was Brinkman's recommendation. Despite being an outlaw, he was an attorney and always well-groomed, and wanted to travel with a person that did not look as though he was a cowpuncher fresh off a cattle drive.

Brinkman was sitting by the window just staring outside watching the countryside go by. He saw a lot of cattle grazing out there on the grassy prairies. There appeared to be hundreds of thousands of longhorns. There were a few large ranches in these parts that controlled most of the land in the Panhandle.

Dakota had his hat pulled down over his eyes and was dozing for a couple of hours while they were traveling through the far north Texas Panhandle, the narrow panhandle of the Indian Territory, and onward into the state of Kansas. When he woke up and looked out the window, Brinkman asked,

"What's your background, Dakota? You seem a little more educated than the other gang members. Well, Colorado may not be educated, but he has good common frontier sense. He's smart enough to take Short's place, but so are you. I think we have a great future together."

"Sir, I don't like to talk about my entire background with anyone. There's a part of it that haunted me for years. It took me a long time to get over it. But here's what I will share with you. I attended a small country school and learned to read and write up in the Sioux country.

Many of our classes were canceled because of the Indian Wars and raids. They came and went like the Canadian geese flocks; although we knew when the geese were going to fly south for the winter or come back home in the spring. The Sioux though, well, they were as unpredictable as the thunderstorms in the summer months. Yes sir, the perils of living in the Dakota Territory were far greater than you could imagine.

Texas had their Comanche and Apache; we had our Sioux and Cheyenne. I grew up killing many Sioux in those days as a teenager. My pa taught me how to shoot at an early age. It was a necessity for us homesteaders up that way. Killing Indians came easy after your first two, I guess. But it was out of necessity. It was either you or them.

However, I never killed a white man unless he pointed a gun at me first. I guess that was because of my upbringing. My ma and pa were good people. They treated me and my brother well."

"I can't say the same for me," Brinkman said. "My pa beat me and Jerod every chance he got. I hated him for that. He drank a lot - he was no good. My ma couldn't do anything about it. He beat her too. One night when he started to beat on ma because dinner was late, I picked up a pistol and shot him in the back. That was the last time he ever laid a hand on anybody. Our youngest brother was only two years old at the time. He never did know pa.

Even when pa was alive, we were poor – we had nothing. Food and clothing were hard to come by. Pa never had a steady job.

I remember you telling Bautista about knowing a few Bible verses. You're a God fearing man, aren't you?" Brinkman asked.

"Yes sir, I guess I am. What about you sir. Are you a believer?"

"Son, I lost my way a long time ago. I'm not sure if I am or not. I guess at one time I was – now, well now I'm probably too far gone to even worry about it."

"Sir, why don't we forget about killing Luke Barnes and his wife Kathleen? I rode jobs with Barnes when he was known as Rusty Blake. He really wasn't such a bad guy. He was just doing a job, trying to earn money for a church in Hays City. He's a preacher now. I don't think I have it in me to kill a preacher."

"He was a no good Pinkerton man!" Brinkman yelled.

Dakota told him to keep his voice down. He realized other folks heard Brinkman and looked their way.

"He and his wife killed my brother. He was the brother I was closest to. I don't know what happened to my other brother, and I don't really care. But Jerod's dead, Barnes and his wife did it, and they're going to pay with their lives. Like the Bible says, an eye for an eye, a tooth for a tooth. That's all there is to it."

"You're taking that out of context, sir. The next verse says that when a person strikes you on the right cheek, turn and offer him the other."

Brinkman laughed.

Dakota didn't say anything after that, but just looked across the aisle and out the window on the other side of the train. Brinkman now had concerns about Dakota's loyalty. He didn't know if he could trust Dakota to go all the way with his plan. Brinkman looked out the window on his side and kept relatively quiet the rest of the trip as did Dakota.

It was obvious now they both had dissimilar views about killing Luke Barnes and Kathleen. This difference in opinions could be resolved, but by what means would be the question. That's what bothered Brinkman all the way to Dodge City.

The train arrived in Dodge City, Kansas on time. After they unloaded their horses, they rode over to the general store to get some supplies for their trip to Hays City. Then they wasted no time. Brinkman wanted to get to Hays City as fast as he could to get the evil deed done. They headed northeast to the small town of Petersburg which would eventually be renamed, Kinsley. It was a one day trip from Dodge City.

There was a hotel in Petersburg called The Cattlemen's Inn. That's where they spent the night. They ate dinner together in the hotel restaurant and then went up to their own rooms. They didn't say much to each other during dinner. Tension was starting to build between the two.

Dakota tossed and turned a couple of hours before he finally dozed off. Brinkman spent some quiet time practicing his quick-draw in front of a mirror. Dakota was always faster than most, but Brinkman's draw was as fast as Doc Holliday's. There were very few who could outdraw Brinkman.

They met for breakfast the next morning and then rode out. The next stop on their journey was La Crosse, the county seat of Rush County, Kansas. It was a small town established in 1876. Again it was a one day trek, but a little further than the previous day's ride. Hays City was only 24 miles away now. Once again they signed into a hotel, and then rode out the next morning.

They could have made it to Hays City on that day if they pressed their horses. However, Brinkman wanted to make one more stop before Hays City and it wasn't because he wanted to give the horses a rest. He wanted to stop at the small town just south of the Smoky Hill River.

The Smoky Hill River – oh if that river could talk. It would tell tales of vigilante hangings from the thick branches of the cottonwood trees along its swift flowing waters. It would remind Dakota how things used to be before law and order moved in along its banks. It would also remind him how he and Pecos first met Rusty Blake (a.k.a. Preacher Barnes) when they broke him out of jail in Hays City just before his scheduled hanging after being judged in a kangaroo court.

The reason Brinkman wanted to stop over in Schoenchen, Kansas was because he wanted to arrive in Hays City in the morning with quick reflexes and a keen eye, and not be tired out from riding 30 miles in the saddle.

Schoenchen was only about 12 miles due south of Hays City. That evening he stood on the banks of the Smoky Hill River and practiced his quick-draw and aim, shooting at logs and branches floating downstream. Dakota just watched and didn't say a word - didn't even comment on some incredible shots Brinkman made.

Dakota gave up trying to convince Brinkman to let Luke Barnes and his wife live. He knew there was no turning back Brinkman's quest for revenge. Dakota had plans to travel all the way to Hays City and see this thing out to the end with Brinkman. However, he had no idea how he would act when it came time for the gunfight in the middle of Main Street.

When morning arrived, Dakota was tense. Brinkman though had determination written all over his face. He didn't say much of anything. He wasn't even interested in eating. He was now focused. This was the day he was waiting for. It was the day he was going to avenge his brother's death.

They saddled up, crossed the bridge over the Smoky Hill River, and rode north to Hays City. It was a gloomy day: cold, cloudy, misting, and with a biting wind – a day made for a killing. At least that's what went through Brinkman's sick vindictive mind.

Brinkman rode out front with his horse traveling at a fast trot most of the way. They arrived at the outskirts of town in just under two hours and brought their horses to a halt. Brinkman then unholstered his pistol and twirled the cylinder to make sure every chamber was loaded. Dakota did the same.

Then they rode onto the south side of Main Street and stopped again. Brinkman looked around to see if he could spot the marshal's office. It was between them and the church, which was at the other end of the long narrow street.

Brinkman looked at Dakota and said,

"Let's get off our horses now and hitch them up here."

After they hitched them to a rail, Brinkman summoned a teenage boy to come over to him. The boy walked over and said,

"Yes sir, did you want to see me?"

"Do you know where Preacher Barnes lives?"

"Yes sir, in that house down there next to the church," the boy said as he pointed to the other side of town.

"Here's a dollar young man for your troubles. Go tell Preacher Barnes that Mr. Brinkman is calling him out. Tell him I am down the street waiting for him. Now, exactly what are you going to tell him?"

"A Mr. Brinkman is calling you out and is waiting for you down the street," the boy said.

"That's right, now go."

The boy was old enough to know the inferences of that message. He ran down the street as fast as he could. When he reached the white picket fence surrounding Barnes's house, he turned around to see if he could still see the two men. He could. He then opened the gate, ran up the porch and knocked on the door.

Luke Barnes opened the door.

"Hi Billy, you've been running. Come on in. What can I do for you?"

Billy walked in and Barnes closed the door. Kathleen had just walked into the foyer to see who was at the door.

"Preacher Barnes, there are two men down at the other end of Main Street."

Billy looked down at the floor and then became quiet. His eyes started to well up.

"Yes Billy, what about those two men?"

"One of them told me to tell you that Mr. Brinkman is calling you out."

"Oh no!" Kathleen said as she put the palm of her left hand to her mouth. Luke stared at Kathleen and Kathleen stared back at Luke.

Luke then walked into his study, opened the top drawer to his desk, and removed his holstered double action Colt M1877 Rainmaker model with a 2.5" barrel - he loaded it up and strapped it on.

"What are you doing?" Kathleen asked. "You can't go down there. He'll kill you."

"I have to Kathleen. We have to end this thing right now."

"This is a job for the law, not you Luke."

"He's calling me out. I have to go out there," Luke said as he opened the door and walked out of the house.

Kathleen grabbed Billy and said,

"Billy, quickly now, run down to the marshal's office and tell Deputy Lucas that the gunmen are here to kill the preacher. Tell the deputy where they are. Tell him the preacher needs help. Now go! Go! Go!"

Billy ran down the street as fast as he could to the marshal's office. He passed up the preacher who was walking slowly down the middle of Main Street.

Brinkman saw Barnes coming and said to Dakota,

"Let's go."

They both began walking down the street as well. Then Dakota looked at Preacher Barnes and then back at Brinkman and with his hand on his gun grip he said,

"I can't let you do this."

Brinkman drew his pistol and shot Dakota. Dakota grabbed his belly and fell to the ground. Brinkman kept walking toward Barnes and Barnes did the same. Now they were about 100 yards from each other.

Then the door of the marshal's office opened and Deputy Marshal Jake Lucas walked out on the street in front of Luke and said,

"Back off son, this is my game."

Barnes stopped, and the deputy continued the slow walk towards Brinkman.

Then they both stopped about ten yards from each other and the deputy said,

"You will have to go by me before you get to the preacher. Make your play."

They stared at each other for a few seconds and then Brinkman reached for his gun but the deputy outdrew him, shooting him in the shoulder and then in the leg. Brinkman fell to the ground. The deputy then ran up to Brinkman and kicked the gun away from him.

Preacher Barnes came running down the street to where Brinkman was doubled-up and moaning. The preacher looked at the deputy and said,

"You're a better shot than that. Why didn't you shoot to kill?"

The deputy looked at Barnes, then down at Brinkman, and then back at Barnes, and said,

"Because he's my brother. Yes, that's right, he's my brother. I'm the third Brinkman brother. I'm really Matt Brinkman. I didn't have it in me to kill my own brother."

Preacher Barnes looked at Matt with a puzzled expression. He was shocked to hear the revelation.

Barnes then looked at Billy and told him to run and get the doctor. Then Barnes walked over to Dakota with his gun drawn. Dakota was still alive. The bullet caught him on the side of the belly and didn't hit any internal organs but he was bleeding profusely.

"Hello Dakota," Barnes said.

"Hello Rusty. I tried to stop Brinkman but he wasn't having any of it."

"I know Dakota. We sent for the doctor. Lie still until he gets here. Are you the one who sent me a telegram a while back warning me that someone was gunning for me?"

"It wasn't me, Rusty."

Kathleen came running down to her husband and gave him a hug that lasted for over a minute. The deputy walked over to Luke and Kathleen. Luke said,

"Honey, I want you to meet Matt Brinkman. He's the Brinkman that saved my life."

After the gunfight, Cole Brinkman and Dakota were patched up and placed in the Hays City jail. The doctor came in everyday for a week to check on their wounds to make sure they were healing up all right. There seemed to be no issues.

Allan Pinkerton was sent a wire and told that Dakota and Cole Brinkman were wounded in a showdown, that they would both survive their wounds, and were now in the city jail.

Pinkerton sent a wire to a couple of people and told them to meet him in Hays City, Kansas as soon as they could.

When Allan Pinkerton arrived in town a couple days later, he signed into the hotel, and then went over to the jailhouse. The cells that held the prisoners were in a back room separated from the marshal's office by a locked door.

The deputy marshal opened that door for Pinkerton who was carrying a chair. He ignored Brinkman and walked over to Dakota's cell. Dakota was lying down but when he saw Pinkerton walk in, he sat up on his cot.

Pinkerton sat down and asked Dakota,

"Do you know who I am?"

"I believe I do. I believe you are Allan Pinkerton."

"That's right. I know who you are Dakota Wilson. I also know your background. I know you were once the deputy marshal in Laramie, Wyoming."

Brinkman looked over at Dakota from the other cell.

Pinkerton continued,

"I also know what happened in Laramie that made you turn from the law. Your wife and child were taken hostage by a notorious gang during a bank robbery. The town and the marshal cowered on you, and your wife and son were killed by the gang. After that you threw away the badge, headed to Deadwood, and became an outlaw yourself.

Now you committed a lot of criminal acts while you belonged to a couple of gangs. We know this for sure. However, I don't believe we can prove that you killed anyone, so I don't think you'll hang for your crimes."

Dakota didn't say a word. He put his feet back up on the cot, stretched out his legs, and laid down again.

Pinkerton then stood up and moved his chair over to the front of Brinkman's cell and sat down. Brinkman ignored him. Then Pinkerton said,

"Cole Brinkman, you don't look so tough anymore. You had us fooled for a while. I must admit, we did not know you were using the name Burns as an alias. It took a while for us to figure that out. But we discovered it all right, while we were playing you for a sucker. Let me tell you how we caught you and your gang."

Brinkman sat up in his cot and said in an arrogant tone,

"All right mister detective, tell me how you did it."

"You were right about Green. He was an undercover agent who I slipped into your gang. He informed us about Dakota and Pecos heading to meet up with Diamond Lil in San Francisco. He went along with them. That was a bad move on your gang's part. Green told us where Lil was in San Francisco. We got to her first and she helped us to set up a trap to catch your gang. Two of my agents met with her during the Open House of her Crystal Palace. We gave her an ultimatum: play our game and get leniency down the road, or be taken to jail now and get life in prison. She chose to play our game."

Now Brinkman was getting more agitated. Just then, the marshal opened the back cell room door and walked in with Mr. Bautista and Harrington. Brinkman looked up and was surprised to see them. Then he smirked and said,

"So they caught you and Harington too, eh Bautista?"

"Not quite," Bautista said.

"No, not quite," Pinkerton repeated.

"You see, Harrington is one of my undercover agents. You probably thought he was killed in Juarez. That's what we wanted you to think. You made the mistake of showing him the location of your hideout. He and my men were waiting for your gang at your hideout after they came back from Juarez. They are all dead except for Doc. He survived.

By the way, we found Slim's body. You thought he was one of ours. He wasn't. He was one of yours. You killed one of your own men. During Dakota's interrogation, he told us how you gunned down Slim after you crossed the Rio Grande and rode back into Texas. He also informed us that you killed Pecos. My only regret is that we won't be hanging him.

And Mr. Bautista isn't really your Mr. Bautista after all. The servant you met named Jose is the real Mr. Bautista. The person you know as Bautista is really Daniel Coit Gilman, a personal friend of mine. He's the president of Johns Hopkins University in Baltimore, Maryland.

He was a member of the secret society known as Skull and Bones at Yale University. He is also an expert on many secret societies. That's why he was able to effectively hornswoggle you into making you believe there was really a secret society called the Illuminati Congrego and that there was an amalgamation of secret societies and their treasures for the purpose of establishing a New World Order.

We made a fool out of you, Brinkman."

Brinkman tried to get up and grab Pinkerton by the throat but he was too sore from his gunshot wounds to move even just a few steps.

"I knew you would fall for the scheme because of your greed and your thirst for power. Your brother Jerod was the same way. I'm happy to know that there is at least one Brinkman brother who has a soul. That's Matt, the one who shot you on Main Street," Pinkerton said as he laughed in Brinkman's face.

Harrington and Daniel Gilman laughed as well. Then those two turned and left the back cell room.

"Hey Pinkerton, what finally happened to Diamond Lil?" Dakota asked.

"Two of my agents picked her up at her Crystal Palace while you guys were in Half Moon Bay at Bautista's. She has already been tried and convicted. She's spending ten years in the Indiana Women's Prison with a chance for parole after five years. By the way, she was the one who sent a wire to Preacher Barnes and warned him that you guys were gunning for him. If Barnes had not received that warning, Matt would not have been here, and the outcome might have been much different."

Pinkerton then stood up and looked at Cole Brinkman and said,

"Yes sir, Cole Brinkman, we made a fool out of you. See you at your hanging."

THE END

EPILOGUE

Allan Pinkerton took a train back to Chicago. He had been ill for a while and could not stay around for Brinkman's and Dakota's trial. He sent a wire to President Chester A. Arthur and asked for an appointment after the trial ended and the sentences were handed down. President Arthur agreed to see him.

The trial lasted about 3 weeks and the verdicts came in. Brinkman was sentenced to be hung. He met his maker 3 days later. Dakota received a sentence of 12 years at the Missouri State Penitentiary with a chance of parole after 8 years. Doc was tried in Pueblo and received 10 years at the Arkansas State Penitentiary. The crooked marshal from Abilene was never found.

After Brinkman's hanging, Allan Pinkerton, with the aid of his son, took a train to Washington, D.C. On the second day after they arrived, they met with President Arthur in his office. The President asked them to sit in the two chairs in front of his desk. Allan's son said,

"I'll wait out in the hall. My father wants to speak with you in private."

"I'll walk you out."

"That's not necessary, Mr. President. I'll close the door when I step out into the hall."

"Thank you," President Arthur said.

After his son left, Allan Pinkerton said,

"Thank you for seeing me, Mr. President. The last time I was here, I told you that I feared there was a criminal network in play. Well I was right. I believe the network is now shut down. Cole Brinkman was hung and most of his gang members are dead. The two who survived are in state penitentiaries."

"I know how you trapped Cole Brinkman's gang," President Arthur said.

"I know you do," Pinkerton replied.

"Well then, was it moved…you know…was it moved safely before the trap?"

"Yes sir…it was moved deeper into Mexico," Pinkerton said. "It's hidden again, it's safe and sound, and it's being guarded by the enlightened ones. You will be informed of its placement on the grid on the 13th of this month.

Daniel Coit Gilman will be your contact man like always."

BONUS SECTION:

Actual Article of the Killing of Billy the Kid

This is an actual article about the killing of one of the most notorious outlaws of the Old West. He was born Henry McCarty on September 17, 1859 in New York City, New York to Catherine (nee Devine) McCarty and Patrick McCarty.

He changed his name to William H. Bonney and eventually became known as Billy the Kid. He was a cowboy, a horse rustler, a ranch hand, a gambler, an outlaw, a gunfighter, and a murderer. He participated in New Mexico's Lincoln County War.

He is known to have killed eight men.

Billy became a wanted man in the Arizona Territory just before his 16th birthday when he killed a blacksmith during an altercation in August of 1877.

His notoriety as an outlaw and killer grew in December of 1880 when the *Las Vegas Gazette* in Las Vegas, New Mexico Territory and the *New York Sun* printed stories about his crimes.

Billy was killed by lawman Pat Garrett on July 14, 1881, at the age of 21. Many people thought Billy the Kid was left-handed. He was actually right-handed.

The article below appeared in the *Salt Lake Herald* on Wednesday, July 20, 1881. It was on page 6 of 8 in the 3rd column.

Billy the Kid's resting place is in the Old Fort Sumner Cemetery.

NOTE: The newspaper articles below include "errors" in punctuation, grammar and spelling because this is how they appeared in the actual articles.

Here then is the first article in its entirety:

"Billy, the Kid"
Particulars of His Daring Capture

Las Vegas, New Mexico…

Positive and reliable information reached this city early this morning at 11:30 by messenger, in regard to the Thursday killing of the notorious "Billy, the Kid" at Fort Sumner, 120 miles distant on the Pecos River.

"Billy" had been stopping with the Mexicans in that vicinity, disguised as one of them, ever since his escape from Lincoln County Jail. Pat Garrett, sheriff of Lincoln County has been on his track for some time, and on the day above mentioned arrived at Fort Sumner, having been put on the track by some Mexicans.

He had to threaten their lives in order to get them to divulge Kid's whereabouts. About 12 o'clock midnight Thursday, Sheriff Garrett entered the room of Pete Maxwell, a large stock owner residing at the fort, and supposed to have knowledge of the fugitive's exact whereabouts.

Garrett had not been in the room over twenty minutes when the Kid entered in his stocking feet, knife in hand, ostensibly for the purpose of buying some meat. He immediately observed Garrett crouching at the head of the bed, and asking Maxwell what that was, drew his revolver.

Maxwell made no answer, but proceeded to crowd toward the foot of the bed. Had he answered giving Garrett's name, "Billy" would have killed him at once, as he is a dead shot. Billy moved slightly, and getting into the moonlight, then shining in at the rough window, Garrett recognizing him, fired, the ball passing through his heart.

He fell backwards, His knife in one hand and a revolver in the other. Garrett, thinking him not dead, fired again, but missed him. Had his first shot failed he would have been riddled with bullets, as the "Kid" is known to have been terribly desperate and very accurate in aim, when in close quarters. His death is hailed with great joy throughout this section, as he had sworn he would kill several prominent citizens and had already killed fifteen or eighteen men.

Note: *The Omaha Daily Bee.*, August 6, 1881 ran a long four column section on page 3 of 9. It seemed to be a more thorough article. It was entitled:

BILLY THE KID
The True History of the Boy-Devil's Terrible Exploits
"He Only Killed Eleven Men That I Know of" –
Details of His Own Death.

Here are just a few paragraphs from that article:

DEATH WAS NOW CLOSE AFTER HIM
Deputy Sheriff Pat Garrett, with two companions, started on his trail, swearing to capture or kill him or die trying. In some way known only to himself Garrett learned that the Kid would probably visit the house of Pete Maxwell, at Fort Sumner, in Lincoln County, sometime during the night of Thursday, July 14. Shortly before midnight Garrett went to Maxwell's and had just seated himself in the dark on the side of Maxwell's bed when the door opened, and

IN WALKED THE KID
Instantly detecting, in spite of the darkness, that there was somebody in the room with Maxwell, he leveled his pistols, exclaiming, "Quien es? Quien es?" (Who are you? or Who's there?) But the delay of asking was fatal. Before the words were off his lips Pat Garrett's bullet was through his heart, and "Billy the Kid" the terror of New Mexico, lay a gasping, quivering corpse while his life-blood dyed the dirt floor of Pete Maxwell's dark adobe hut. Eleven gory ghosts stood waiting to escort him to eternal shades.

IN PERSONAL APPEARANCE
The Kid was anything but a desperado or a monster. He was very small and slender, being 5 foot 2 inches tall, and weighing scarcely 120 pounds. He had a plain but pleasant face, with thin, sharp features, blue eyes, and light hair. He was calculated to make friends, and strange as it may seem, left many who sincerely mourned his death. One of the best men of the territory, who though identified with the opposite faction, knew him well, said to me this morning, "Do you know I couldn't help feeling sorry

when I heard that boy was killed." He was a splendid horseman and a dead shot, and at the time of his death was only about 22 years old.

The hero of the hour in New Mexico now, the king lion of the territorial menagerie, is Patsey Garrett, the slayer of the kid…

Bibliography

Newspaper article of Billy the Kid
http://chroniclingamerica.loc.gov/

Newspaper articles in the Author's Foreword
http://chroniclingamerica.loc.gov/

Ark
http://www.biblestudytools.com/dictionary/ark/

Daniel Coit Gilman
https://en.wikipedia.org/w/index.php?title=Daniel_Coit_Gilman&oldid=763152054

Blue Duck (outlaw)
https://en.wikipedia.org/w/index.php?title=Blue_Duck_(outlaw)&oldid=744630344

Cynthia Ann Parker
https://en.wikipedia.org/w/index.php?title=Cynthia_Ann_Parker&oldid=765315489

Charles Goodnight
https://en.wikipedia.org/w/index.php?title=Charles_Goodnight&oldid=752898190

Quanah Parker
https://en.wikipedia.org/w/index.php?title=Quanah_Parker&oldid=765315154

Comanche
https://en.wikipedia.org/w/index.php?title=Comanche&oldid=765262411

Muscogee Native Americans and President Andrew Jackson
https://en.wikipedia.org/w/index.php?title=Muscogee&oldid=765192714

History of King Solomon's Temple
http://www.templeofkingsolomon.com/Site/TempleHistory/Default.asp

King Solomon's Temple and the Ark of the Covenant
The New American Bible, Catholic Bible Publishers, Wichita, Kansas

Famous Masons
http://aasrvalleyofjax.org/famous_masons.htm

Main events in the history of Jerusalem
http://www.centuryone.com/hstjrslm.html

New World Order
http://www.jeremiahproject.com/the-new-world-order/

Illuminati
https://en.wikipedia.org/w/index.php?title=Illuminati&oldid=759424640

New World Order (Conspiracy theory)
https://en.wikipedia.org/w/index.php?title=New_World_Order_(conspiracy_theory)&oldid=759282360

Freemasonry
https://en.wikipedia.org/w/index.php?title=Freemasonry&oldid=764592337

Knights Templar
https://en.wikipedia.org/w/index.php?title=Knights_Templar&oldid=764582786

Convento de Cristo, Convent of Christ (Tomar)
https://en.wikipedia.org/w/index.php?title=Convent_of_Christ_(Tomar)&oldid=756171129

Order of Christ (Portugal)
https://en.wikipedia.org/w/index.php?title=Order_of_Christ_(Portugal)&oldid=761131781

Knights of the Golden Circle
https://en.wikipedia.org/w/index.php?title=Knights_of_the_Gold
en_Circle&oldid=761321712

Mesilla, New Mexico
https://en.wikipedia.org/w/index.php?title=Mesilla,_New_Mexico
&oldid=764169457

Medicine Lodge, Kansas
https://en.wikipedia.org/w/index.php?title=Medicine_Lodge,_Ka
nsas&oldid=763913289

Pueblo, Colorado
https://en.wikipedia.org/w/index.php?title=Pueblo,_Colorado&ol
did=765099836

Billy the Kid
https://en.wikipedia.org/w/index.php?title=Billy_the_Kid&oldid
=764944618

Secret societies
https://en.wikipedia.org/w/index.php?title=Secret_society&oldid
=765048930

Iberian Union
https://en.wikipedia.org/w/index.php?title=Iberian_Union&oldid
=756114874

James Black (blacksmith)
https://en.wikipedia.org/w/index.php?title=James_Black_(blacks
mith)&oldid=762586081

Gold Rush
https://en.wikipedia.org/w/index.php?title=Gold_rush&oldid=76
5239742

Timeline of San Francisco History
http://www.zpub.com/sf/history/sfh2.html

Stanford's Nob Hill Mansion
http://www.sfgenealogy.com/sf/history/hgoe02.htm

Barbary Coast, San Francisco
https://en.wikipedia.org/w/index.php?title=Barbary_Coast,_San_Francisco&oldid=765375348

History of San Francisco
https://en.wikipedia.org/w/index.php?title=History_of_San_Francisco&oldid=761666203

Juarez
https://en.wikipedia.org/w/index.php?title=Ciudad_Ju%C3%A1rez&oldid=764330683

Medieval torture devices
http://opishposh.com/15-gruesomely-painful-medieval-torture-devices/

Lloyd's Lights and Shades of San Francisco 1876 (book)
https://en.wikipedia.org/w/index.php?title=History_of_San_Francisco&oldid=761666203

Belle Starr
https://en.wikipedia.org/w/index.php?title=Belle_Starr&oldid=763707853

Knights of the Golden Circle
http://knights-of-the-golden-circle.blogspot.com/2011/12/albert-pike-freemasonry-and-kgc.html

Conspiracy Theories
https://en.wikipedia.org/w/index.php?title=Conspiracy_theory&oldid=771089473

CPSIA information can be obtained
at www.ICGtesting.com
Printed in the USA
FSOW02n0437060417
32718FS

9 781681 111728